INTRODUCTION

The Marrying Kind by Kathleen Y'Barbo
Texas native Rafe Wilson's life as a small town sheriff held little excitement beyond the occasional cattle rustling or stagecoach robbery until Peony Potter moved her dressmaking business to Cut Corners. Who would have known that such a tiny woman would turn out to be such a big problem?

Here Cooks the Bride by Cathy Marie Hake
Lacey Mather breezes into town to help out at Millie's Diner until her great-aunt's broken arm heals. Blacksmith Jeffrey Wilson knew a man had to have a cast-iron stomach to eat at the diner—until that gal arrives. It's downright entertaining to watch lonely men woo her—until Jeffrey realizes he's developed a taste for a sweet thing he can't let go.

Unexpected Blessings by Vickie McDonough
Anna Campbell sets out to deliver two small orphans to their uncle. Erik Olson knows it's impossible for those cute little pests to be his brother's and refuses to accept them—regardless of Anna's persistence. Little do they know that behind the scenes, Erik's uncle Lars and his buddies are doing a little matchmaking, hoping to give the children a father and a mother.

A Christmas Chronicle by Pamela Griffin
Vivian Sager wants more out of life than to marry and raise babies, that is if any man would have her. Travis McCoy is sure no woman would want to share his nomadic lifestyle of chronicling the West with a camera. Can God provide for them a new picture, one that includes the two of them traipsing through life together?

LONE STAR CHRISTMAS

Someone Is Rustling Up a Little Holiday Matchmaking in Four Delightful Stories

KATHLEEN Y'BARBO
CATHY MARIE HAKE
VICKIE MCDONOUGH
PAMELA GRIFFIN

BARBOUR
PUBLISHING

Prologue

by Kathleen Y'Barbo

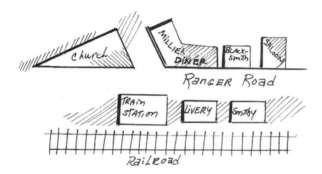

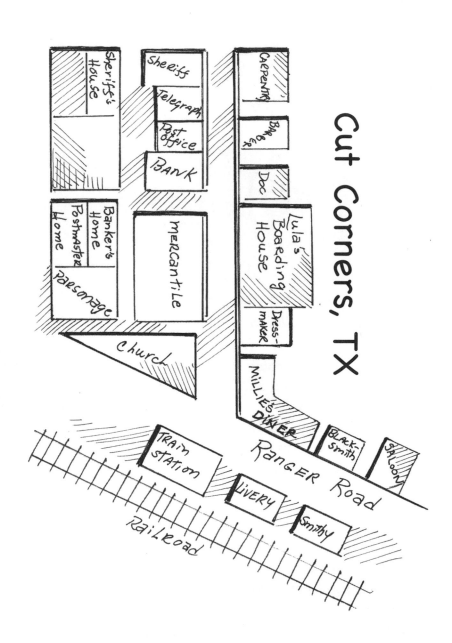

Prologue

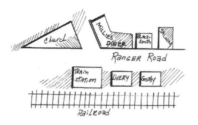

San Antonio, Texas
Christmas Day, 1851

Texas Ranger captain Ebenezer "Eb" Wilson swiped at his eyes with the back of his hand and knelt at Carolina's bedside. On the other side of the closed door, his firstborn, Rafael Ebenezer, wailed in the capable arms of his grandmother. His wife had given him a strong, fine son, a lad with his mama's dark hair and his papa's talent for howling at full volume.

If only he'd been there when. . .

"Eb, promise me. . . "

Jerking his attention back to the tiny form beneath the blankets, Eb felt the tears threaten again. His beautiful fiery wife, the delicate counterpoint to his big, clumsy self, lay so still and pale that he barely recognized her. The very life seemed to flow from her as the clock at the bedside ticked.

She reached for his hand, but her fingers fell limp on the

quilt just shy of their mark. Eb grasped her tiny hand in his and lifted it to his lips. "Anything, Lina. Anything."

For a moment, fire flashed in Carolina's eyes, a reminder of the saucy senorita he'd met and married in a whirlwind courtship barely one year ago. "Don't let my mama take our Rafael to raise. Get him another mama, someone young and strong who'll love him like me."

"No." The sharpness of his tone startled him, but it seemed to have no effect on Carolina. "I'll never marry again. I—I couldn't."

Her fingers slid from his grasp to wipe a tear off his cheek. "Then I will only pray you will consider it."

"I'll try, but you'll be everywhere I look. How's a man going to find a new wife like that?" His poor attempt at humor fell flat, but Carolina, bless her soul, chuckled anyway.

"Leave San Antonio then," she said softly. "The city is no place to raise a child."

"Maybe I will, Lina," he said, although he had no idea how he, a ranger captain, would ever settle somewhere and raise a baby. His life and his command were here. So was the extended family that would help him care for his son. People like Lula Chamberlain and Millie, his wife's best friends, would never let him leave.

Right now, however, he would promise her the moon and all the stars in the sky if she asked. Setting up housekeeping somewhere quiet and raising a baby seemed minor in comparison. "It might take me some time," he amended. "A man has to plan these things."

"You and your plans. Do you think I don't hear you and your friends when you speak of the things you will do when you are no longer rangers?" She caught his gaze, and her eyes narrowed. "Find some land. Start a little settlement up north where the weather's cooler. Put down roots someplace nice and safe from the *banditos*. Did you and those three *compadres* of yours not say this?"

"Well now, we might have mentioned it a time or two."

Indeed, he and fellow rangers Stone, Swede, and Chaps had jawed about doing just that for a while now. They even had a name for their little town: Cut Corners, Texas. Of course, that was just fool talk, part jest and part wishful thinking. He hadn't actually thought about the reality of it, and he doubted the other three had either.

"Then make your Cut Corners a reality, *mi amour*. Promise me."

"I promise." He paused to add a dash of reason to the statement. "Just as soon as we're done rangering, me and the boys'll see there's a Cut Corners on the map."

Carolina nodded, and her satisfied look made him wish he believed the promise would come true as much as she seemed to. As far as he was concerned, however, he'd be a Texas Ranger until the day he died, and he knew the others felt the same way. Cut Corners would most likely stay a dream, but he would never admit that to Carolina.

"Second, make Christmas special for our Rafael. He and our Savior share a birthday, and I want you to make a grand celebration of the day, you hear?"

"Of course."

Now *that* he could do. He'd always been big on celebrating the Lord's birth. The only wrinkle in that plan would be figuring out how to get through the day without missing his Carolina. Eb shifted positions to lie beside her. If only he could stop the clock, take away time's ability to move forward.

"Lina," he said as he buried his face in her dark hair, "I love you."

His wife sighed. "No better husband ever drew a breath than you, Eb Wilson. I do not ask this last thing of you out of spite but rather out of love. Do you understand?"

"Yes," he managed.

"Mi amour," she said as she peered at him, "our son must never ever be a Texas Ranger."

The hardest words Eb Wilson ever said were, "I promise."

The Marrying Kind

by Kathleen Y'Barbo

Dedication

To Meg Shaheen. . .for taking Hannah under your wing and into your carpool so I could write on Thursday nights. And to Evie for being a forever friend to Hannah.
May God bless you as much as you have blessed me.

And he said unto them, How is it that ye sought me?
Wist ye not that I must be about my Father's business?
LUKE 2:49

Prologue

Cut Corners, Texas
Christmas Day, 1871

S ure feels good to finally keep my promise, even if it did
take nigh on twenty years. Guess it goes to show you can't
rush the Lord. It all happens in His time, don't it?"

Eb Wilson sat atop his favorite horse and stared at the
beginnings of the town called Cut Corners. None of them
could remember which of the four former rangers had come
up with the name, but they all agreed it fit the little spot on the
north Texas prairie to a *T*.

Now, with a light dusting of snow, Main Street and its collection of finished and partially finished buildings looked prettier than ever. From the train station to the little church where
they would worship that morning, signs of progress abounded.

Tomorrow the work would continue, but this day, the
Savior's birthday, was reserved for celebration. After church
they would celebrate Rafe's birthday, too, just as Eb had done

every year, keeping his promise to Carolina.

Carolina.

Eb swallowed hard and cast a glance skyward. *I miss you, mi amour. I only hope Rafe and I have made you proud.*

"*Ja,*" Lars Olson, better known as Swede, said under his breath. "Cut Corners. Can you believe it is finally real?"

Eb cast a glance over his shoulder at his nephew, blacksmith Jeff Wilson, who drove the buckboard filled with gifts for the town's few children. Beside him, Rafe wore a grin.

The two of them were quite a pair, cousins and friends but raised like brothers. More often than not, they were partners in crime, as well, although their adult years and the fact that Rafe had agreed to act as sheriff of Cut Corners in the coming year had slowed their antics a bit.

"It's not done yet," Rafe said as he climbed out of the buckboard and helped his cousin secure the horse. "Won't be for a long time."

"That's the truth, Son. We still have a long way to go," Eb said, "but with hard work and prayer, it's going to be done before we know it. Then all we'll have to do is ask the Lord and our new sheriff to keep it safe."

From inside the little church building, a chorus of voices rose. Eb checked his watch. Straight up eleven, and time for services to begin. The new preacher sure was prompt.

"Onward then," Charles P. "Chaps" Smythe said as his boots hit the ground. "We have a church service to attend. I'd hate to think the four distinguished gentlemen who had the vision to found this town would be late to its first Christmas morning service."

"Are we late already?" Stone Creedon asked. "My watch must be slow."

"No, we're right on time," Eb said, being sure to speak into his slightly hard-of-hearing friend's good ear.

He let the young men walk ahead of the group, allowing them to disappear into the church building before he spoke. "Gentlemen, I'd like to thank you all." The lump in his throat almost kept him from finishing what he had to say. Almost but not quite. "There's not a one of us who can take more credit than the other for getting this town started up, but I feel like I'm the one you all did a favor for."

"How so?" Stone asked.

"Well, if it weren't for my Carolina, rest her soul, I'd probably have been content to dream about this place until the Lord took me home."

Chaps clapped a hand on Eb's back. "Sometimes a man needs a nudge to get going on what the Lord intends him to do. For you, your wife's passing was that nudge." He paused to look at the others before turning his attention back to Eb. "For the three of us, it was a friend and fellow ranger's promise."

"Ja, that's right," Swede said. "When you think of it, we are all fulfilling a promise to serve the Lord and the state of Texas."

"That we are," Stone said. "I say we dedicate this town to Him right here and now. What say you, fellow rangers?"

"I'm in on that." Eb held his hand out, and the others clasped theirs atop it. The four former rangers, comrades on the trail and friends in retirement, huddled together.

Rafe appeared at the church door. "Preacher's waiting," he said. "You can't miss the first Christmas service."

"Indeed. Shall we reconvene this meeting of the founding fathers at a later hour, say over dominoes after lunch tomorrow?"

"Who are you now, the mayor?" Swede asked Chaps with a grin.

"Actually I hadn't considered the office, but if you're offering it, then I'll heartily accept."

"After you, Stone, Swede, Mr. Mayor," Eb said with a sweep of his hat. "Save me a spot down front."

As the last of his fellow rangers filed past, Eb paused to once again look toward the sky. "Thank You, Lord," he said softly. "I do indeed dedicate this town and all that takes place here to Your glory. Keep those who live here safe from harm. And if You think about it, could You tell my wife, Carolina, that I love her and I sure do miss her?"

Chapter 1

Christmas Eve, 1877

I t was Christmas Eve, and when I opened my mouth to sing, a hymn came out. Mama sent me to my room so the gentlemen callers wouldn't hear. No doubt the Lord wasn't as welcome as the other menfolk in Mama's parlor."

Peony Primrose Periwinkle Potter shifted positions and dabbed at the perspiration on her brow with her mama's best silk handkerchief, no doubt a gift from some hapless fool bent on taking Mama away from a life she had no intention of leaving. Despite the chilly winter temperatures outside, the tight confines of the railcar made the room feel more like summer.

The train's horn sounded, and Peony sighed. "No trifling with men for me. I plan to open a dress store, you know. A nice establishment with lace curtains and a pretty mirror for the ladies to see themselves in. I've been collecting scrap fabric ever since I was a little girl for just that purpose."

Peony peered over at her traveling companion, unsure as

to why she'd just rattled on to him about the intimate details of her life as a New Orleans bawdy house owner's daughter. Perhaps it was because the sweet old man was stone-cold deaf and fast asleep.

Mr. Connor snored softly, his head gently bobbing with the rhythm of the train as it headed west. Peony smiled to think of how the Lord had arranged it so that she went out to fetch water at just the right time to overhear one of Mama's customers lament at having to take his valuable time to escort his elderly father out west.

"So I volunteered to see you safely to your destination, Mr. Connor. Mama didn't dare go against her best customer." Peony shrugged. "The way I see it, the Lord heard my prayer, and the rest is history."

She squared her shoulders and closed her eyes. As bad as her days with Mama had been, things could have turned out much worse. *Thank You, Lord, that Mama never wanted me to be one of her "girls."* Still, after seeing what she'd seen and living as she'd lived, Peony knew she might never be considered fit for decent folk.

All the more reason to start over somewhere new.

Visions of silks and satins danced across her mind, chased by silver thimbles and golden threads. Finally, her skill at hemming the dresses of Mama's girls and adding ruffles and flourishes to their lacy underthings would come in handy.

To think it all seemed so far from her grasp mere days ago. Next Christmas she'd celebrate her Savior's birthday in style—or at least in safety. Back home in New Orleans, Christmas had been just another day on Mama's busy social calendar. When Papa lived with them, it had been a day to gamble and play cards.

For a moment, Peony allowed her thoughts to wander toward memories of her beloved papa. She had vague recollections of a dark-haired man with a tickly beard who could lift her over his shoulders and toss her into the air with ease.

Later she knew this same man as a down-on-his-luck shadow of his former self, a man so broken by the weight of his habit that she could scarcely recognize him. Finally, somewhere around her fourth or fifth year, he'd disappeared entirely. That's when Mama began using the big house on Royal Street for something other than a home.

How she despised gambling in any form.

She settled back and watched the Texas landscape roll by until she could no longer hold her eyelids open. Somewhere between the purple fingers of dawn and the bright noonday sun, the train shuddered to a stop. Peony blinked hard and shook away the grogginess.

Placing a gloved hand atop her charge's blue-veined one, she stifled a yawn. Someday soon, she'd be sleeping in a real bed in a room with a door she didn't have to bar with a kitchen chair to keep Mama's clientele from "accidentally" trying to climb beneath her covers.

She shuddered with the memory, then purposefully turned her thoughts back to the elderly gentleman beside her. "The sign at the depot says we're in Dallas, Texas. It's a lovely day. Shall we take this opportunity to step outside, Mr. Connor?"

No response. Of course. He was fast asleep and couldn't hear her.

She shook his hand. "Mr. Connor?"

Nothing. Trying again, she got the same result. Despite her best efforts, the old man continued to sit head down, his chin resting on his narrow upper body.

Peony leaned closer and touched her palm to his chest. No response.

"Oh no," she whispered. "Mr. Connor, you're dead."

Muffled voices drew near, then passed by, oblivious to Peony's plight. She dabbed at her temples, her gaze darting from the open door to the open window. Which one offered the safer means of escape? The door beckoned but offered the added chance she might be spotted by someone while traversing the passageway. To slip out the open window seemed her only option.

Gathering her things, Peony prepared to make good on her escape. She swung her traveling bag onto her shoulder and put one foot on the bench. Using the window's frame for balance, she climbed up and prepared to slip out the window. The tracks were deserted in either direction, and the fall seemed to be one that she could survive. She'd walk away bruised, but at least she would walk away.

There would be nothing to connect her to the dead man. Nothing to hinder her from creating a new and respectable life.

The conductor called, "All aboard!" off in the distance as Peony leaned over the window's wooden frame and prepared to drop her bag onto the tracks. A pang of conscience hit her hard. What would happen to Mr. Connor?

One last look over her shoulder and Peony knew she couldn't just slip away and leave the kind old man to an unmarked grave on some Texas version of Boot Hill. She let the bag fall at her feet and climbed off the bench to retrieve a pen and writing paper from her reticule. Hurriedly scribbling a note for the conductor to find, she identified Mr. Connor's son by name and address, then wrote simply, "He died of natural causes, I promise."

"There, Mr. Connor," she whispered as she placed the note in his lapel pocket. "Now I'll know you're going to be taken care of."

She smoothed the fabric back into place, then paused. What was that? Reaching deeper into his pocket, past the note she'd just placed there, she found quite a surprise. Money. A fat wad of it, folded in half and secured with a red ribbon.

Peony counted the stack, then stifled a gasp. "Seven hundred dollars."

Carefully replacing the bills in the old man's pocket, she fell back against the hard wooden bench and closed her eyes. "Think," she whispered. "What do I do?"

The urge to run still bore hard on her. She tamped down her panic and allowed logic to take over. By the time the conductor arrived at the door, she had a plan—and seven hundred dollars in the waistband of her skirt.

It took her all of ten minutes to convince the authorities of her grief, scarcely longer than that to be driven to the undertaker in the sheriff's buggy to purchase a suitable casket and a plot in a nice cemetery atop a green hill near town. Declining the undertaker's offer to find lodging beneath his roof, Peony settled for a small room at a boardinghouse near the station. As darkness began to gather in the corners of the little room, Peony spread her remaining funds on the threadbare bedspread.

Just over six hundred dollars remained after the day's carefully budgeted expenses. A fortune to her—nothing, she was certain, to the younger Mr. Connor.

Exhaustion tugged at her senses, and it was all Peony could do to slip the money back into her waistband and rise to head outside once more. She reached her destination in a few steps, the telegraph office being the only building standing between the rooming house and the train station.

Obviously accustomed to discretion, the Western Union clerk barely blinked when Peony handed over three hundred and seventeen dollars and forty-three cents along with a note addressed to Robert Walker Livingston Connor III of New Orleans. She'd labored over the words, ultimately telling the younger Mr. Connor where he could find his father and why. She gave a full accounting of the monies she spent buying a proper casket and burial plot. Finally, she added a note of condolence and a receipt for payment of three hundred dollars, exactly half the money she'd agreed to.

After all, she'd only accompanied him halfway.

Half an hour later, she returned to her room and fell atop the narrow bed, not bothering to remove her traveling clothes. She would need them soon enough.

Chapter 2

Christmas Day, 1877

Rafe Wilson stepped away from his birthday celebration to cast a glance out the back window of Millie's Diner. Pop and his three constant companions raced across the broad expanse of space to slip behind the privy.

He chuckled. Like as not, the four of them were plotting trouble. Well, they'd earned the right.

Together the men formed the backbone of a ranger unit that, in its heyday, struck fear in the hearts of outlaws from San Antonio to the Brazos River and on up to the Oklahoma border.

Slowed by age, the four had lost none of their ranger camaraderie. They had, since entering retirement, shifted their focus from clearing Texas soil of evildoers to arguing the finer points of nearly everything while presiding over the town of Cut Corners. For the past seven years, the quartet and their various friends and acquaintances had turned their little place on the Texas prairie into a right fine home for God-fearing folk.

If he weren't so anxious to leave, he'd be glad to call the place home. Why, it would be a nice place to set up housekeeping with a pretty girl, maybe raise up a passel of young'uns.

Too bad he wasn't the marrying kind.

"I don't care what the captain says. Rafe's not joining up with the rangers, and that's that."

"He's a full-grown man, Eb. Older than you were when you took the oath," Swede said. "I don't see how you can stop him if he takes a notion to go."

"Don't worry. I've got a plan."

Eb leaned away from his hiding place behind the privy and checked to see if the coast was clear. Thus far, no one inside Millie's Diner had noticed the absence of the town's four original citizens. From the laughter drifting toward them, the dual celebration of Christmas and Rafe's birthday was still going strong.

Soon Millie would insist Rafe make a birthday wish and take the first slice of cake. That's where the party usually went south. While everyone in Cut Corners loved Millie, her cooking left something to be desired. Too bad she put all the sugar in the pot roast and none of it into her birthday cakes. Even though her pound cake could pound nails, Millie had practically raised Rafe and his cousin Jeff, too. Leaving her out of the family party that always followed the Christmas service at church never entered Eb's mind.

Setting her kitchen afire so she couldn't offer up her grub at the festivities—now that had occurred to him on more than one occasion. Too bad he was a law-abiding citizen and a God-fearing man.

"You've always got some sort of plan, Eb." Chaps jabbed his ribs with a sharp elbow. "I hope this one's better than the time you set the hogs on the preacher's garden. I thought we never would catch those critters once Rafe scattered them with buckshot."

"Well, it worked, didn't it? Before he lit out after those hogs, my son had about as much interest in his sheriffing as he did in learning to knit purty. Ever since then, he's been walking with a spring in his step and acting like he's useful around here." He paused. "Until lately, that is."

"Late?" Stone, deaf as a doorpost in one ear, turned to walk away. "We don't want to be late. We might miss the birthday singin'. The cake, now that's another story."

Eb caught his friend's elbow and spun him around. "We're not late yet," he said into the man's good ear.

"Well, why didn't you say so?" Stone grumbled. "I don't want to be late lessen it's for the cake eatin'."

"So you really think your harebrained scheme will work?" Swede asked. "Maybe we should just have a talk with the boy, explain to him that his mama didn't want him to be a ranger, and leave it at that. That makes sense, ja?"

Eb had pondered that possibility for years. Setting the boy straight on his mama's bias against rangering seemed like a tempting prospect, one that would certainly get him off the hook. While the finer points of the plan were obvious, Eb never could get past the idea that somehow the knowledge that his mama went to her reward with a dislike for the rangers might make Rafe think less of her. One thing Eb Wilson would never do was tarnish the memory of his beloved Carolina.

No, he had to keep his peace about the promise he made to her. The Lord and his ranger friends would have to help him out on this one.

"Trust me," Eb said. "This plan's foolproof."

Chaps leaned back against the rough wall of the privy and peered up at Eb from beneath the brim of his bowler hat. "That's what I'm worried about, my friend."

"What do you mean?" Eb narrowed his eyes. "Don't you want Rafe to stay in Cut Corners?"

"Of course I do," the Englishman said. "But I am a bit concerned about being shot in the process. If you'll recall, he didn't miss when he aimed at the pigs."

"Yes, I do recall that. Who do you think taught the boy how to shoot?"

"Millie, actually," Chaps said. "So what's your point?"

Eb ignored his friend's joke and offered a knowing smile. "The point is that even though Captain Phelps keeps me posted on things, I can't help but wonder when Rafe's going to come around to talking to him about joining up. You know he's taken quite an interest in my boy."

"Phelps is a good man," Chaps said, "but if Rafe decides to join up, there's not much he can do. Your boy's a born ranger, and any company would be lucky to get him. If Phelps won't take him, one of the other company commanders will."

Swede nodded. "Ja, I see how that might cause you to worry about your promise to Carolina, but the boy's a man now. How can we interfere?"

"Well, we won't exactly be interfering," Eb said. "I like to think of it as helping the Lord along with His plan."

"Sounds like meddlin' to me," Stone said.

Eb narrowed his eyes and stared at each of his friends in turn. "Well then, any of you fellows object to being called meddlin' men?"

"Nope," Stone said.

Chaps smiled. "Not I."

"What about you, Swede? You mind being a meddler?"

"In this instance, I don't mind."

"Well then, it's settled." He hit the high points of a strategy so brilliant he couldn't believe he'd thought of it. "Now, the thing is, until we know for sure that he's making plans to sign up with the rangers, we just keep the scheme on the back burner. Deal?"

Stone shook his head. "Burning? Somebody say something's burning? That Millie must of done gone and set the kitchen afire." He chuckled and slapped Eb hard on the back. "That there's an answer to prayer."

"No, my friend," Chaps shouted. "The kitchen's fine."

The former ranger looked about as happy as a long-tailed cat in a room full of rocking chairs. "Well now, that's too bad."

"Eb Wilson, are you and those friends of yours out there? You better get in here afore Christmas and your only boy's twenty-sixth birthday is done over and gone."

"Uh-oh, it's Millie." Eb paused and looked at his friends. "Look, are we agreed on this? We wait until the time's right, then we implement the plan. In the meantime, we pray Rafe doesn't get some wild idea and take off for San Antonio and the rangers."

Daylight sliced across Peony's sore eyes. Something jabbed her in the ribs, and with care, she leaned away from the offending spring to reach for the edge of the mattress. Where was she? Shaking off the cobwebs of last night's disturbing dream, she placed her feet on the floor, fully expecting to feel the rocking of the rails beneath her and hear the roar of a train's engine. Instead, she heard a loud rap at the door.

"Management," a female voice called. "It's high noon and past time to go."

Gathering her wits, she stumbled toward the door and threw it open. A rather surly-looking woman of advanced years stood inches away.

"Noon?" she said as she stifled a yawn. "Already?"

"Yes'm, it's nigh on half past, actually, and ya gotta vacate, hon," the woman said. "Room's been rented." She took a step back and gestured toward the stairs with her thumb. "That'un there paid me for a whole month. I'll hold him off a minute or two so's you can change."

An older fellow, spry but graying, headed their way at a fast clip. Peony looked down at the wrinkled mess she'd made of her only traveling dress. Although she looked a fright, there was no one in Dallas she needed to pretty up for.

"No, really," she said as she stepped away from the door. "Let me just fetch my bag and I'll be out of your way. I meant to be on my way to the train station hours ago."

"Ain't no train till late this afternoon," the older woman said. "Like as not you'll find the benches hard down at the station. 'Sides, it's Christmas. Nobody's gonna be keeping to a schedule today."

Christmas. Peony's heart sank. She'd all but forgotten. Back home, the bells on the cathedral would be ringing out the good news of the Christ-Child's birth. At Mama's place, however, it would most likely be business as usual.

"Where you headed, anyway?"

"West. North. I haven't exactly decided, although I've prayed about it quite a lot." She shrugged. "Anywhere a good seamstress is needed and reasonably priced storefront space can be had."

"Now isn't that interesting?"

Peony whirled around to see the elderly gentleman standing in the doorway. He held a battered hat in his hand and carried a valise under his arm. His linen suit belied the fact that Dallas had awakened to the coldest day in the month of December so far.

"Thomas Holcombe," he said with a smart nod. "Pleased to make your acquaintance."

She returned the greeting, then offered a weak smile.

Mr. Holcombe gave her a quick shake of his head, then addressed the proprietor of the hotel. "I'll not be responsible for putting this gentlewoman out on the street on Christmas Day." Dropping his valise at his side, he crossed his arms over his chest. "I insist she be allowed to stay. I will remain in the dining room until the lady can secure a ticket and be escorted to the train. If she cannot make arrangements until tomorrow, then so be it. I'll take lodging elsewhere."

The woman snorted. "Only empty rooms in Dallas on Christmas Day's at the jailhouse, and that ain't for certain."

"No, really, I insist." Peony stuffed her feet into her shoes and slipped the handle of her bag onto the crook of her arm. "I've missed breakfast, and I'm about to miss lunch, too." She slipped past the linen-clad man to address the proprietor. "Would it be improper for a single woman to sit alone in your dining room?"

The older woman gave a most unladylike snort. "Hon, this is Dallas. You come on downstairs with me, and I'll see you're not bothered."

A few moments later, Peony found herself settled at a

corner table near the kitchen and under the watchful eyes of the proprietor's son, an overlarge man of middle years. While her stomach offered the dual complaints of hunger and queasiness, her heart offered only one—desperation. She closed her eyes and offered a blessing over the plate of home-cooked fare, finishing with a plea more centered on her future than on the meal presently before her.

Lord, You led me out here—I just know it. Why have You left me high and dry in Dallas, Texas, on the very day Your Son was born? This was supposed to be my best Christmas ever. Now what do I do, Lord?

Chapter 3

The sound of a man clearing his throat broke into her prayer. Peony opened her eyes to see Mr. Holcombe standing before her.

"I'm very glad to see you're still here," he said. "I feel just terrible putting you out of your room, especially with it being a holiday and all."

She waved away his concern with a sweep of her hand. "Think nothing of it, sir. I assure you I'll be heading for. . ." Peony paused. She peered up at the gentleman, who now stared at her expectantly. "Well, I'll be heading out of Dallas very soon."

Touching the corners of her lips with the rough napkin, Peony hid her frown. Perhaps the man would leave if she acted disinterested. She stabbed at a salted hothouse tomato slice and took a bite. He stood watching her chew until she swallowed both the tomato and her fears and asked him to join her.

Peony gave the dapper Mr. Holcombe a sideways look, smiling despite herself as he winked and said, "I assure you

I'm far too old for anything other than dinner. I'm nothing but an old reporter looking to change my ways. I'm working on a book, you know."

"A book?" She set her fork down and narrowed her eyes. The wrong answer would send her scurrying for the train station for sure. "What's your book about, sir?"

He shrugged and rested his elbows on the gently worn checked tablecloth. "My adventures," he said. "All those years chronicling the ways of Texas seem to be paying off. I'm actually being paid a livable wage this time, to boot."

"But don't you have family you'd rather spend time with today?"

His answer lay in the expression on his face.

"Oh, I'm terribly sorry. I shouldn't have asked," Peony said.

"Actually I don't mind the question. It's the answer that's difficult." The reporter offered a weak smile. "You see, I was once a family man with a wife almost as pretty as you."

"What happened?" The question was out before she could take it back. She winced. "I'm sorry. Again I've overstepped the bounds of propriety."

"Nonsense," he said. "The nomadic life of a reporter didn't set well with my bride. She took our little girl and went home to her mama some years back."

"You simply have to go to them." Once more she'd spoken before her good sense could stop her. "Forgive me. Perhaps I'm speaking out of turn because it's Christmas Day and I'm here in this place without a family of my own. It's just that I know—or rather, I can imagine—that it would be most difficult for a girl to grow up without her father."

Mr. Holcombe's face grew solemn, and he seemed to give

great thought to her words. The pain of the memory of growing up without her own father burned almost as bright as the shame of thinking she might have accidentally told someone about it.

"Just consider it," she said quickly. "Think about making things right with your family."

A smile lit the older man's face. "If I didn't know better, I'd think you were some sort of Christmas angel sent to guide me home."

Peony laughed out loud at the thought of her being any sort of angel. "I don't know that the Lord has any use for the likes of me, but if I've given you something to think about, I'm grateful to Him for providing the words."

"Well, you have." He paused. "So, why don't you tell me more about what brings you to this worthy establishment on Christmas Day?"

Peony winced. "I'd much rather you tell me your story than to bore you with mine."

Moments later, the gentleman was entertaining Peony with tales of his two decades of newspapering, the most recent centering on a place called Cut Corners, Texas.

Somewhere along the way, Peony managed to finish her lunch and two of the best cups of coffee she'd had all week. She also confided her hopes for a future designing dresses, making him the second stranger in as many days with whom she'd shared her carefully guarded dreams.

By the time Mr. Holcombe pulled a gold pocket watch from his lapel, she'd all but forgotten she had no plans beyond lunch save the short walk to the train station. She hadn't considered whether the train would be heading east or west, and she told him so when he asked.

"Perhaps I can provide an impetus to set you aboard a train going north."

"North?" She placed the folded napkin beside her coffee cup and topped it with a few coins.

He looked away and seemed to be considering whether to speak. Finally, his gaze met hers. "My dear, I do believe the town of Cut Corners is in dire need of a dressmaker." He leaned forward. "And I am in dire need of someone to purchase a certain empty newspaper office set right on the main thoroughfare."

Peony gathered her traveling bag into her lap. The most she could spare would be a meager one hundred dollars, a sum so low she dare not mention it for fear of offending the kind man.

"I'm sorry, Mr. Holcombe, I don't have the money to—"

"You'd be doing me a great favor." He waved away her protest, then removed a slip of folded paper from his linen jacket and set it on the tabletop between them. With gnarled hands, Mr. Holcombe smoothed out the document, a deed, and turned it toward Peony. "Could you afford one hundred dollars?"

Ten months later, on the last day of October, Peony stepped out of the train station and stopped at the edge of the platform, taking a moment to look over the peaceful little town of Cut Corners, Texas. Not much to it, just as Mr. Holcombe had warned, but still it fairly resembled the image she carried in her mind. She reached into the pocket of her traveling dress and pulled out the key to her future.

Giggling at the pun, she set off toward Main Street and the old newspaper office, soon to be the home of her new dressmaking shop. The first of several trunks of essentials was due to arrive from Dallas in a few days, so until then, she would have to make do with what she'd managed to fit into the carpetbag at her side.

And make do, she would. After working as a maid at the boardinghouse in Dallas since the day after Christmas, she'd finally scrimped and saved enough to purchase a proper inventory for her dressmaker's shop. She'd even managed to purchase a used Singer sewing machine.

Offering a smile to the dapper man at the telegraph office, she marched across Ranger Road onto Main and strolled along until she stood in front of the building—her building—situated between a boardinghouse and a diner with a hand lettered sign reading MILLIE'S DINER. A stiff north breeze kicked up the hem of her skirt and blew a strand of hair into her eyes as she fitted the key into the lock.

"Thank You, Lord," she whispered. "Without Your intervention, none of this would be possible." Adding a promise to dedicate all she did to God, Peony threw open the door and stepped into her—

She froze.

The place was a mess. Dark streaks decorated one wall, and the residue of printer ink hung heavy in the air.

Against her better judgment, she stepped over the threshold into her new life, a life so far removed from New Orleans that it made her smile despite the mess surrounding her. Setting her carpetbag beside the door, she knelt right there and again thanked the Lord for bringing her to Cut Corners.

"Well, I declare. Looks like I've got me a churchgoin' woman for a neighbor."

Peony stumbled to her feet and swiped at the mess she'd

made of her already dusty traveling skirt. A woman of fifty-something stood in the doorway, her iron gray hair pulled off her face and captured in a messy knot atop her head.

Shaking the older woman's outstretched hand, Peony offered a smile and a soft "Yes, ma'am."

"Well now, that is an answer to prayer." She placed her hands on her hips and shook her head. "Old Man Holcombe hasn't gone on to the Lord, has he?"

"Mr. Holcombe? Oh no. He's fine. I last saw him in Dallas. He is working on a book about his travels in Texas."

"Is that right?" A broad grin split her lined face. "Well, you don't look much like your daddy, but I sure am glad he finally found you." Confusion must have etched Peony's face, for the woman gave her a sideways look. "You are Tom Holcombe's long-lost daughter, aren't you?"

"No, ma'am," she said. "He's still looking for her."

The woman made a clucking sound. "A pity, that situation. I told him he oughtn't to stop until he finds that girl and her mama."

"I told him the same thing." Silence fell between them, punctuated by the shrill call of the train's whistle. Funny how just moments ago she had been on that train, and now here she stood in her store with her neighbor.

Back in New Orleans the decent folk they had for neighbors didn't speak to Peony or her mama. At least not in public.

"Goodness, where are my manners? I'm Millie from next door. I run the diner. Nice to meet ya."

"I'm Peony. Peony Potter." She cringed when she said the name aloud, as she always did. Why Mama hadn't named her something sensible like Mary or Jane, she would never know. If she ever had daughters of her own, they certainly wouldn't be strapped with a moniker as silly as Peony Primrose Periwinkle Potter.

"Where you from, Miss Potter?"

"New—" She clamped her lips tight. Better not to give even a hint of her background. "I just arrived on the train from Dallas," she said. "And please, call me Peony."

Chapter 4

Y ou aim to open up another newspaper?"

Peony breathed a sigh of relief that Millie hadn't seemed to give her unusual name or her faltering explanation of her hometown a second thought—or perhaps she thought it rude to comment. She and the older woman would be fast friends if this was any indication of Millie's character.

"No," she said. "My intention is to open a dressmaker's shop. I sew, you see."

"Well now, isn't that nice?" She looked past Peony to the room beyond. "Looks like you've got a job ahead of you."

Nodding, Peony turned to follow Millie's gaze. "Yes, well, I wasn't expecting something so. . .so, well. . .in need of a woman's touch."

Millie cackled with laughter. "That it does," she said. "Actually, I'm thinking it might need some male attention first."

"How so?"

The older woman pointed to the jumble of tables and

shelves stacked at the back of the room. "That there used to be where old Tom would put together his paper. If'n you take that big old board down, you'll find a right nice window. And those shelves, well, wouldn't they look nice up here in front with your goods stacked on them all purty?"

Peony pictured the changes in her mind. "Yes," she said. "That sounds wonderful. Perhaps you might know someone with some carpentering skills."

Her guest frowned and crossed her arms over her chest. "You don't have a husband to help you? A purty young thing like you?"

"No, ma'am," she said.

"You a widow already?"

"No, ma'am. I've never been married."

"Well, isn't that something." Millie took a step back to stare at Peony. "Looks like you haven't seen a full plate in a coon's age. Why, I bet I've got something simmering on the stove that'd put some meat on your bones. Why don't we step next door and I'll fix you a bite to eat? Then we can talk about how you're going to get this little place shining like a new penny."

A good meal would be a welcome distraction and a nice beginning to her new life in Cut Corners. "Thank you," Peony said as she shouldered her carpetbag. "I'd like that very much."

"Set your suitcase down, honey," Millie said. "Ain't nobody going to mess with it. You're in Cut Corners now. We don't have any crime. Sheriff Wilson sees to that."

"What does Sheriff Wilson see to?"

Peony looked past her new neighbor to see her doorway filled with a dark-haired man. His uniform told her he was the law in Cut Corners, but his demeanor and slow Texas drawl told her he'd seen his fill of silly women like her. At least that was the impression she got as she felt his gaze sweep past her to focus on Millie.

A lady would have been offended. Unfortunately, she was still learning how to be a lady.

While she waited for the outrage she knew she should feel, she studied the breadth of his shoulders and the deep dimple in his clean-shaven chin. By the time she focused her attention on his velvet brown eyes, she knew this was a man who could pose a serious threat. Not only was he the law in Cut Corners, and thus a man in a position to find out much more than she wanted him to know about her past, but he was also a thief.

One look at him and he'd stolen her breath. What would five minutes in his presence do?

Perhaps she should leave now, walk out of Cut Corners with her finances in ruins but her heart still intact. She'd only had to hear Mama's story of lost love, desperate circumstances, and wrong choices once to know that retreat was often the best option.

Luggage still in hand, she should march right back to the depot and forget she'd ever seen eyes so brown and hair so blue-black. If the Lord got her out of New Orleans, then getting her out of Cut Corners, Texas, would be simple.

Getting that dimple out of her mind, well, that would probably take a bit longer.

What am I thinking?

Peony clutched the carpetbag to her chest and stared at the ink-streaked floorboards beneath her feet. This was her dream, her destiny. Whatever this silly feeling of butterflies in her stomach meant, it surely wasn't going to keep her from what the Lord intended for her to do.

No, she would not take off running like a scalded cat just because some man turned her mind to mush and set her heart beating double time. Unlike Mama, she planned to set down roots and live a respectable life earning a respectable living without turning the fool over a man.

Peony squared her shoulders and stared head-on into the face of the man she would have to begin thinking of as the enemy—the enemy of her heart, anyway. She'd already sunk her savings into this little piece of Cut Corners; she had nowhere else to go. All she had to do was learn to avoid Sheriff Wilson at all costs, and she would be fine.

"Well now," Millie said. "You see what I mean. Speak of the law, and there he is. Come here, Rafe Wilson, and meet Miss Potter." She turned to Peony. "Miss Potter, this here is Sheriff Rafael Wilson. He's in charge of keeping the peace in Cut Corners."

"Ma'am." Rafe tipped his hat to the piece of fluff, then returned his attention to Millie, who'd obviously just paused to take a breath. Uh-oh. She looked like she'd caught hold of an idea and was just about to let loose with it. *Probably ought to head back where I came from.* He knew from experience that when Millie chewed on something, she stayed at it awhile.

"Miss Potter's gone and bought this building from Tom Holcombe. She's gonna make a dress shop out of this place. Aren't you, hon?"

The woman smiled and nodded but said nothing. Interesting. A female who didn't rattle on. And a pretty one, at that.

"Rafe here's been the sheriff for, well, how long's it been?" He jabbed his fists into his pockets and forced a smile.

"Nigh on to seven years now."

"Seven years," Millie repeated. "My how time does fly."

Seven years of presiding over a town where the most exciting thing that happened was the occasional drunk rolling out of the saloon to shoot up a couple of windows or a pig getting stuck in a well. While other sheriffs were dealing with Indian uprisings or outlaws, all Rafe Wilson had to worry about was whether the loose nail in his chair was going to poke his backside during his afternoon nap.

Millie's giggle drew his attention away from the new dressmaker. The older woman shrugged. "Has it been that long? Seems like yesterday we were holding church up the street for the first time and thanking the Lord we didn't have to live in tents anymore."

Millie stopped her jawing and took a step back, crossing her arms over her chest. For a second she studied the both of them, and then she grinned.

Something was up, and Rafe already knew he didn't like it. Time to make his escape.

He thrust his hand in the dressmaker's direction in an attempt to make good on his exit. She lifted her gaze. It collided with his, and he felt the jolt down to his toes. At that moment, something inside him shifted, and his heart did a big old flip-flop while his throat froze up tighter than a puddle of milk at the North Pole.

He couldn't be sure what it was or why it happened, but Rafe knew that trouble was brewing. What sort of trouble remained to be seen, but he felt confident it had everything to do with the new dressmaker.

A chorus of male voices tumbled toward them on the east wind. The object of his thoughts raised her pretty brows, then turned her pink lips into a frown. Dropping her carpetbag, Miss Potter moved toward him.

Rafe scooted out of the way just as she brushed past to step out onto the boardwalk. She smelled pretty, this little lady, and it was all he could do not to inhale deep one more time after she'd passed by. Instead, he followed her outside like a pup on a rope. When she stopped, so did he.

"What are they doing?" she asked in an agitated tone.

"Hmm, what?" He followed the direction she pointed.

A few feet away Pop and his ranger friends had set their pickle barrel and board contraption up in a small sliver of sunshine. Stone and Chaps were busy setting up the domino game. Pop and Swede stood nearby jawing about whose turn it was to cut firewood for the church stove Sunday morning.

"Looks like a regular Tuesday morning in Cut Corners, ma'am."

"Gambling and wayward men? Is that what this town supports? Well, I never."

Pop caught sight of him and waved, and Rafe returned the gesture. "Wayward men? Those four? Hardly."

Rafe smiled down at the feisty female, hoping to either rile her further or placate her. Both options promised to offer an entertaining result.

What was left of his good humor began to fade as all four former rangers turned to stare in his direction. Pop said something to Stone, who needled Chaps. All four roared with laughter.

"Great," Rafe said under his breath. By supper the whole town would know he'd paid a visit to the new dressmaker. Pop would ride him about it for ages. So would Jeff.

"Aren't you going to do something about them?"

Rafe forced his attention back on Miss Potter. His heart still went *ker-thunk* when he looked at her, but his brain had the good sense to remind him womenfolk were nothing but trouble to a man with one foot on the train to San Antonio and ranger headquarters.

Rather than get all riled up, he shrugged. "Like as not someone will complain about someone else taking too long to make a move, and the four of them will end up at Millie's before noon. Most days that's how it happens."

The woman crossed her arms over her chest and gave him a look of disgust. "Surely you don't expect decent folk to be exposed to the likes of those—those. . .criminals." Squaring her shoulders, Miss Potter leaned toward him. "You're the sheriff. Do something." She turned up her pretty nose as the word left her lips.

The minute he laughed, Rafe knew he shouldn't have.

Chapter 5

With not so much as a how-do-you-do, the little dressmaker whirled around and headed inside, passing him with such force that his hat went flying.

"Hold on there," Rafe called. "What do you expect me to do?"

The woman practically skidded to a stop, then whirled around to stalk back toward him. Stopping inches away from his nose, she rose to her tiptoes and regarded him through narrowed eyes. "Sir, as the law in this town, you are expected to make the streets safe." Rafe cast a lazy glance to the left and then to the right. "Well, Miss Potter, maybe you'd know better than me, but I believe the streets look just fine. Course we've only got two of them here."

For a minute, she looked like she might speak. Rafe started thinking of what he'd say in response. Should he point out that the very criminals she was worried about were the same men who'd kept this part of the prairie safe for the better part of three decades? Maybe he ought to tell her real plain that if she didn't like the daily domino game in front of her establishment, she ought to pick another place to set up shop.

Before he could say a word, she turned on her heels and stormed away.

Out of the corner of his eye, he saw Millie smile. "What?" he asked as he grabbed his hat off the boardwalk.

"She's right. You ought to do something."

He watched the swirl of blue skirts swish around the corner and disappear into the back room. "You know as well as I do that there's nothing to be done with the likes of those four."

"I wasn't talking about your daddy and his ranger friends." Millie nudged Rafe, then shook her head and pointed inside the shop. "You really ought to go on in there and do something about her. She's liable to hurt herself."

A crash sounded somewhere in the depths of the future dress shop. Rafe took a step back from the door and whistled under his breath. "Miss Millie, I've never backed down from man or beast, but I believe I'm going to walk away from this fight before I find myself bested."

Tipping his hat, he turned to head for Erik's workshop. If his friend wouldn't take him on as a part-time employee, maybe he'd turn him loose with a hammer and bag of nails and let him pound away his riled-up temper on the scrap wood out back.

Another crash and Millie went skittering toward the diner like a scalded cat. Rafe was tempted to go back and make sure Miss Potter hadn't buried herself under an avalanche of old newspapers or fallen through the staircase that led up to the storeroom.

He stopped and waited. The only sound he heard was the cackle of Pop and the men laughing. Then the laughter stopped.

Rafe watched in disbelief as the town's new dressmaker appeared in her doorway wielding something that looked like a large stick. No, he decided, it was a broom she held.

"Gentlemen, I am going to ask you nicely to leave the premises immediately and take your gaming apparatus with you. I intend my dress shop to be a decent establishment, and I will not have my customers see such goings-on at my doorstep."

To her credit, she spoke nicely, but her face and the way she held that broom told another story. The little lady looked capable of breaking up the domino game by force at the slightest provocation.

Rafe leaned against the hitching post to watch the show. "This just could be the most fun I've had all day."

Chaps rose first and gave Miss Potter a courtly bow. No doubt back in England, he'd charmed his share of the ladies. The dressmaker, however, seemed oblivious.

"My friends," Chaps said as he collected the dominos, "I do believe it is time to reconvene this meeting of the town council elsewhere as the lady has requested."

"Yes, sir, Mr. Mayor." Pops lifted the board off the pickle barrel, then offered Miss Potter a smile. "Welcome to Cut Corners, ma'am. You sure do pretty up the place."

Rafe knew for a fact that Pop had done his share of lady charming in his day. Once again, the lady in question was not amused, however. Rafe chuckled at the sour face she made.

"Might I suggest though," Pop added, "that you take to carrying a pretty little reticule or a parasol of some sort? It's not that you don't look fetching holding it over your head like that, but something a little less threatening than a broom might better impress the menfolk."

"I give her a week and she'll be on the train out of town,"

Rafe said under his breath.

Stone gathered up the remaining stools while Chaps hefted the pickle barrel onto his shoulder. "Onward, men," he said as he led his band of brothers across Main Street.

"Don't forget it's my turn," Swede called.

She must have seen him laughing, for the dressmaker started his way. Rafe rose to his full height and squared his shoulders. He adjusted his holster, then fiddled with his badge to be sure it glittered just right in the morning sun.

A glance in her direction told him she'd neither slowed her pace nor dropped her broom. Rafe frowned. Surely she didn't intend to sweep the boardwalk with the sheriff of Cut Corners.

Not in broad daylight on Main Street.

"Sheriff Wilson?"

He met her halfway, then tipped his hat and looked down his nose at the prettiest sight that ever decorated the middle of Main Street. Her eyes were blue-green. Now how about that? He'd have sworn they were blue. And here in the sun her hair had the prettiest shades of honey mixed in with the brown. Her lips, now they were still pretty and pink just like he'd noticed back in the—

"Sheriff Wilson."

Rafe shook his head to clear his thoughts. "Yes, ma'am."

"Sir, you are the law in this town. Am I correct?"

He stared at the broom instead of the woman to keep his brain from running off and leaving him again. "You are."

"And you work for the law-abiding citizens of Cut Corners?"

"I do."

There he went looking at those eyes again. Rafe stared past her to the boardinghouse where Lula stood on the porch jawing with Ticks McGee. When Lula lifted her hand to wave, he responded with a nod.

Then he noticed the crowd gathering at the windows of Millie's place. It looked like half the town was watching them instead of eating. Of course, it was pot roast day, and that alone could have kept the diners from raising their forks.

She shook her broom and narrowed her eyes. My but she still looked pretty, even riled up like a banty rooster.

"Then, as a citizen of Cut Corners, I demand you end the lawlessness that seems to pervade this town."

Rafe watched the crowd gathering on the boardwalk outside Jay Harris's barbershop and frowned. Something had to be done about this menace to his peace and quiet.

"Do tell," was all he could manage.

"Indeed. You are needed, Sheriff. What will you do about it?"

A nagging voice reminded him that just this morning he'd prayed for the Lord to do something about the fact that he never seemed to be needed by the citizens of Cut Corners. When he uttered that prayer, he'd thought he was asking God to give him clear rein to join up with the rangers.

Now he had to wonder if the Heavenly Father didn't have a sense of humor.

"Well, ma'am, a man doesn't go into a fight unarmed, if you know what I mean." She obviously didn't, but he pressed on anyway. "So what I'm going to do is go back to my office and think on this. I'm going to get me a plan. How about that?"

She seemed to be chewing on the idea of complaining further. Finally she nodded. "I think that's a good idea."

"Well, praise the Lord. Now if you'll excuse me."

With that he turned tail and headed for the quiet confines of his office and the nap he planned to take just as soon as he calmed down. This afternoon he'd go see Erik. If the carpenter wouldn't take him on for free, he'd just have to pay Erik to work there.

The extra work ought to keep him busy and out of reach of the dressmaker's complaints. It would also serve to make the time pass quickly until he could make a trip to San Antonio.

If Peony Potter was putting down stakes in Cut Corners, it was time for him to pull his up.

Chapter 6

The first day of November dawned bright and clear, but Peony's eyes were anything but. She'd spent half the evening and into the night clearing out reams of old paper and scrubbing down windows and walls. Today she planned to tackle the ink-streaked floor and the dusty shelves. By the time her supplies arrived from Dallas, her shop would shine like a new penny.

Peony sipped gingerly from the steaming cup of coffee and gave thanks that Lula Chamberlain, owner of the boarding-house that had become her temporary home, made the best around.

"Miss Potter, might I join you?" A man of considerable stature stood beside the empty chair. "I'm Thaddeus Seymour. I'm the banker in these parts."

She nodded, and the fellow sank onto the chair. "Welcome to Cut Corners, Miss Potter."

"Thank you," she replied.

Rafe Wilson stepped into view, and her heart jumped.

What a handsome man. A pity he was such a grump.

"As I was saying, your monies are more than safe in our little bank. Why just yesterday I was speaking to a fellow banker on the train back from Dallas, and he said. . ."

The fellow's mouth kept moving, but Peony heard none of what he said. Instead, she watched the sheriff pour a cup of coffee and disappear into the kitchen. A few seconds later, she heard the unmistakable laughter of Lula Chamberlain followed by a deep rumble that could only belong to Sheriff Wilson.

"Miss Potter?"

Peony tore her attention away from the kitchen door and focused on her companion. "Yes, I'm sorry. What were you saying?"

Mr. Seymour let out a long breath and smiled. "I was explaining how our system of compounding your interest. . ."

Interest. Yes, that's what she felt, but not in anything the banker said. More than anything else, she was interested in what was so funny behind the kitchen door. Twice now she'd heard the sheriff's laughter and, more than that, a giggle from Lula Chamberlain.

Why, the woman was old enough to be that man's mother. Surely the pair weren't, well, a pair.

The objects of her thoughts spilled through the door with the sheriff in the lead. He stopped short when his gaze met Peony's, causing Lula to run into him. His glass of milk went flying, and so did the pan of biscuits Lula held. The end result was a mess that landed partly on the floor and mostly on the banker.

Mr. Seymour clambered to his feet, howling at the indignity of cold milk trickling down his back and decorating his expensive suit. Lula rushed to placate the banker while Rafe winked at Peony. "Looks like we're both out of luck for breakfast," he said.

Peony nodded, stomach growling. With the biscuits a total ruin, the only alternative was the fare at Millie's place. If only she'd saved some of the jerky she'd purchased for her trip from Dallas. Unfortunately she'd eaten the last of it yesterday evening. At the time, it had seemed sensible to continue her work without leaving to dine at the boardinghouse.

"Miss Potter, are you as hungry as I am?"

Peony jumped and clutched her napkin to her chest. For a large man, Sheriff Wilson certainly could move quietly. Of course, the banker's howling would have drowned out all but the most careless of patrons.

Meeting his gaze, Peony noted the lawman had a glorious smile. "Actually I'm famished. Perhaps you could tell me whether Millie is still serving breakfast."

"Yes, she's still got breakfast cooking, but I have to warn you, good food's as scarce as hens' teeth over at Millie's place." The sheriff cringed. "I love her like my own mother, but what that woman does to biscuits ought to be illegal."

Peony giggled. "I did find yesterday's lunch quite interesting."

"Ah, the Monday lunch special. Pork chops and apple dumplings."

She nodded. "Funny, but I never knew a cook to put molasses in pork chops."

"And onions in the apple dumplings?"

"Exactly."

Rafe sighed. "Like I said, Millie's got a special place in my heart. It's her food I can't stomach. Pardon the pun." Silence fell between them, broken only by the thud of the banker's retreating footsteps and Lula's chuckle as she headed off to the kitchen, promising more biscuits in half an hour.

"Half an hour's a long time," Rafe said. "How about I make up for ruining your breakfast by offering you a little something I've got over at my office? I keep a supply of jerky for emergencies." He gave her a sheepish look. "I couldn't help notice you like jerky."

"How would you know that?"

"Well, you see, I happened to be strolling past your shop last evening around sundown and noticed you having a picnic amongst the rubble." He looked pained at the admission. "I wasn't spying. I'd actually thought I might. . ."

"Might what?"

The sheriff frowned. "Well, now, I thought I might apologize for my rude behavior yesterday. See, I'm the law in Cut Corners, and as a citizen, you had every right to complain about the goings-on on your boardwalk. I guess I didn't do a very good job of explaining things."

"Explaining things?" She gave him a sideways look. "What things?"

Warning bells went off in Rafe's brain as the words he spoke hung in the silence. He'd been smoothing out her ruffled feathers with his sweet talk, and now this? With one sentence he'd set their relationship back to square one.

Not that they had a relationship, of course.

"What I mean is, I didn't tell you that the fellows were harmless and that they just like to play dominos for fun. There isn't any gambling going on—at least not that I know of—so you can leave your broom in the closet."

Well, that did it. The pretty girl's smile went south, and the bristle returned to her backbone. "I thank you for that apology, Sheriff Wilson, however backhanded it turned out." She folded her napkin pretty as you please and set it on the table beside her coffee cup. "Now if you'll excuse me, I have work to do."

Rising, she beat a quick path to the door.

"What?" he called after her. "What did I say? Can't a man apologize?"

Lula came to the door, her hands white with flour. "Rafe, if I didn't know better, I'd think you meant to get off on the wrong foot with that girl."

"I did no such thing," he said. "Besides, I was just trying to tell her I was sorry."

Without comment, she turned and headed back to the kitchen, leaving Rafe to contemplate the unfairness of it all. Then he spotted the biscuit under the table.

There it sat, perfectly preserved atop a napkin that had fallen under the banker's chair. Neither milk nor humans had touched it, or at least it looked that way as he scooped it up and set it before him.

He was hungry as a bear and had the growl in his gut to prove it. And there sat the butter and honey. Two minutes later the biscuit was in his hand and his boots were heading down Main Street.

"Miss Potter," he called as he trod lightly on her freshly mopped floor. "You in here?" A sound from the back of the building told him he wasn't alone. "Miss Potter?"

He set the biscuit on the first clean shelf he could find and headed off in the direction of the noise. This time he crept softly, not caring to let whoever was hiding there know he was coming.

To be safe, he palmed his revolver. As he felt the cold metal touch his palm, his heart kicked up a notch. The last time he used his gun, it had been for target practice. He hadn't missed then, and he wouldn't miss now.

Regulating his breath to cause the least amount of noise, Rafe hunkered down behind the counter and readied the weapon for firing. No common criminal would get away with trying to steal from Peony Potter.

Not with Rafe Wilson on duty.

Chapter 7

Pulse racing, Rafe slowly moved toward the back of the store. Again he heard movement—this time just beyond a large stack of newsprint.

"One last chance to come out before I have to carry you out."

"Sheriff, what are you doing?"

Rafe nearly jumped out of his skin. He whirled around to see Peony Potter standing behind him. "Get down and be quiet," he stated firmly.

To her credit, she complied without question.

A rustling sound preceded a loud crash, all taking place in the back of the store. Rafe touched his finger to Miss Potter's lips to indicate he needed silence in order to rid the shop of its intruder.

The next series of events happened in a blur. Rafe rushed the back room, gun ready. A movement caught his attention, and he aimed. Before he could shoot, someone or something knocked the weapon out of his hand. He fell, and a blur flew over him. His revolver skidded to a stop against the far wall, and Rafe scrambled after it.

By the time he retrieved his weapon and prepared to fire, he stood alone. Slowly he made his way through the debris into the main room. "Miss Potter?" he whispered.

No answer.

He clutched the weapon and strode toward the door. If the creep had harmed Miss Potter, well, Rafe would not be responsible for what he did when he caught up with him.

Two steps from the boardwalk, Peony Potter raced in and slammed into his chest. The collision sent him reeling backward while the dressmaker fell forward. Rafe rolled out of the way just in time to miss being landed on.

His gaze met hers, and to his surprise, she began to giggle. "What's so funny?"

Rather than respond, she pointed to a spot behind him. Rafe rolled over to see a fat orange cat with mismatched ears perched on a shelf.

"A cat?" The lop-eared feline looked about as happy as a woodpecker in a petrified forest. Peony continued to giggle, and Rafe joined her. "I nearly shot a cat."

"Actually I think the cat won the battle." She pointed to his face.

Rafe swept the back of his hand over his cheek and came away with a smear of blood. Peony offered him a lacy handkerchief, which he reluctantly accepted. Replacing his revolver in his holster, Rafe leaned back against the counter and dabbed at his cheek.

"Miss Potter," he said as he exhaled, "this is by far the most exciting breakfast I think I've ever had."

"Breakfast?" She shook her head. "We missed breakfast, remember?"

Rafe searched the room for signs of Lula's napkin, finally spying a glimpse of the fabric beneath the overturned stack of newsprint. He reached to reclaim the treasure, only to find it hadn't survived the near-battle with the cat.

Inside the folded napkin, Lula's tasty biscuit had become a puddle of crumbs.

"Well, I tried," he said with a shrug.

Peony nodded. "I appreciate the effort, Sheriff. Remind me to call you if I need my breakfast smashed or my cat frightened to death."

He waited to see if she was making a joke, then laughed when her expression showed she was. "I wish I'd known you had a cat."

Peony shrugged. "I didn't know I had one either."

Silence fell between them, giving Rafe time to study his companion. Indeed she was prettier than a newborn calf. A fellow could get used to looking at a woman like her.

Sure, they'd hit a rough patch early on in their getting-to-know-yous, but she looked as though she'd forgotten all about the little run-in with Pop and his ranger buddies.

Maybe it was time to let her know he'd felt something from the first time he laid eyes on her. He'd have to go slow, obviously, because a woman of Miss Potter's breeding probably wouldn't take kindly to a big oaf declaring his infatuation after such a short time.

No, he'd speak kindly of her first, greasing the path to her heart with a little flattery and a smile. He began with the smile. Obviously she liked what she saw, because it seemed she leaned a bit closer. He did his part and scooted in her direction. Between the leaning and the scooting, they soon found themselves side by side.

Oh, but she did smell good. A gentleman shouldn't wonder what it would be like to kiss a total stranger. But then, he and Miss Potter had been properly introduced by Millie, and she'd been approved of by Lula.

She had told him so in the kitchen just a short while ago. He'd laughed then. He wasn't laughing now.

Neither was she.

"Miss Potter, I want you to know that as sheriff of Cut Corners I've seen my share of—"

"I tell you, Stone, if you don't pay attention you're going to lose."

Pop.

Rafe groaned and inched a bit closer to the dressmaker. "As I was saying, Miss Potter, I've noticed that when you—"

"Honestly, gentlemen, a meeting of the town council's a serious matter. Why are you two worrying about the pickle barrel?"

Chaps this time. Miss Potter's face told Rafe she'd heard him, too.

Rafe sucked in a deep breath and let it out slowly, then debated stealing a kiss right then and there. He decided to show his gentlemanly side instead. "Miss Potter, what I'm trying to say is—"

"Now there you go trying to cheat, Eb Wilson. Didn't you think I'd notice?"

Swede.

No need to look at Miss Potter to know how cold the room had turned. He chanced a glance anyway. Any thoughts of stealing a kiss fled. Yep, better to make a quick exit than to sit here any longer and be thought a fool.

"I ought to be moseying on then," he said as he climbed

to his feet and cast about for his hat. He found it on the floor beside the ladder and jammed it on his head.

Rafe had nearly made his exit when Miss Potter called to him. She remained seated on the floor, leaning against the counter, and he had to backtrack his steps to see her properly. To his amazement, the orange menace had jumped down from its perch on the shelf and made itself at home in her lap. She sat there scratching its good ear, a blank look on her face.

"Sheriff," she said as she met his stare, "thank you for breakfast."

Relief flooded him. "You're most welcome. I just wish I'd delivered it in one piece."

She nodded. "Yes, well, I appreciate the thought anyway."

Nodding, Rafe stood waiting for further praise or a word of any kind. Instead, the woman who'd set his heart to thumping remained quiet.

"Well then, I'll just be going."

Again she nodded. This time he got all the way outside before he turned to see her standing a distance behind him. "Sheriff," she said as she walked slowly toward him, "I'd appreciate it if you'd do me one favor."

By now she was close enough to smell her, and she smelled like lilacs. "What's that?" he asked.

"Seeing as how you take your job so seriously, I'd appreciate it if you'd do what you ought to and rid the streets of those four."

He didn't have to look over in the direction of where she pointed to know she referred to Pop and the boys. "Miss Potter, you're a fine lady, and I have thoroughly enjoyed most of the morning I've spent with you, but I believe you're out of line in asking me to remove the founding fathers of Cut

Corners while they're holding a council meeting." He tipped his hat. "Now if you'll excuse me, I'll just go find some real law work to do. And to think I almost kissed you."

She huffed and puffed and stormed inside. "To think I almost let you."

Chapter 8

December 4, 1878

The Lord must have known Rafe wasn't meant to put down roots in Cut Corners, or He wouldn't have made the week in San Antonio such a productive one.

Rafe thought he probably should have signed the induction papers while he was there, but Captain Phelps urged him to take them home and think on it a spell first.

To his mind, there was nothing to think on. He was born to be a ranger; the Lord made him to follow in his father's footsteps. Why, then, did he feel as jumpy as a frog on a hot skillet about leaving the place he'd spent the past seven years?

True, Captain Phelps had given him the lecture about how hard it was to be a ranger and a family man. Well, he knew about that firsthand, but spending long periods of time with Pop away on duty hadn't killed him.

Could be his strange inability to get Peony Potter out of his mind. While he'd managed to steer clear of her for the better

part of a month, his brain went goofy and his heart thudded whenever he thought of her. On those occasions when he found himself in the vicinity of her or her dress shop, he took pains to keep from having any actual conversations.

Trouble was, whenever he looked at her, he thought about kissing her. Whatever had transpired between them in the rubble of the old newspaper office had long since been forgotten by the dressmaker. That much was obvious on those rare occasions when he caught sight of her and she crossed the street to keep from having to say hello.

Rafe stepped off the train and waved to Ticks McGee over at the telegraph office. Making a passing glance in the direction of the dressmaker's shop, Rafe noted that in his absence the dressmaker had added a fluff of lace curtains in her front window and a neatly lettered sign reminding the ladies the time was at hand to order dresses for the Christmas social season.

What Christmas social season? Little did the silly Miss Potter know, but the closest thing Cut Corners had to a holiday social gathering at all was the Christmas Eve pot roast special at Millie's Diner. Given the skill of the cook, or rather the lack of same, that postchurch gathering could hardly be described as a social event. The family party to celebrate his birthday generally didn't fare any better, as Millie tended to keep her cake recipes too high on the shelf to go by most years.

Bless her heart, dear Millie did try though, and thanks to her, he'd never spent a birthday feeling unloved or alone. Christmas Day was the one day of the year Pop and his buddies were always home.

As for Millie's pot roast, however, a single man ate what he could batch up in his own kitchen before he succumbed to the

infamous Christmas Eve lunch, often seasoned up with sugar and other things your average cook wouldn't think of throwing in the skillet. But then Millie was not your average cook. The only reason tradition held was because being with others suffering the same fate seemed a slight bit better than suffering through another Christmas Eve alone in bachelor's quarters.

Rafe heard his father's laughter before he rounded the corner and caught sight of his pa and the others. Seated at their usual spot, the men looked to be plotting trouble—their usual state of affairs. Rafe slowed his pace and absentmindedly palmed the barrel of the revolver strapped to his hip.

The gun still saw less use than a mirror in a pigsty, but as sheriff, he wore it all the same. Actually he did shoot the thing occasionally in the line of duty. Just last year he'd had to fire off a round to scare a half dozen hogs that were feasting on the remains of the preacher's garden. Before that, he'd be hard-pressed to think of the last time he used a bullet on anything more dangerous than the tin cans he kept around for target practice.

A sorry state of affairs for a man who called himself a sheriff.

"Well, I don't see another way around it." His father again. "He simply ain't gonna be convinced lessen we take action."

"Who's not going to be convinced?" Rafe looked down into four of the guiltiest innocent faces he'd seen all week. "And what action are you planning to take?"

He turned first to the guiltiest of the lot, his father. "Pop, have you been reading my mail again?"

Eb Wilson had the decency to look offended, except that the expression didn't quite make it to his eyes. They twinkled with glee even as he frowned.

"I've been busy all morning and hardly had a chance to sit down." His nudge of the fellow sitting to his left was almost imperceptible.

Almost but not quite.

"Ja," Swede said. "Eb's been helping me set fence posts all morning. We've barely had a chance to sit down."

"Is that right?"

A chorus of agreement rose among the men. Rafe turned his attention to Stone and Chaps. Neither would look him in the eye. Finally he swung his gaze back to Pop, who suddenly found a great interest in studying the domino in his palm. The edge of a telegram peeked out of his pocket, evidence to Rafe's mind that Eb Wilson and his pals had been meddling again.

"You're a full-grown man, Son," his father said. "Why in the world would I want to waste my time poking my nose into your business?"

"Because you've been meddling in my business ever since I was out of knee pants, Pop. So have the rest of you." He paused to let the others express their halfhearted outrage. At least his father hadn't denied the accusation. "Look, I'm full-grown and able to make my own decisions on whatever—"

The rest of his statement caught in his throat as Peony Potter, dressed in something pink and pretty, appeared in the window of the dressmaker's shop. He struggled to capture his escaping thoughts and herd them back in the direction they were supposed to go. Unfortunately, gaining his voice and speaking anything other than nonsense was like trying to scratch his ear with his elbow. It just couldn't be done.

Peony looked over in his direction, and for a moment he thought she might wave. Instead, she looked past him to the four old rangers, then slammed the curtains shut.

"That girl's about as sociable as an ulcerated back tooth." Rafe didn't realize he'd spoken the comment aloud until the four meddling men hooted with laughter.

"She's as harmless as a bee in butter, Son." Pop rose to slap Rafe on the back. "All she needs is a little attention from the right man, and she'd be sweet as honey." He glanced down at his partners in crime, then winked at Rafe. "Maybe you ought to be the fellow who turns her attention to something besides criticizing decent folk for minding their own business on a public boardwalk."

Chuckling, Rafe pointed to his father. "You're the one with all the answers, Pop. Why don't you go smooth talk her?"

"I would, Son, but out of respect for the young, I thought I might give you a chance." He settled back into his chair and looked up at Rafe with a smug grin. "Lessen you don't think you're up to a challenge."

Any other challenge he would have taken in a split second. This one, however, he knew he'd never meet. Peony Potter had taken a dislike to him that time had not changed one lick. Better the subject moved on to something less ticklish.

"So, Pop, what's that in your pocket?"

Eb Wilson patted his chest. "This? Why, it looks like a telegram."

"Anything I ought to know about? Maybe something that beat me here from San Antonio?" He gave his best shot at looking like a lawman deep in the midst of a serious investigation. "I know you and your buddies at the ranger command post are still thick as thieves. You got something you want to 'fess up to?"

The older man seemed to consider his question for a moment. His pals watched him without expression. Rafe had to give it to the four of them. These old rangers might be slowed by age, but not a one of them showed any signs of weakness when questioned.

"Something to 'fess up to? I don't reckon so." His father's grin widened. "Besides, we all know Ticks McGee can't keep a secret. If it was anything important, you'd have heard about it before you stepped out of the depot."

This much was true. The telegraph operator could best any woman in town in a gossiping contest.

"You all in agreement with Pop? Nothing new I need to hear about?" The other three nodded, although Rafe noted that none of them could quite look him in the eyes. "Then I guess you aren't interested in what I told your old buddy Captain Phelps when he asked me if I could report for duty with the rangers the first Monday in January."

With that, he tipped his hat and walked away.

Chapter 9

Peony stepped back from the curtains and watched the sheriff move with purposeful strides toward the building that housed the jail. "That man makes me so mad."

Peony spoke to the orange lop-eared cat that had taken up residence in her shop during the former owner's absence, the same cat that had almost lost its life to the sheriff's bullet. Naming the feline Tabby, Peony appreciated the fuzzy guest's listening ear. Who else could she complain to about a man who was obviously the paragon of virtue and respect in Cut Corners?

She'd mentioned to Mrs. Chamberlain, the owner of the boardinghouse, that she'd been irritated at the lack of concern the lawman showed in ridding the streets of the riffraff only to find out the woman had practically raised him and thought he hung the moon. A discussion with Millie over breakfast regarding the men who insisted on gambling within earshot of her establishment resulted in bitter coffee and cold flapjacks. Of course, in dear Millie's case, that could have been the norm and not any sort of statement regarding her opinion.

Sighing, Peony lifted a stack of neatly folded fabric onto the shelf nearest the door, then stood back and admired her handiwork. In no time, she'd managed to get the former newspaper office clean and orderly and had even pried the boards off the window in the back to allow the morning sun to shine in.

That last feat had been accomplished with ease. It was amazing what a woman could do when she was angry. Why, if she lived to be a hundred and ten, she never would understand men.

Especially that man.

Shuddering at the reminder of the cranky lawman, she forced her mind to the task at hand. Soon a pretty yellow calico dress wore bright green buttons and a thick set of seams down the side. The newly expectant farm wife who ordered the garment would have plenty of room to let it out once her belly began to swell.

Peony allowed the dress to slip from her fingers. For a moment, she allowed herself the luxury of imagining what it might be like to be some man's wife, some child's mother. As quickly as the image appeared, she chased it away with thoughts of the next project on her list: unpacking the newest parcel of fabrics from Dallas.

She pushed the ancient rolling ladder—a welcome leftover from the previous owner—closer, then climbed to reach the topmost shelf. Peony settled a stack of multicolored calicos atop the shelf and climbed down to retrieve a basket of thread.

Unfortunately Tabby had taken up residence inside, and she complained bitterly when Peony ousted her onto the floor. The cat gave her an irritated look, then turned tail and headed for the crate that held Peony's unpacked sewing machine.

A cackle of male laughter followed by four distinct voices all speaking at once assailed her through the front windows. Those awful gamblers again. This time, due to threatening skies, they seemed to be headed for Millie's Diner.

"Believe me, we all have our irritations, Tabby," Peony said as she hefted the basket onto her shoulder and stepped onto the ladder. "At least you can find another place where you won't be bothered. I don't have that luxury."

Not with the sheriff refusing to do his job.

His job. Peony shook her head. Well, of course the man wasn't doing his job. The ringleader of the gamblers was his father. She'd found that out over breakfast one morning in the diner.

And the other three, well, to hear Lula tell it, they were practically family, as well. Of course the man was loyal to those he cared for, an admirable trait under most circumstances. Oh, how she disliked admitting he had good traits.

"Excuse me, ma'am, but might I have a word with you?"

Peony looked up to see Eb Wilson standing on the porch looking in. He seemed out of place, a rough man among laces and calico, and his demeanor showed he felt that way, too.

Mama might have done a lot of things wrong, but one thing she did right was to teach Peony respect for her elders. "Please, do come in," she said, rising to meet him halfway. "Would you like some tea? I was just about to make myself some."

The older man clutched his hat in his hands and studied the boardwalk. "No, ma'am, and if you don't mind, I believe I'll just stand out here. Fancy stuff makes me nervous."

Suppressing a smile, she took a few steps forward. "How can I help you, Mr. Wilson?"

"Well now, it's me who's aiming to help you, actually." He lifted his gaze to meet hers. "It's about my boy, Rafe. I believe you two are acquainted."

Irritation rose. "Yes, we've had several conversations," she said.

"And I feel bad about that, ma'am. I believe my friends and I are the source of those conversations, and I'd like to apologize right now for that."

"You would?"

He nodded. "You see, it's come to my attention that the friction between you and my boy might be the cause of him not telling you his true feelings."

Ticks McGee appeared in the doorway of the mercantile across the way. Peony offered the man a polite wave, then turned her attention back to Mr. Wilson.

"What do you mean 'his true feelings'?"

"Miss Potter, I'm a single man myself, have been for nigh on twenty-seven years now, but when my Carolina was alive, rest her soul, well. . ." He paused to clear his throat. "Let's just say I remember what it felt like to be in love, and I feel terrible that I might be keeping you two apart."

"I assure you, Mr. Wilson, you are not keeping us apart."

Eb Wilson let out a yell that caused the horses tied in front of the bank to skitter and complain. He took a step inside to clasp Peony's hand and shake it with vigor. "Now that's the best thing I've heard all day."

"It is?"

"Yes, indeed. Thank you for clearing that up, Miss Potter." He set his hat back firmly on his head. "I believe I'll go let Rafe know he doesn't have to hide his affections any longer." With a wink, he added, "You have a lovely afternoon, you hear?"

Peony stood in the door and watched the elder Mr. Wilson cross Main Street with a spring in his step. Tipping his hat to Ticks McGee, he headed in the direction of the sheriff's office.

A plaintive meow reminded Peony that she wasn't alone in the dress shop. She turned to see Tabby sunning herself beneath the lace curtains and knelt to scratch the soft fur behind the cat's right ear. The cat stretched and nestled against her hand.

"Now that was an interesting conversation."

Rafe leaned back in his chair, resting the heels of his boots on his desk. He need not worry about disturbing the contents of its surface with his big feet. There hadn't been anything of value sitting on the scarred wooden surface since he took the job back in '71.

Hearing from the rangers had been the only bright spot in his week—his year, actually—and just thinking about getting out from behind this desk to ride with them gave him a smile. Only his pop's strange reluctance to discuss the matter kept him from jumping for joy.

Why Eb Wilson couldn't be proud that his only son wanted to join the family business was beyond him. It was a plain fact that Pop and his buddies only left the rangers because the government folks disbanded the units and sent their men off to fight in the War between the States. Pop never talked about why the three of them chose to settle in Cut Corners and take up the ordinary life of gentlemen farmers and such after the war ended. When pressed to comment, Eb's response was always the same: "I made a promise."

What sort of promise or to whom remained a mystery to

this day, one Rafe had chosen not to try and solve. For whatever reason, his father gave up a life of adventure and purpose to loll about a small town with little to do but play dominoes with his buddies and rehash the old days. The funny thing was, this man who once captained a unit of fearless lawmen seemed perfectly content sitting in front of the old newspaper office until it got too dark to see the checkerboard.

Only a heavy rain or Sunday services broke up the rhythm of the day for the old codgers. Worse, they seemed to like it that way.

"Well, that's not for me," Rafe muttered as he leaned back a notch farther and settled his hat over his eyes to begin his morning nap. "This man's going places."

"Well, not today, you ain't."

Chapter 10

Rafe jerked to attention and caught his hat before it hit the floor. His pop stood in the doorway. He half expected at least one of Pop's cronies to be standing with him. The fact that he showed up alone could only mean one thing.

Here it comes. The lecture about being content. So much for the nap.

With a heavy sigh, he placed both feet firmly on the floor. Resisting the urge to speak, he merely stared. As much as he loved his father, he had no desire to have his good mood ruined by the contentment lecture. Come Christmas Day, he'd be twenty-seven years old. If that wasn't too old to be told what to do, then he'd eat his hat.

Besides, he was content, wasn't he? There were only a few things in his life he really wanted to change. If a man was looking to hang his hat somewhere besides Cut Corners and to get his pay from someone other than the mayor of this fair city, where was the fault in that?

"Ain't you going to ask what's wrong, Son?"

"I reckon you're going to tell me whether I ask or not." Once again, Rafe sighed. At times like this, he wished he hadn't heard the Lord's command on honoring your father. He loved Eb Wilson more than anything on this earth, but the man could sorely try his patience. "Why don't you come on over here and sit a spell and tell me what's on your mind?"

"Maybe I will."

Pop sauntered over and stood a minute before settling himself into the chair on the other side of the desk. He made a fuss of rubbing the stubble on his jawbone before turning his gaze on Rafe. "You really aim to do it this time, don't ya?"

"Do what, Pop? Sign up for the rangers?" When his father nodded, Rafe continued. "I wish you'd just come right out and tell me what's so bad about your son following in your footsteps."

"I'll admit I'm right pleased that you would consider the rangers, but it's just that. . ." His father lapsed into silence, a pained look on his face.

Understanding dawned, and along with it, anger. Rafe rose and steadied himself with a firm grip on the corner of the desk.

"Say it, Pop," he managed through clenched jaw. "You don't think I can make a ranger of myself."

Eb Wilson fairly flew out of his chair. "That's the most ridiculous thing I heard come out of anyone's mouth. I'm proud as I can be of you."

Rafe frowned. His father looked like he was about to bust his buttons. "You sure about that?"

"Son, if anybody was cut out to be a ranger, it was you. Why, from the time you were knee-high to a grasshopper, you could ride and shoot with the best of 'em."

"That's because I learned from the best, Pop." He shrugged. "So, you admit I'm qualified. What's your beef with me signing up?"

His father looked like he planned to jaw on that question awhile, so it surprised Rafe that he spoke right up. "Well now, there's two things wrong with the plan. First off, you're needed right here in Cut Corners." Before Rafe could protest, Pop held up his hand to silence him. "You asked; now hear me out. This town needs a lawman who will keep the criminal element out. It can't be helped that the place is as quiet as a Monday morning church house. You ought not complain because you're doing such a good job. Come January if you're not here, what do you think will happen? You think anyone's going to protect Lula and Millie and Miss Potter and the others like you do? I say not."

"I never thought of it that way, Pop."

A satisfied look crossed the older man's face. "Well, you chew on that thought awhile. "You'll be missed. In fact, the boys and I are so sure that you're needed that we drew up a little something we'd like you to sign." He pulled the folded sheet of paper—the one Rafe had thought was a telegram—out of his pocket and thrust it in Rafe's direction. "It's a little contract Chaps drew up. We'd all be obliged if you'd sign it."

"Now hold on a minute. I don't know about this. Since when does the sheriff of Cut Corners operate under a contract?"

Pop shrugged. "Since this morning." He stood. "Look here, boy, I know you're aiming to feel your oats, but I got a notion that what you want isn't out there on the trail. No, I think the thing to set your heart to thumping ain't a thing or even a job. I think it's a woman."

"What are you talking about? Captain Phelps thinks—"

"Son, I don't care what Captain Phelps thinks. Until you handle things with Miss Potter, you're not going to be worth the saddle you ride in. You'll be forever trying to prove something." Regret washed over his wrinkled features. "I love you, boy, but you need to find out your heart's right here before you go running all over Texas looking for it and missing out on what's right here."

"Pop, you're talking foolish now."

"Am I? That woman's crazy about you, and I can't help but see that you feel the same way. There, I've said it." With that, he stormed outside and left Rafe with his mouth hanging open.

"Hold on a minute, Pop." Rafe jumped to his feet and followed his father out the door. "You really believe all that, or is this just one more case of meddling?"

Eb Wilson stopped and whirled around, nearly causing Lionel Sager's sister, Vivian, to plow right into him. Sidestepping the girl, Pop headed back in Rafe's direction, only stopping when he was practically under Rafe's nose.

The two men stood eye-to-eye. Neither blinked.

"Rafael Wilson, you are a good man, born of good stock, and well loved by your mama, who's now in heaven, rest her soul. I've loved you and cared for you, and I've been blessed to have the help of Lula and Millie to raise you. In all those years, have I ever meddled in your affairs?"

"Yes. Frequently."

"Fair enough. In this case, however, I'm going to step back and give you just enough rope to hang yourself. That contract on your desk is the key to your happiness, boy. You're a better lawman than any ranger who ever rode, me included, but that don't mean you have to leave the ones who loved you and raised you. Your talents are needed right here. Why, you never know when there's going to be some big threat to your loved ones. Where will you be when that happens—here or somewhere else?"

He paused to catch a long breath. Rafe dared not speak. He didn't like the choice of words floating around in his brain. Half were disrespectful, the rest downright frightening in that if he said them he'd be agreeing with Pop.

"Now, the other thing. I aim to state that youth is wasted on the young. Why, if I had a pretty filly like Miss Potter watching my every move, I sure wouldn't be spending my spare time over at Erik Olson's carpenter shop hammering nails and sawing table legs."

"Pop, you don't know what you're talking about. That woman hates me. She's made that fact plain enough."

Pop chuckled. "I repeat. Youth is wasted on the young. Why do you think she pays so much attention to you if she isn't sweet on you?" He shook his head. "Why, your mama, rest her soul, gave me such grief when I first started showing up on her doorstep that any sane man would have turned tail and run."

"Is that right?"

"That's right. Now the question is, what do you think about that girl? You sweet on her? I bet you can't look into her eyes without your heart going pitty-pat."

"Yes I can." Lately, anyway. But then, he'd made it a practice to avoid her.

"Well, you answered that awful fast. What is it Shakespeare says—'Methinks thou dost protest too much'?" He clapped a hand on Rafe's shoulder. "Look, I don't aim to tell anyone about how you think Miss Potter's prettier than a new calf on a spring morning. I do think maybe you ought to let her know that."

"But I don't think that," he said as he watched Pop's back disappear down the boardwalk. "I really don't think that."

But did he believe what he said? There was only one way to find out. He'd take Pop up on his challenge. He'd go right down there to the dressmaker's shop and look her in the eyes and prove to himself and Pop that Peony Potter was the last woman in the world for him.

First he ought to head home and change shirts.

"Well?" Chaps said. "What happened? Did you talk to him?"

Eb smiled and leaned across the checkerboard. The other three followed suit.

"I spoke my piece." He paused for effect. "To both of 'em."

Stone's eyes narrowed. "How'd they take it?"

"About like I expected." Eb turned to Chaps. "Everything set?"

Chaps nodded. "Ticks ought to be getting the telegram any minute."

"Why'd you send Ticks a telegram?" Stone asked.

"I didn't." Chaps grinned. "I sent myself one. You know how Ticks is. The news of that secret gold shipment will be all over town before sundown. The rest of you done what you were supposed to?"

The three men nodded. "I predict there will be a veritable crime spree in Cut Corners in short order."

"Hello, Miss Potter." Eb smiled at the dressmaker as she passed them on the boardwalk and stepped inside her shop. "Lovely afternoon we're having, isn't it?"

Peony Potter paused to glanced over her shoulder. Without

saying a word, she gave him a look that left no doubt she'd heard everything they said. Eb waited for the woman to say something.

To his surprise, she merely smiled and disappeared inside the shop.

He reached over to slap Chaps on the back. "I like that girl," he said. "She's going to be good for Rafe."

Chapter 11

You didn't hear it from me, Miss Potter, but there's a secret shipment of gold headed through Cut Corners."

Peony looked up from her needlework to offer Ticks McGee a smile. He had wasted no time delivering the telegram to the British fellow, but it seemed as though he might spend the rest of the afternoon sitting in Peony's shop. Unlike the elder Mr. Wilson, this man had no reservations about sipping tea in such a feminine setting.

Perhaps she shouldn't have offered him that second cup. She couldn't help herself, as the man was a wealth of information. Today his topic was the safety of Cut Corners and Rafe Wilson's ability to defend the entire town from marauders should the need arise.

"Why I've seen that man fend off a dozen wild boar with a single-shot rifle." He fiddled with the chain of his pocket watch, then smiled. "Very impressive if I do say so myself."

"Now Ticks, you know there were only a half dozen of them, and they were hogs, not wild boar." Rafe tipped his hat and nodded toward Peony. "Afternoon, Miss Potter."

"Mr. Wilson."

Ticks scrambled to his feet, very nearly upsetting the contents of his teacup.

"Might I have a word with the lady, Ticks?"

The telegraph officer nodded and continued to sip his tea.

"Alone," Rafe added.

With that, Ticks set his cup on the table and beat a path to the door. As soon as they were alone, Rafe's expression softened.

"Miss Potter, I thought I ought to tell you that I've come to a decision about my future. You see, I—"

"Rafe, is that you?"

He turned to wave at a blond-haired gentleman. As he neared the door, Peony recognized Erik Olson.

"Am I interrupting something?" he asked.

The sheriff shook his head, and a look of relief flooded his face. "Naw, I was just passing the time of day with Miss Potter. Miss Potter, do you know my friend Erik? He's the carpenter here in town."

She nodded. "Yes, in fact, he's working on some plans for the shop, aren't you, Mr. Olson?"

"Ja," the blond giant said. "Well, I have come to speak to Rafe, but I can do that another time."

"No, really, I was just leaving," Sheriff Wilson said. "Best regards, Miss Potter."

Before she could respond, he and the carpenter were gone. "Thanks," she heard him say as she skittered to the window to watch them walk away.

"For what?" the carpenter responded.

The sheriff's reply was drowned out by the cackle of the

men sitting at the domino table mere feet from her window. Closing the lace curtains with a huff, she headed to the back of the shop to find something, anything, to do.

"My friend, you are the best employee I have ever had. I do not even mind that you are only here to hide from Miss Potter."

"That's not true, Erik. I like working with my hands. It feels good to accomplish something." Rafe looked up from the chair he'd just nailed back together and smiled. "Well, I admit that Miss Potter hasn't thought to look for me here, but I am the only employee you've ever had, and I work for free." He righted the chair, then sat in it. "And I'm not hiding from Miss Potter. I just don't happen to want her to find me anytime soon."

"Is she still complaining about the rangers?" Erik chuckled. "It seems as though someone should have explained the situation to her by now. Those four men are the reason Cut Corners exists. If they want to set up a checkerboard and play a few games, they ought to be left alone to do it."

"You and I think so, but the new dressmaker disagrees. And because she disagrees, I haven't had a decent nap in more than two weeks."

"Well now," Erik said as he shook the wood shavings out of his hair, "I thought you were here because you wanted something constructive to do with your spare time. I did not realize it was insomnia that drove you across the street."

"Just don't get used to the extra help. I'll be gone before you know it."

Erik stopped his sanding work on Parson Clune's new pulpit and straightened his back. "You are really going to join up with the rangers?"

Nodding, Rafe slapped his knees and rose. "What? You look like you swallowed a bug, Erik. You know I'm expected at headquarters after the first of the year. Did you think I'd change my mind?"

"Actually, I did." His friend began to chuckle. A moment later he rose to slap Rafe on the back. "Rafe Wilson, a Texas Ranger. Now that is something to celebrate."

Rafe held up his hand. "It's a little early to celebrate. I haven't officially accepted yet."

"Accepted what?" Jeff strolled into the workshop. "Did I miss a good story?"

"Rafe is joining up with the rangers," Erik said. "Evidently he is not happy repairing chairs and building bookcases for a living."

"I'm a lawman," Rafe said, "and I need to go where a lawman is needed."

Jeff shook his head. "Your pop's not going to like this."

"My pop's going to be so proud of me that he can't stand it." Rafe pushed the chair out of his way and settled his hat back on his head. "Besides, we talked about it when I came back from my visit with Captain Phelps. He was fine with it then, and he will be fine with it now."

"If that's so, why haven't you told him when you're leaving yet?" Jeff asked.

"I'll tell him soon enough." Rafe strode past his cousin to regard his friend. "I appreciate being put to work here, Erik. Good, honest labor makes a man feel useful."

And I haven't felt useful in a very long time.

"Where are you headed?" Jeff called as he trotted to catch up.

"I thought I might have a word with Pop," Rafe said as his cousin fell into step beside him.

Jeff nodded. "Want some company?"

He pondered the question for a moment. "I probably ought to do this by myself. I don't know what's gotten into Pop, but every time I try to mention talking to Captain Phelps or joining up with the rangers, he changes the subject. It's downright perplexing."

"I've noticed he is a might tight-lipped on the subject," Jeff said. "Maybe he's missing the good old days when he and the others rode with the rangers. Have you ever wondered what they'd be doing now if the rangers hadn't been disbanded back in the sixties?"

"Mr. Wilson."

Rafe and Jeff turned in unison to see the dressmaker standing on the boardwalk a few feet away. Rafe suppressed a groan. For the better part of two weeks, he'd managed to avoid the tiny terror; now there she stood. Too late to turn tail and run, not that retreat ever set well with him.

So far, however, he'd managed to either hide or head for the hills every time she came around the office complaining. Someone must have told her by now that the sheriff and the chief offender at the checkers table were father and son. Did she honestly expect him to run Pop and his buddies out of town on a rail?

"Sheriff Wilson."

"That's what I was afraid of," Rafe muttered. Out of the corner of his eye, he saw Jeff slink away toward the blacksmith shop and wished he could join him. "How can I help you, Miss Potter?"

"Rafe! Rafe Wilson, come on over here right now. There's been a robbery!" Millie trotted toward him, both hands in the air. "Come quick, Rafe; someone's done stole my pies."

"Rafe Wilson, is that you?"

Rafe whirled around to see Parson Clune standing on the boardwalk behind him. The preacher looked more flustered than Millie, a rare state of affairs for the sedate man. "Rafe, someone's stolen my tomato plants right out of the ground. Why, I just put those plants in the ground two days ago. Come with me, and I'll show you the scene of the crime."

"Begging your pardon, Parson Clune," Millie said, "but the scene of the crime's over at my place. Three pies gone right off the counter."

"Sheriff, I really must have a word with you," Miss Potter said.

"Well, wait your turn," Millie scolded. "I've got a crime scene in my diner."

Parson Clune pointed over his shoulder to the church. "Forgive me, Millie, but I've got a crime scene in my garden, too."

"Rafe, is that you? Would you mind stepping over here a minute?"

He swung his attention to the mercantile where Lionel Sager stood on the boardwalk waving. "Yes, it's me," he said. "I'm a little busy right now, though."

"Well, I'm in need of the law, and you're the only law in Cut Corners."

Rafe pushed his hat back a notch on his head and focused on the mercantile owner. "What do you need the law for, Lionel?"

"Pickles. Someone took 'em all. Every last one of them."

"Excuse me, Sheriff," the dressmaker said.

Suppressing a frown, he let out a long breath. "Not now, Miss Potter. Your complaints can wait. We have real crimes here."

"Actually, that's exactly what I was going to tell you." She peered up at him from beneath the brim of a ruffled bonnet just a shade darker than her eyes, eyes that looked like they were about to fill with tears. "Perhaps you and I might continue this conversation at a later date. Much later. In fact, I think I'd rather not have a conversation with you at all, thank you very much." With that, she swung her skirts toward the dressmaker's shop and disappeared inside.

"Sheriff!"

Chapter 12

December 17, 1878

It took Rafe the better part of two weeks to solve the mystery of the crime wave in Cut Corners. At first he only had his suspicions, but when each of the crime victims awoke on Sunday morning to a bag of coins in the amount of their loss, he knew it had to be Pop and the boys. While the trouble they went to flattered him, he was tempted to throw them all in the jailhouse for a night to keep them from doing it again.

Instead, he settled for a formal apology from each one, in writing, and given to the crime victims in the middle of Main Street. The only citizen of Cut Corners missing that day was Peony Potter. By the time he got around to noticing, the event was over and the crowd had dispersed.

He ought to go make peace with her. If he did, he might end up losing out on the biggest adventure of his life. No, better to remain at odds with Peony Potter than to risk turning down Captain Phelps and the rangers in favor of spending more time with the pretty dressmaker.

"Sheriff, you got a plan for what's gonna happen when the stage rolls through on Christmas Eve?"

Rafe looked up from his musings to see Ticks McGee standing in his office. "If I got a plan, do you think I'm going to share it with you?"

Actually he only had the beginning of a plan, but he'd never admit that to Ticks. The gold shipment described in the telegram he'd received last Friday was so large, it would need four men to protect it. With Cut Corners set squarely on the trail to the gold's final destination, Rafe would be entrusted with seeing it safely through town.

He folded the telegram and slid it into his shirt pocket. As much as he hated it, it sure felt good to be doing some real sheriffing.

Of course, he'd be living the life of a real lawman soon enough. In the meantime, he had plans to make. The stage would be rolling through a week from today. Other than deputizing the four former rangers, his cousin Jeff, and Erik Olson, he hadn't had a chance to make good on any of the other details of the plan to protect the stage.

Rafe sighed as he unrolled the maps Pop had loaned him. This was going to be a big job, but he was up for the challenge.

"Excuse me, Sheriff Wilson." Peony Potter stood in the doorway. "May I come in?"

He motioned for her to come in, then returned his attention to his maps. When she settled in the chair opposite him, he realized he was in for a longer conversation than he'd hoped.

Ignoring her had never worked in the past, so he decided

to get the confrontation out of the way right off. "Yes, I know, Pop and his buddies have been up to no good. File a written report and be on your way, please."

He was totally unprepared for her giggle. "You have no idea, Sheriff."

Leaning back in his chair, he regarded her from beneath the brim of his hat. "What are you talking about, Miss Potter?"

When she told him, he fairly fell off the chair. "So this is all a fake?"

She nodded. "It seems as though your father and his friends are trying to show you that you belong in Cut Corners by creating some excitement that will culminate with a stage holdup."

"How do you know this for sure?"

"Remind me, Sheriff. Where do these men sit every day for hours on end?"

Rafe smiled. "Miss Potter, I would like to apologize for my father and his friends. It seems as though they have been up to no good, and I've allowed your customers to be exposed to it."

"You know, I believe I will accept your apology. Now what are we going to do about this?"

Ticks McGee ambled in with a telegram in his hand. "Sorry, folks, I was just passing through, and I had this telegram for Miss Potter and, well, I thought. . ."

Rafe rose and strolled to the other side of the desk, casually resting on the corner as he regarded the telegraph operator. "You thought you were going to catch me with Miss Potter?"

"Yes, actually," he said with a gulp.

Rafe looked down at Peony and winked. "And what did you think you would catch us doing?"

"N—n—nothing at all, Sheriff," he said as he backed out of

the office and headed down the street.

"Miss Potter, I have a plan."

She rose. "Do you?"

He nodded. With your help, we are going to expose these old coots for the meddling men they are."

"I like that," she said.

"There's just one thing," he added.

"What's that?"

Rafe smiled. "I'm going to have to kiss you first."

"I thought you might say that."

"Any complaints if I do?"

"If I do, I'll put them in writing like you asked," she said as she leaned up on her tiptoes.

"Fair enough," he whispered just before their lips made contact and he lost his heart to Peony Potter.

Chapter 13

H ere it comes," Eb shouted. "There's the stage—right
on time."

Rafe nodded and pointed to the west. "Jeff, you
and Erik go that way. Pop, you and the fellows fall in behind
the stage and escort it through town and on into the next
county. I'll ride ahead and scout for trouble."

As the men rode off on their respective assignments, Rafe
smiled. *Pop always has a plan. Let's see how he likes my plan.*

Just over the rise, Rafe spotted a pair of would-be robbers poised to hold up the stage. He'd pegged them as former
ranger friends of Pop's, owing to his long memory and the
recognizable faces of the pair.

A quick conversation with them along with an explanation and the pair were more than happy to deviate from the
plan. Rafe waved as he passed the men, who now hid behind
a stand of trees. As the stage rolled past, the two fellows gave
chase.

The real fun began when Pop and the boys rode up behind the group and dismounted beside the stage. Hidden in the underbrush, Rafe watched the scene unfold. Pop jumped to the ground first and strolled toward the two fake robbers with the other three in hot pursuit. Just about the time the meddling men had gathered around the stage, they found themselves held at gunpoint.

"What are you doing, fellas?" Pop inquired as he was handed into the empty stage. "This isn't how the plan was supposed to work."

"Ja," Swede said. "You're not supposed to be taking us prisoner."

"Shut up and get inside," the taller of the pair shouted as he emptied the rangers' weapons of their bullets and tossed them into the bushes.

As the last of the men fell into the stage, the pair bolted the door and turned the stage north. "Where are you taking us?" Pop called.

On cue, Rafe rode up alongside the stage. "Hey, Pop," he called.

Eb Wilson stuck his head out of the stage and frowned. "What're you doing out there, boy? You turn crook on me?"

Rafe grinned. "Well, actually—"

A round of gunfire interrupted his words. The driver halted the stage as a pair of masked gunmen rode toward them.

"Very funny, Rafe," Chaps said. "But I think turning our own two against us was enough. You didn't have to add more actors to the game."

Rafe froze. "I don't know what you're talking about. I didn't have anything to do with those two."

A bullet zinged past, snaking a hole in Rafe's best hat before it lodged in the side of the stage. With the four former rangers disarmed and the two false robbers carrying guns that held no bullets, Rafe was the sole possessor of a working weapon.

The first bandit rode up at lightning speed, leveling his weapon as he passed. Rafe had no trouble knocking him out of his saddle with the first bullet. When the second criminal appeared, he too was felled by Rafe's revolver.

Releasing the four rangers from the confines of the stage, Rafe hung back and let Pop take a look at the two bad guys. "Yep, they won't be robbing any stages anytime soon," Pop said as he looked up at Rafe with admiration in his eyes. "That's some nice shooting. You brought 'em down but didn't kill 'em. Like as not, they'll wish you did after they stand trial." Pop reached up to shake Rafe's hand. "Son, you've proved to me you're more than fit to ride with the rangers."

"Pop, I appreciate that, but I was wondering something."

"What's that?"

He smiled. "I was wondering if one of you meddling men had a copy of that contract you gave me awhile back."

"Why's that?" Pop asked.

Rafe shrugged. "Oh, I don't know. I kind of thought I might stay right here in Cut Corners and see what sort of trouble I can get into."

Up ahead a buggy came over the rise. Rafe recognized it instantly as Lula Chamberlain's rig. Riding beside Lula was Peony Potter.

"And here comes that trouble now," Rafe said as he urged his horse into a gallop and met his future bride halfway.

At least he hoped she would be his future bride. First he had to ask her.

Epilogue

Christmas Day, 1878

R afe, there are things about my past you don't know."
Peony leaned against the tree just past the privy and
stared up at the light flakes of snow as they dusted the
sheriff's blue-black hair. "Things that might surprise you."

Rafe wiped a snowflake off Peony's nose and smiled. "I
can't imagine a thing that would make me love you any less."

He'd asked her to marry him just yesterday, presenting the
idea of the two of them living in Cut Corners and raising a
family only a few minutes after he signed the contract agreeing
to be sheriff for another year. Peony had said yes after joking
that he was only spending the day with her to avoid the bachelors' pot roast at Millie's Diner.

She'd been elated yesterday, but now she worried he might
change his mind once he heard the full truth about her past.

Peony sighed. "I'm not really from Dallas like I led you to
believe. I was raised in New Orleans, and my mama, well. . ."
She paused to regard the man who'd stolen her heart. "If, after

you hear this, you want to call off the wedding, I'll understand."

Stealing a quick kiss, Rafe shook his head. "I won't, but go ahead and tell me anyway."

So she did, starting with her papa's leaving them, her mama's occupation, and finally telling him about the dead man on the train headed for San Francisco. When she'd told the entire tale, she sat back and waited for Rafe to break the engagement.

Instead, he sat in silence for a moment. Finally he turned to face her. "Sounds like we both come from interesting families," he said as the sound of Pop and the boys echoed around them. "Now how about you and I go inside and have some birthday cake?"

"Millie's cake?"

He nodded.

"Can't we just stay out here a little longer?"

He stole one kiss, then two more. He would have stolen another except that he heard Millie calling his name. "Be right there, Millie," he said. "Just one more kiss."

"Happy Birthday, Rafe Wilson," Peony whispered. "And Merry Christmas. Looks like you are the marrying kind after all."

CHRISTMAS EVE BACHELORS' POT ROAST

2 tablespoons olive oil
1 clove garlic, minced
½ onion, chopped fine
Beef or pork roast, any size
Carrots, peeled and cut in 2" lengths
Onions, cut in eighths
Potatoes, quartered
2 cans golden mushroom soup

Place Dutch oven on burner set at medium-high. Heat olive oil and add garlic and onions. Sauté. Brown roast, then cover with vegetables and reduce heat. Prepare 2 cans mushroom soup per package directions, then pour evenly over roast and vegetables. Cover and let simmer 1–2 hours, depending on size of roast. Serve with rolls or corn bread.

KATHLEEN Y'BARBO

Kathleen Y'Barbo is an award-winning novelist and sixth-generation Texan. After completing a degree in marketing at Texas A&M University, she focused on raising four children and turned to writing. She is a member of American Christian Romance Writers, Romance Writers of America, and Writers Information Network. She also lectures on the craft of writing at the elementary and secondary levels, and conducts distance-learning classes on the university level.

Here Cooks
the Bride

by Cathy Marie Hake

Chapter 1

September 1879

E xcuse me, sir."
Jeff halted mid-motion, his shovel full of coal. Black dust swirled around his thick boots as he glanced at the young lady. Oh, and she was definitely a *lady*. Judging from her so-very-proper Boston accent, the Daddy-has-money traveling suit with all the fuss and bother, and her wide hazel eyes, this gal wasn't just out of place; she was lost.

"Might I impose for a moment to inquire as to the location of your local diner?"

He dumped the coal into his wheelbarrow and stood to his full height. "Diner's closed. Best hop back aboard the train and try Meadsville."

The feather in her stylish hat swayed back and forth as she gave her head a small shake. "I fear I did not make myself known. I'm Lacey Mather, and I've come to help my great-aunt

Millie at the diner."

"Millie's your great-aunt?" Jeff couldn't hide the surprise in his voice. On her better days, Millie looked as if she'd been caught in a whirlwind. Most of the time, she looked like she sorted bobcats for a living. No man in his right mind would imagine Millie as kin to this dainty blond beauty.

"Yes." Miss Mather folded her white-gloved hands at her waist and gave him a charming smile. "I'm eager to reacquaint myself with her. Could you please direct me to her place?"

"Sure. Go on through the station here, and you'll see Main Street turning off to the west from Ranger Road. Millie's is the first place on the right side of Main."

Miss Proper-and-Pretty leaned forward ever so slightly. "Would west be to my right or left?"

Jeff tamped down a groan. Helpless. The woman wasn't just lost, she was utterly helpless. What kind of assistance did she think she could give Millie, clear out here in the wilds of Texas? He heaved a sigh. "Give me a minute. I can show you the way—long as you don't mind coal dust."

Laughter tinkled out of her—from behind her gloved hand, of course. "Sir, after riding a train for the past three days, I assure you, I could shake out my skirts and fill your wheelbarrow!"

The woman had a point. He nodded, then directed, "There's a bench over yonder. I'll just be a minute."

Chestnut brown skirts whispered as she turned to walk away. The whisper might as well have been a shout, because the narrow-cut front of that fancy dress hadn't prepared him for this view. Row upon row of ruffles draped over a sassy bustle and spilled to the ground. Dainty, swaying steps led her away from the bench and toward a trunk, valise, and hatbox.

She really does plan to stay.

The realization made Jeff groan aloud. Bad enough that Millie couldn't cook a lick. Put both women in the kitchen, and most of Cut Corners would probably die of food poisoning. Resigned to continue to prepare his own meals, Jeff dumped more coal into his wheelbarrow and muttered, "Lord, I know I'm not supposed to question Your wisdom, but seems to me a homely old spinster who knew her way around a stove would be a much better choice for us here in Cut Corners."

The train whistle blew, adding an exclamation mark to his opinion.

"You've been too kind." Lacey clutched the cording from her hatbox and smiled at the stranger. He'd not yet introduced himself. These western men were a rough lot—rough but strong. He'd filled the biggest wheelbarrow she'd ever seen, then hefted her trunk across the handles as if it weighed no more than a pillow. Shoving the heavy burden through the rutted streets didn't even leave him breathless. He'd stayed in the street but next to the boardwalk so she'd not have to contend with the hazardous road any more than necessary.

"Open the door. I'll tote in your belongings."

Lacey rapped on the door to what appeared to be the residential portion of the diner.

"Open it," he ordered as he lumbered up. "Millie's probably knocked out from the laudanum Doc gave her."

"Oh. I see." Though it felt intrusive to barge in, Lacey understood the necessity. "Very well." The door creaked open to reveal a jumbled mess. Lacey yanked the door shut. "If you'd be so kind as to leave the trunk here, I'll drag it inside later."

"You couldn't drag this thing if it were empty. Get the door."

She shook her head. "I'm dreadfully sorry. Truly I am. I'm

not trying to be difficult, and I appreciate your strength. It's just that. . .oh, dear. Well, Aunt Millie's hurt. She simply hasn't felt up to tending to matters."

Her trunk thumped loudly on the boardwalk. The man looked at her like she'd taken leave of her senses. "Suit yourself." He wrapped huge, blackened hands around the handles of his wheelbarrow and trundled back across Ranger Road to the smithy. Suddenly the width of his shoulders and his uncommon strength made perfect sense. Lacey tilted her head to read the sign. JEFFREY WILSON. BLACKSMITH.

"God, please bless Mr. Wilson."

"Which one?" a frail, raspy voice asked from behind her.

Lacey whirled around. From the wild wisps of her gray hair to the tattered hem of her dressing gown and the sling on her arm, the woman looked positively ghastly. "Aunt Millie?"

"In the flesh. Which Mr. Wilson?" She motioned with her good arm for Lacey to enter.

Lacey gripped her hatbox and valise as she stepped over the threshold. She'd never seen a place in such a sad state. Afraid she'd blurt out something hurtful, she grasped at the slim thread of conversation. "How many Mr. Wilsons do you have in this town?"

"Three. The old codger who used to be a ranger, the sheriff, and the blacksmith."

"I see. The blacksmith just escorted me from the train station." She set her valise and hatbox on a nearby table and patted the woman's good hand. "I'm here to help you now."

"Imagine that." Aunt Millie quirked a lopsided smile. "So why don't you tell me who you are?"

The question nearly felled Lacey. Then she recalled the blacksmith mentioning how the doctor gave Aunt Millie laudanum. No wonder the poor dear soul was a bit confused! "I'm Lacey, Tobias's daughter. I've come to help you since you hurt your arm."

The old woman squinted, then bobbed her head. The tortoiseshell comb holding up her wispy gray bun slid lower, and her topknot loosened into a precarious nest of tangles. "I remember you. Last I saw you, you were clinging to your mama's fancy ball gown and missing your front teeth. I see good, sound ones filled right in."

Having her teeth remarked upon as though she were a mare under consideration for purchase stunned Lacey. Then again, poor Aunt Millie dealt with gruff men all day long. No doubt, now that she had feminine companionship, the gentler side of her nature would shine. "How kind of you to remember Mama. I only hold a few memories of her. Perhaps, after you rest, you could share some of your recollections." Lacey took her aunt's arm and led her toward an open doorway. Surely this must lead to the residential portion of the building.

"You hungry, girl?"

"I confess, I am. Perhaps you'd like me to prepare us lunch."

"Then we're headed the right direction." Aunt Millie shuffled ahead and blocked Lacey's view for a moment. When she stepped to the side, pride rang in her voice. "How do you like it?"

A fair-sized kitchen spread before Lacey. Well, she thought it was a kitchen. Pots, pans, kettles, and roasters lay stacked on the stove and counter and hung from the ceiling. Towers of plates listed perilously close to the edge of what she supposed was a sink. Glass canisters formed a jumble in the center of a table, and a cat lazed across the far side of that table, soaking up warmth from a sunbeam. Pretending to ignore the sad state of the room, Lacey pulled off her gloves. "It's plain to see you have a well-equipped establishment. I'll get to work. Is there anything in particular you'd fancy?"

"Jeff."

The hammer clanged down on the horseshoe one last time; then Jeff set the piece back into the fire. "Yeah?"

Two old men hovered by the rail in his smithy. No one stepped beyond that rail—he'd established that rule straight off, and never once had he regretted it. It kept folks from getting hit by the hammer, sparks, or worse. It also kept them from meddling with him when he worked.

Not that anyone ever managed to keep what the town collectively called "the meddling men" from sticking their noses into other folks' business. Four retired Texas Rangers had founded the town after they'd spent the bulk of their adult years directing and fixing issues and problems. Now, in a peaceful town, the old guys couldn't limit themselves to dallying with dominoes or grumbling over checkers. From their vantage point on the boardwalk, they were worse busybodies than a pack of gossipy widows.

And here two of them were. His uncle Ebenezer leaned forward and cleared his throat. "Pretty filly you were escortin' down the avenue this morning."

Big old Swede nodded his silver-blond head. "Ja. So, what is this? Did you send for a bride?"

"A bride?" Jeff burst out laughing. "Not a chance."

"It's past time you married up," Uncle Eb declared. "Your cousin's happy as a clam now that he married up with Peony."

Mentioning Peony and clams in the same breath seemed

daft, but Jeff didn't bother to share his opinion. The less he said, the better off he'd be. Once someone took a mind to challenge the meddling men, the old men took it as a personal affront and reckoned they had to defend their honor by proving themselves right.

"So who is this pretty girl?" Swede asked.

"Millie's kin. Gustavson's mare threw a shoe. I need to get her shod before he comes back."

"Millie's kin, huh?" Swede crammed his thumbs into his belt and rocked to and fro. "Think she can cook any better than Millie?"

"Anyone can cook better than Millie," Eb said in a wry tone.

"No telling," Jeff said gloomily. "Could have inherited Millie's recipes."

All three men sighed. Jeff used his pinchers to pull the horseshoe from the fire and hooked it over the conical end of the anvil, then started pounding it into shape again.

"A man has to have a cast-iron stomach to survive Millie's food. I suppose I'd better keep payin' Lula at the boardin'-house for chow." Swede frowned. "Even my nephew cooks better than that."

Jeff purposefully clanged his hammer extra loud just to drown out their conversation. After all, the two men were directly responsible for matching up his cousin Rafe with Peony, the dressmaker, last Christmas.

Ever since then, the bachelors in Cut Corners had been manipulated into any number of situations wherein the meddling men tried to match them up with anyone in a skirt.

"Of course he will, won't you, Jeff?" his uncle half shouted.

Jeff knew better than to agree when he hadn't heard what

they'd said. He shoved the horseshoe back into the fire and picked up the awl so he could drive holes into the shoe and be done with it. "Don't know what you were jawing over."

Swede harrumphed. "No offense, you understand."

Jeff looked to his uncle for an explanation.

"We were discussing how you've sorta let yourself go. It's the heat and coal and all. . .but I'm sure now that we've called it to your attention, you'll spruce up a bit."

Even though he stood right beside the forge, Jeff's blood ran cold. "I'm not trying to impress anyone."

"Didn't say you had to." His uncle pretended to be interested in a sample brand burned into the wall. "But you'd do well to take your Saturday night bath—"

"And get your hair trimmed," Swede tacked on for good measure.

They were reaching for something to needle him about. Because of the grime from the smithy, Jeff bathed every day, whether he needed to or not. Why, he probably bought more soap from the mercantile than a family of eight. Instead of saying a thing, he snorted.

"You've been keepin' company too long with horses, son. Snortin' and tossin' your mane like a riled stallion."

"Jay Harris took his shears to me just last week."

"Humph." Swede managed to use that sound to great advantage. Jeff wondered how long it took him to cultivate just the right tone to make it dismissive and disparaging all at the same time. Probably did it for survival's sake, because he had that lilting tonal quality as part of his accent that made him seem more like an affable farmer than a gritty Texas Ranger.

Jeff grabbed nails and stuffed them into the pocket of his leather apron, then slung the horseshoe on the anvil and closed one eye as he measured and punched the holes with a steadiness borne of experience. Done with that, he plunged the shoe into the water bucket and relished the satisfying hiss it produced.

"You men'll have to excuse me." Jeff nodded curtly toward them and headed out the side door to the corral attached to his place.

"Forget about that mare and think about the pretty filly across the street!" his uncle called.

Jeff scowled. "Why don't you go tell Swede's nephew about her?"

The two old men exchanged a conspiratorial look and hot-footed out of the shop.

Jeff went over to the mare, stooped, and held her leg fast between his knees. In no time at all, she boasted a perfectly fitted shoe.

He straightened up, gave the mare a chunk of carrot, and chuckled. "I ought to feel guilty about sending them to Erik, but it's every man for himself."

"Excuse me, sir."

He tensed at the sound of that soft feminine voice. Silly Boston woman. Exact same words she used early this morning at the train. Was that her standard greeting? Jeff turned. "Yes?"

"Aunt Millie tells me you deliver coal to her. Could I trouble you to bring over more?"

"Sure."

The woman had changed into a simple calico dress, but it looked anything but plain on her. Judging from the damp tendrils corkscrewing around her flushed face, she'd been busy. She smiled—a friendly, sort of shy smile. "Thank you ever so much."

"I'll be by shortly." There. That served as a polite dismissal. It was the best he could manage. She might be pretty as a picture and smell sweeter than a rose garden, but Jeffrey Wilson wasn't looking for a wife, and with Uncle Eb plotting and scheming, the last thing Jeff wanted was to be seen near Millie's niece. He wanted her to go away. The sooner the better.

Chapter 2

"W"onderful! Thank you." Lacey stood to one side as Jeff brought in a full scuttle of coal.

"Don't mention it."

She inched back a bit farther and stood on tiptoe to swipe a smudge off the wall. "You've been so kind. Would you care to join us for supper?"

"No."

He answered so quickly, Lacey wondered what she'd said to offend him. She hid the soiled cleaning rag behind her back and offered, "Maybe another time."

He hitched his shoulder and headed out the door.

Lacey didn't dwell on his terrible manners. She had too much to accomplish, and troubling herself over his surly ways would be a waste of time. She'd dealt with fractious children and found it wisest to ignore such dark moods. Most often, they blew away like a bank of unwelcome thunderclouds. Not that he was at all like the little girls she'd worked with. Mr. Wilson belonged to that mysterious gender with whom she'd rarely interacted. Growing up in a young ladies' academy severely limited her ability to associate with men. To be sure, with his imposing physique, deep voice, and unmistakable strength, Mr. Wilson was the epitome of masculinity.

Still, it would have been nice for him to notice what she'd accomplished.

But he didn't see the place. *I shut the door so he wouldn't know how Aunt Millie let the place fall to rack and ruin. Well, no matter.* Lacey felt the satisfaction of a job well started. Certainly she couldn't consider it well done. Too much remained on her to-do list.

The list lay on the table—the clean, catless table—weighted down with two of the freshly scrubbed canisters. Every last dish, pot, and pan now rested neatly in a hutch, cabinet, or crate. She'd used sink after sink of water and half a cake of soap to wash them all. The windows and floor shone.

So did her nose.

Lacey giggled at herself for that vain thought. No one here in Cut Corners would give a fig for what she looked like or how she behaved. They'd simply be glad Aunt Millie had help and the diner offered decent meals. It would be fun to do this—sort of a holiday. All the other young ladies at the school got to go on trips and vacations, but she'd always remained on the premises. Father never managed to arrange his important business schedule in such a manner as to be home during the school term breaks. Well, this was her vacation. Once Aunt Millie healed, Lacey would pack her trunk and head back to Boston, where a more prestigious school had offered her a very flattering position.

In the meantime, plenty needed doing. Poor Aunt Millie was behind the times. She'd never read Beeton and didn't live according to the all-important maxim that ruled a woman's world. "A place for everything and everything in its place," Lacey quoted as she strove to decide how to make a place for the hundreds of unmatched knives, forks, and spoons she kept unearthing in odd nooks and crannies. So far, she'd resorted to dumping them into three buckets she'd set on a table in the diner.

The diner. She shuddered. The place was a veritable pigsty. No one had come to help clear the tables from the meal Aunt Millie had been serving the day she broke her arm. It had taken every scrap of Lacey's fortitude to collect and scrub those dishes. Bless Aunt Millie's heart, she'd slept through the day thanks to a dose of laudanum. Before the poor old woman woke, Lacey still had several things she wanted to accomplish. If she stayed on the schedule she'd set for herself, Lacey estimated she'd have the diner open for business the day after tomorrow.

"Excuse me, sir. Could I trouble you to fill this?"

There she goes again. "Excuse me, sir." Her pretty little head must be full of manners and empty of brains. Jeff told himself he wasn't going to turn, but he did. Resplendent in a light purplish dress, Miss Mather handed a list to the grocer. Jeff couldn't decide whether the grocer smiled because of the woman's charm or because the long list would make for a profitable day. Either way, Miss Mather had just made herself a friend in Cut Corners.

"No trouble at all." Lionel Sager beamed at her. "I'll have it done in a trice. I heard tell we had a new lady in town. No one mentioned you were so lovely."

"You're too kind."

The way her thick lashes lowered might well be a practiced

response, but Jeff couldn't deny that the fetching blush filling her cheeks was genuine. She acted as if men didn't shower her with compliments all the time. He grew angry with himself for paying any attention and spun back around. Soap. He'd come to get more soap.

A moment later, Miss Mather stood by his side. A wooden basket was looped over her arm, and she'd already put two cakes of lye soap inside. She stood on tiptoe to look farther back on the display. "Good morning, Mr. Wilson." She helped herself to two more bars of soap—fancy ones. Larkin's Sweet Home and Larkin's Oatmeal Toilet Soap.

"Morning." He grabbed an ordinary bar of Pears.

"It's a pleasure to see Cut Corners boasts such a well-stocked mercantile."

He nodded, then headed toward the counter. Gordon Brooks walked past him, leaving a choking cloud of Hoyt's cologne in his wake. The smirk on the saloon owner's face left nothing to the imagination, and Jeff spun back around. He didn't want his name paired up with Miss Lacey Mather's, but he couldn't leave a poor, defenseless lady to the schemes of a rogue.

"Gordon Brooks at your service." Brooks doffed his hat.

"Thank you," Lacey said as she added knitting needles to her basket, "but the storekeeper has already offered his capable services."

Jeff watched in amusement as she breezed around a corner and busied herself with choosing a ball of string. Brooks followed. "I was merely introducing myself. Here in the untamed regions, a man learns to introduce himself to a lady. Otherwise, someone else will beat him to her since ladies are so few and far between."

"Sir!" Lacey pressed a hand to her throat and gave him a

shocked look. "I saw several God-fearing women as I came down the boardwalk and must protest the slur you've made upon their good character."

"I did say there were a few," Brooks said in a placating tone. "I meant no offense. My intent was merely to make your acquaintance and ask you to supper."

"I'll have to refuse your invitation."

"Why?" Brooks looked flummoxed that his oily charm hadn't worked on her.

"Because I must."

Jeff didn't bother to smother his smile. She actually made that flimsy excuse sound like a reason. He'd thought the little lamb needed to be rescued from the wolf, but that wolf was starting to resemble a whipped puppy. Still, it wouldn't be wise for her to make an enemy of such a man. Jeff cleared his throat. "The lady is being discreet. Fact is, she and her aunt already asked me to supper."

"Yes, yes, we did." She gave Jeff a look of sheer gratitude.

Lionel Sager rounded the corner with a bag on his shoulder. "Miss? This is the last of my sugar. I'll wire for more on the next train, but if you don't mind, I'd like to split the bag so I can keep some stock."

"Please do." She edged farther away from Brooks. "I don't believe I have beans on my list. Do I?"

"Come take a look."

As she walked to the counter, Jeff growled at Brooks, "Leave her alone."

"You Wilsons are all cut from the same cloth—think you run the town." Brooks shook his head. "You got it all wrong. Money is power, and I'm the one in Cut Corners with more of it than most of you put together."

"To my way of thinking, the important things can't be bought."

"Maybe not." Brooks paused, then tacked on, "But that's because those are the things you win." He tugged a pack of poker cards from his vest pocket, then shoved them back down. "Anytime you want, there's room for you in a game."

Jeff grinned. "Sitting at a supper table's my style. Card tables don't hold any appeal."

Vivian Sager approached them. "Pardon me, but I need to get a tin of lard for Miss Mather's order. It's behind you, Mr. Brooks."

Gordon Brooks's suave facade slipped as he scrambled out of Vivian's way. Known for being clumsy, she managed to drop or bump things with disconcerting regularity. He straightened his coat and headed for the door. On his way out, Brooks began to whistle.

"The Girl I Left Behind Me." Vivian identified the tune as she grabbed the bucket of lard. "He'd better not be whistling that about me."

"Allow me." Jeff grabbed the five-gallon tin from her before she crippled one of the two of them by dropping it. He took it to the counter and set it with a rapidly growing pile of groceries.

Lacey stood by the spice display and kept chucking tins into her basket. "Since you're here, Mr. Wilson, perhaps you could tell me if you prefer stewed tomatoes, butter beans, or succotash for supper."

Succotash. He loved succotash. Then again, no use spoiling one of his favorite things by having her massacre it. "Whatever's easiest."

"It's all the same to me."

I'll bet. Just like it is to Millie. How did I rope myself into eating over there tonight?

"I have asparagus," Lionel suggested. "End of the season. Won't be in again until next year."

Jeff shrugged. "I'll leave the menu up to Miss Mather." In all actuality, he hated asparagus. Never did seem quite right, gnawing on something that looked like a bloated, sickly pencil. Then again, he'd be needing bicarbonate after the meal anyway.

Miss Mather set her basket on the counter. The thing overflowed with a crazy collection of luxuries and nonsensical things. Soap, knitting needles, string, paprika, cloves, thyme, tooth powder, and two licorice ropes. "I think this is the last of it."

Vivian scratched off the last thing on the long list and squinted through her thick glasses. "If you think of anything else, you can run back. It's not like Boston where you'd have to take a buggy and need an escort."

"You must enjoy that freedom." Lacey's voice carried a tinge of longing. "It's so refreshing to be here."

"I'll put this on Millie's account." Lionel added the last few items and circled the total.

"Oh no." Miss Mather promptly pulled a small purse from the bottom of the basket and drew out a dozen or more ten-dollar greenbacks.

"Perhaps you'd like to go to the bank and deposit that," Lionel half choked.

"I've already been to the bank," she said blithely.

I had this woman pegged from the start. Daddy has money. That confirmation felt like the last nail in Jeff's coffin. No woman from a wealthy family learned to cook. He silently set a bottle of Peabody's Seltzer on the counter.

Chapter 3

I declare, Aunt Millie, you'd think that man's been starving for a decade," Lacey said as she finished washing the supper dishes. Jeffrey Wilson had come over, asked a nice blessing over the food, then taken very modest portions. After the first few bites, he'd practically inhaled the remainder of the food on his plate and accepted seconds with gusto. . .then taken thirds.

Aunt Millie rested her elbow on the table and propped her head in her hand. "Barely said a word, but his mouth was full."

"So he's usually more talkative?"

"Not much." The cat jumped up into Aunt Millie's lap. "He's got a weakness for critters, though. Talks to horses, dogs, and cats. Isn't that right, Tiger?"

Tiger purred in response.

"Oh, that plate you're washing belongs to Peony Wilson. She brought over some meals for me. I'm surprised she hasn't bustled over to meet you."

Suds splashed everywhere as Lacey dunked the plate. "Don't tell me I asked her husband or brother here for supper and didn't invite her!"

"No, no. She's married to Rafe—the sheriff. He's Jeff's cousin. That's a mighty fancy apron you've got on."

Lacey didn't bother to glance down. She owned four aprons—all of them cut off the same pattern, each with a different floral pattern embroidered across the bodice. "All of the young ladies learn needlework at the academy. This is an everyday one. There's another that's my Sunday-best."

"You'd better plan on wearing mine. Stains'll never come out of that white cotton."

"Madame taught us how to handle each type of spill." Lacey smiled. "But I thank you for your generous offer. What time do you normally serve breakfast?"

"Half past six, I unlock the door. Folks wander in whenever they've a mind to. Wouldn't expect too many to come tomorrow. They won't know the diner's open for business again."

The next morning, Lacey cracked the very last egg she'd bought into the skillet. She'd planned for those eggs to last three days. They hadn't lasted three hours! Aunt Millie tromped into the kitchen and wedged two more plates into the crate beside the sink. "Erik Olson wants another order of flapjacks."

"Another!" Lacey flipped several on the griddle, then shuffled the spatula beneath the egg and slid it onto a plate that held a sizzling slab of ham and handed the plate to her aunt. "I'm out of eggs."

Aunt Millie headed toward the dining room and called over her shoulder, "Not to worry. Just whip up some more flapjacks."

"More flapjacks? But I don't have eggs!" Lacey chased after her. "We'll have to close till lunch."

The entire noisy dining room suddenly went silent. Lacey stood in the doorway and stared at the shocked faces of what looked like the entire population of Cut Corners. Four older gentlemen glowered at her. One thumped his coffee cup on the table. "Can't do that. It's criminal."

"Don't worry," Aunt Millie said. "I told her to just make more flapjacks."

"I don't have eggs to make more batter for—" Lacey shrieked, "The flapjacks!" as she whirled around and ran back to the stove. Half of them were acceptable. The others— She scraped them off and winced.

"Finally got 'em cooked all the way through. I wasn't sayin' anything, but those others looked half-raw to me." Aunt Millie shoved out a plate and set the charred ones aside. "Crispy ones taste the best. 'Specially with apple butter on 'em."

"Bless you," Lacey said softly. Her great-aunt showed great consideration by speaking such kind words when those pancakes were only suitable for—

"Well?" a deep male voice asked. Lacey looked over and started to laugh. Half a dozen men crowded the doorway. She wasn't sure who had asked. "I believe Aunt Millie said Erik Olson ordered flapjacks. He has five coming to him. There are. . ." She took quick inventory and reported, "Seven more left."

"I'll pay a nickel apiece for 'em!"

"I'll pay a dime!"

"I'll wash the dishes," a woman said from the other entry, "if you share your recipe."

Four old gents hunkered over the barrel and pretended to study the checkerboard. Ebenezer Wilson said, "Can't let this one get away."

"Only had breakfast," Stone Creedon muttered. "Don't know if she can cook anything else yet."

"Who cares? I'll settle for breakfast."

"We must come up with a plan." Chaps reached over and methodically jumped his checker. "King me."

Swede grumbled, "Ja, ja. I king you."

Eb lowered his voice. "Swede, your nephew liked her flapjacks. If we tie her apron strings to a man here in town, that'll make sure she stays at the stove!"

"Erik saw her. Says she's pretty but she talks funny."

No one made mention of Swede's accent. Then again, no one made a comment about Chaps's English accent, either. Stone let out a snarling sound. "He can get used to her accent if he likes her cooking."

"It would be wise to have other gentlemen express interest," Chaps mused. "Nothing makes a woman more attractive than the fact that other men want her."

"Who cares about other men wanting her? The fact that she knows her way around a kitchen is recommendation enough."

"It doesn't matter what we think," Eb Wilson said. "We gotta convince some young buck here in Cut Corners to pay her court."

"Your nephew's a good prospect." Chaps leaned back and smirked at the checkerboard. "He's the first man to see her, and he's already been a supper guest."

"Eb and me, we already tried to convince him." Swede's

voice dragged with disappointment. "He isn't interested in her much."

Stone kicked the toe of his scuffed boot against the edge of the boardwalk to dislodge a dirt clod. "Who cares if he don't like her mush? She can cook plenty of other stuff."

Ignoring the fact that his old crony's deafness had him speaking nonsense, Swede announced, "I know what to do."

"What?" Chaps and Eb asked in unison.

"This." Swede leaned forward, took a checker, and hopped it across the entire board like a cricket on desert stones. Scooping up all of Chaps's pieces, he slapped his knee with the other hand and chortled. "You got the king, but I got the game."

"Crazy old coot," Stone muttered. "I thought he figured out something important."

Eb watched as Lacey sashayed down the boardwalk and into the mercantile. Every last bachelor either stared or followed after her. "Fellas, we might not have to do much a'tall. Seems Miss Lacey Mather might need our help to fight off the men instead of us draggin' 'em to her doorstep."

The doors to the diner didn't stop swinging. From the moment the folks in Cut Corners discovered Lacey Mather could cook, they'd beat a path to her door. Morning, noon, and night, she'd dash out with chalk in her hand, write up a menu in the fanciest script ever seen, and run back to her stove. Well—to Millie's stove. Only no one wanted it to be Millie's. They all loved Millie just fine, but her cooking could gag a skunk. Even now, folks could tell what Lacey prepared and what Millie made. Lacey's biscuits rose to fluffy perfection; Millie's would make fine sinkers if someone planned to go fishing. Lacey's batch of gravy could coax a full sentence of praise from grumpy old Stone Creedon; Millie's had lumps big enough to fool a man into thinking he got a dumpling.

Clang, clang, clang. Jeff worked on repairing Heath's plow. He'd sharpen it free of charge. Though it took a little extra time, he always wanted his customers to feel they got a good deal. Besides, he could sit outside the smithy by his large whetstone and watch the parade of swains going to eat at Millie's. The food tasted great, but word around town was the bachelors had more than just a full plate in mind. Many intended to court the pretty little gal. Lacey might think they were claiming their steak; Jeff knew they were staking their claim. There went Harold Myers, hair slicked back and a string tie, and it was just an ordinary Tuesday night. Bay rum wafted clear across the road as Ticks McGee headed into the diner.

Yup, no doubt about it. I've got a front-row seat for first-class entertainment.

"Hey, son." Uncle Ebenezer sauntered over. "Ain't it 'bout time you cooled off, cleaned up, and chowed down?"

"In a while."

"Best you not wait. Miss Mather might run outta grub again." Uncle Eb's head jutted forward as he imparted, "Happens 'least once a day."

Jeff jabbed his thumb back toward the forge. "Beans already on the fire."

"You're fixin' to eat your own cooking?" Eb shook his head. "Heat from that forge must be fryin' your brain."

"You taught me how to make 'em," Jeff replied. "They've been good enough all these years."

"Son, when you ain't got nuthin' but a mule to ride, you ride it. Only a fool keeps on a-riding that flea-bitten old beast when someone offers him a high-steppin' filly."

"You're assuming I aim to go somewhere. I'm happy to stay put."

"I'm flattered, sir, but I simply cannot." Lacey refilled Ticks McGee's coffee mug and moved on down the table, topping off the mugs.

"Why not?" Mr. McGee demanded. "You'd never want for nothing. I'd treat you real good. My job at the telegraph even comes with the upstairs rooms for us."

Everyone in the diner awaited her answer. Lacey hadn't realized the men were being more than friendly until Ticks just proposed to her in front of everyone. She'd thought the gangly telegraph operator had been joking. He wasn't. *Men are fragile creatures—their pride is easily damaged.*" Madame's words echoed in her mind. Lacey set down the big blue enamel coffeepot and gifted Ticks with a gentle smile. "You've honored me with your offer, sir. Truly, I'm flattered, but I cannot accept because I'm set to take a position at Le Petite Femme Academie once my aunt is better."

Angry roars and denials ripped through the diner.

"The matter is settled." She headed toward the kitchen for refuge.

"What was all that noise?" Aunt Millie asked as she sat at the table and made another bowl of coleslaw. "And where's the salt?"

Lacey scooted a cup toward her aunt. "Here. I measured this out for you already." The fact that the cup held sugar instead of salt—well, Lacey had to do something. Aunt Millie seemed to have very. . .unique notions about her recipes. Rather than offend her aunt, Lacey simply started supplying bowls with already measured dry ingredients so her aunt could still be helpful. So far, the solution had worked wonderfully.

"How about adding a little kick to this with some chili powder?" Aunt Millie asked after adding the sugar and taking a taste.

Chili powder in coleslaw? Public marriage proposals from near strangers? Lacey shook her head in disbelief.

"No?" Aunt Millie looked disappointed.

"Raisins. They'll complement the pork roast, don't you think?" Lacey swiped the chili powder from the spice rack and slipped it into her apron pocket. No use leaving temptation on hand. "You've made a wonderful suggestion, though. We could make chili and corn bread for lunch tomorrow."

Mollified, Aunt Millie dumped raisins into the coleslaw. "Best you get plenty of peppers from Sager's. These men are Texans. They like their chili hot."

Aunt Millie's idea of hot would no doubt have every last man in Cut Corners on his knees, praying for redemption. With that concern in mind, Lacey hovered over the stove the next day. Jeff Wilson lumbered in with more coal. As he filled the box and added more coal to the stove for her, he sniffed. "What is that?"

"Chili." She smiled at him and tapped the edge of the enormous pot on her left. "This one is regular. The other is hot."

"Hmm." He washed off at the pump, dried his hands, and swiped a spoon. After taking a taste of the hot pot, he gave her a patient look. "Miss Mather, back in Boston you fix beans with brown sugar and molasses. That's all well and good, but you're in Texas."

"Why, of course I am."

"Texas chili doesn't use beans—but just this once, we'll overlook that."

Another peculiar thing about Texas. At least he was nice about telling me. And the chili tastes perfectly fine the way it is.

"The real problem is, that stuff's milder than kissin' your sister." Jeff grabbed a bottle of Tabasco and upended it over the pot. "Millie, head on over to the mercantile. Grab up half a dozen more bottles, a mess of peppers, and grab me a ginger ale while you're at it."

"Sure thing!" Aunt Millie shot Lacey an I-told-you-so look and rushed out the door.

Horrified at how he blithely spoiled a perfectly decent pot of chili, Lacey spluttered. Just the fumes from the Tabasco had her gasping for air.

"Now that she's gone," Jeff said, continuing to give the bottle emphatic shakes to empty it, "I'm going to talk turkey. Your aunt's a fine woman, but she's a miserable cook. I heard tell you plan to leave once she gets better. Take pity on us all and teach her your recipes, will you?"

Staring at the pot in utter dismay, Lacey said, "You seem to share her chili recipe."

"Simple rule: In Texas, you make the chili so it blows off the top of your head when you take a taste." He grinned. "Then you triple the hot stuff." He gawked at the spice rack. "Where's the chili powder?"

Lacey pulled it from her apron pocket. "I had to hide it from Aunt Millie so she wouldn't put it in the coleslaw last night."

His features looked pained. "So that's what she does to it." He dumped an eye-popping amount into the first pot, then as much into the second, and finally set down the tin. "At least she won't be able to do it again until you buy more."

"You emptied the chili powder and Tabasco into it!"

"Yup." He stirred the pot.

Aunt Millie returned so fast, Lacey suspected she'd already sent word to the mercantile to have everything ready. Lacey couldn't even cut more peppers. Her eyes, nose, and fingers already stung. Jeff grabbed a knife, hacked the peppers into an unsightly mess, and dumped them into the chili as Aunt Millie merrily shook Tabasco into the second pot.

Lacey put another pan of corn bread into the oven and wondered how she'd ever explain to the hungry patrons that the main dish had been spoiled.

Jeff tilted his head toward the icebox. "Now get yourself some milk."

"Would you care for a glass?"

"Don't need it." He waited until she had a glassful. "Now taste this."

Lacey didn't want to sample it. Then again, she didn't want to be rude. At least he didn't have a lot on the spoon. She opened her mouth.

Chapter 4

O h. Ohh." Lacey's hand went up to her mouth. The strangled sound coming out of her made Jeff drop the spoon and grab the milk from her.

"Here. Drink." He lifted the glass and tried to peel her hand from her mouth. Her big hazel eyes filled with tears that overflowed and spilled down her cheeks.

"It'll help. Drink!"

Both of her hands clamped around his. The poor woman could scarcely breathe, but she took a sip and fought to swallow.

"Drink it all. Fast." Jeff hadn't ever seen such a pitiful sight. Proper little Lacey Mather broke out into a full-on sweat, and her face rivaled a tomato for color. Tears poured down her face, and she kept making a sound of pure anguish.

"Wa—" She tried to scramble away. "Wa. Ur."

"Oh no. No water!" Millie stood in front of the pump by the sink.

"More milk." Jeff sloshed milk into the glass and shoved it back at Lacey. "Milk cools the fire." She couldn't decide what to do or where to go, so he yanked out a chair and shoved her into it. As she drank the milk, Millie flapped a dish towel to cool her off.

"I gave her a taste out of the milder pot," he said to Millie.

Lacey said something—it sounded sort of like "murder," but he wasn't sure. Maybe it was "mother."

"Millie, let's have her lie down." Jeff half lifted Lacey from the chair. She clutched the milk bottle for dear life. "Yeah, princess. You bring that along."

With Millie as chaperone, it would be decent enough for him to escort Lacey back to the bedchamber, only Lacey didn't cooperate. They'd scarcely gotten into the parlor when she pulled away and sank onto the horsehair settee and gulped more milk—directly from the bottle.

"She can't breathe," Millie said as she shoved at his shoulder. "You go on back and stir the pot."

Jeff took his cue and left. Women and their stays. Once Millie loosened Lacey, then she ought to improve. Or so he hoped. He stirred the pots, tasted each, and couldn't fathom why she'd reacted at all. They were still blander than rattlesnake. Well, Lacey wouldn't try another taste, so he might as well go ahead and finish seasoning the pots so they'd be ready for the lunch crowd. She'd done fine with the garlic and onion, but the woman didn't have a hint on how much zing and heat to add. Satisfied he'd salvaged lunch, Jeff decided he'd better try to rescue the fair maiden.

"How's she doing, Millie?"

"Hot," Lacey croaked.

Jeff tore open the icebox and chipped out a chunk of ice. His bandanna wasn't exactly clean, but it would have to do.

He wrapped the ice in it and ventured back into the parlor. Ever since she'd arrived, the woman always looked like a page straight out of that *Godey's Lady's Book* his aunt used to pore over. Not any longer. Hair askew, clothing loosened, and apron off, Lacey looked like she'd been dragged through a knothole backward. The sight of her melted his heart.

"Ice." He slid it across her forehead. "Millie, I'll just put the pots on the table and let folks serve themselves today. Why don't you put the corn bread out?"

Lacey grabbed his wrist. "No. Dumb. Keyhole."

"Princess, I'm not going to dump it out. It won't kill anybody." The accusation in her eyes had him squirming. "Just drink a little more milk. Trust me."

Her pretty round jaw dropped open in shock, then clamped shut. Jeff figured it was a good thing she couldn't talk much right now.

Lacey stood in church and held the hymnal, but she didn't sing. Couldn't sing. Ever since yesterday's chili debacle, her tongue and throat belonged to a dragon. A whole day now. An entire day of not being able to speak much, taste at all, or sing a note. And the men! Every last bachelor in town—except Jeffrey Wilson—wouldn't leave her alone. They'd tasted that pot of bubbling brimstone, declared it the best they'd ever eaten, and vowed they'd never let her leave Cut Corners. Unable to deny any responsibility for that vile dish, she'd become a celebrity.

Jeff Wilson—that rascal—didn't let on. No, he didn't. Neither did Aunt Millie.

Both of them ought to visit the altar and confess their dirty deeds.

Only staying mad didn't make sense. Truly this group was

a lot of fun. They managed to find the good in just about any-thing. The fact that they'd eaten every last bit of that dread-ful chili proved her point! But they helped one another out. Peony Wilson had come to the diner the first morning it was open and helped wash all of the dishes. Vivian Sager dropped by each morning to see if Lacey needed anything from the mercantile. The old gents who whiled away their days on the boardwalk playing games all kept watch on the children as they darted across the road on their way to and from school. Jeff brought over coal and sharpened her knives. Aunt Millie, for having a painful arm, still kept a cheerful attitude and did her best to help.

When the last chord on the piano died out, Lacey sat down between Aunt Millie and Peony on the bench. Rafe had gotten called to go check something and worried about his wife, so he'd brought her by to "help" get Aunt Millie ready for church. One glance told Lacey why he'd fretted so. Peony alternated between blanching and taking on a peculiar green tint. No wonder Rafe started showing up for breakfast at the diner! Her new friend deserved to reveal the wonderful news when she took a mind to—and not a moment earlier. That being the case, Lacey opened her silk fan and managed to waft it more toward Peony as the parson approached the pulpit.

"We are all part of the family of God," Parson Clune said. "Working together for the betterment of one another and to promote the kingdom of God."

Aunt Millie reached over with her good hand to give Lacey's leg a loving pat. Ever since Mama had passed on and Father had sent her to the academy, Lacey hadn't been part of a family. She didn't have anybody. Well—back in Boston, she didn't. Here, she had Aunt Millie. If it hadn't been for Father's housekeeper sending the telegraph message on to Lacey, she wouldn't have known her great-aunt still lived.

"Instead of considering it a duty to help our brothers and sisters, it is a privilege and honor to serve them in the name of Christ. Christ displayed an attitude of humility by washing the disciples' feet. You can't get any more down-to-earth than that."

Folks in the congregation caught the pun and chuckled.

Parson Clune smiled and continued, "We want to be like the Savior. That means caring for each other in the everyday, mundane, little matters. . . ."

As the sermon continued, Rafe arrived. He scooted onto the bench next to his wife and slid his arm behind her. She immediately leaned into him and relaxed.

A lady sits upright at all times. Back straight. No slumping. Only a lazy woman rests against the back of her chair. . . ." Madame's lessons darted through Lacey's mind, and for the first time they all seemed petty and nonsensical. Rafe cherished his wife, and she wasn't feeling her best. To support her back while she sat on this hard old bench was—well, it was an act of everyday love. It's like in the fairy tales. A happily-ever-after kind of love. *And they're going to have a family.*

After the service, Lacey couldn't get that image out of her mind. Something tugged at her—a longing she couldn't escape. How wonderful it would be to have someone to love and to be loved by! Oh, if she wanted to, she could accept the very next marriage proposal and become a wife within a week. Men asked for her hand with stunning regularity. *But none of them love me, and I don't love them. I can't live day in and day out when there's no love beneath the roof.*

But a small voice inside taunted, *You already have—all your life at the academy.*

Lacey shoved that thought aside. It was untrue. The younger girls flocked to her, and she adored them. And she admired Madame. If anything, the sermon opened her eyes. She could love in Christ's name and by His example in dozens of tiny ways each day. But that plan didn't take away the odd feeling that she was missing out on finding her own happily-ever-after.

Chapter 5

H oo–oo–ey!" Jeff finished filling the coal bin, took out his bandanna, and flapped it in the air. "Now that you can fire up the stove, I'll open the door and air out this place."

Millie winked. "Long as I've been here—and I'm one of the founding folks of Cut Corners—Ticks McGee never put on any airs for me."

"Put on airs!" Jeff hooted. He opened the door and fanned it back and forth to dispel the overwhelming scent the telegrapher had left in his wake. "The man did a backstroke through bay rum to deliver that telegram."

"Oh, stop that." Lacey continued to peel potatoes, but laughter tinged her voice.

"I don't dare." Jeff kept fanning the room. "If this place isn't aired out by supper, folks'll all think you got a polecat under the planks."

"Not with all the flowers," Millie said in a droll voice as she stood on tiptoe over at the spice rack. "I'm flat running out of jars for 'em."

"They look pretty on the tables," Lacey said as she set aside a potato, got up, and smoothly took the tin of spice from her aunt. "I'd like to save these cloves for the ham, Aunt Millie. I hope you don't mind."

Millie frowned. "Then what're you going to put on the roast beef?"

"I was thinking maybe we ought to do something together. Madame taught us to mix spices and jar them so we'd have ready-made seasonings specifically for chicken, pork, fish, or beef. It saves a lot of time. After I leave, it'll simplify things for you."

"Great idea!" Jeff beamed at her. "Tell you what: I was fixin' to go to the mercantile to get a few things. I'll bring back some of those nifty Ball-Mason jars. What spices do you need?"

"I'll make a list. We can write the recipes down, too." Lacey smiled at her aunt. "And you can be sure to give me your cowboy cookie recipe and that sweet cornmeal mush. The girls at the academy will love it."

Jeff grinned at her. Lacey Mather exhibited more tact than anyone he'd ever known. She hadn't even spoken a cross word when Jay Harris and one of the Baxter boys both brought in goldenrod and had everyone in the diner sneezing all day. Men kept bringing her posies, and she'd have her aunt stick them in jars on the dining tables—along with everyone else's. That way, according to Lacey, everyone could enjoy the beauty of Texas. Far as all those men were concerned, Lacey was the Beauty of Texas. But Beauty never once showed the least bit of interest in any of the men.

Millie and Peony did a fair job of sitting on either side

of Lacey at worship services; otherwise, a passel of lovesick cowboys all practically trampled the poor woman in hopes of having the honor of sitting by her side. Ticks McGee actually knocked over a bench in church in his rush to be near her.

That wasn't all. She'd befriended the women in town, and even old sourpuss Lula Chamberlain sang her praises. Youngsters were crazy about her, too. Why, she'd taken to baking cookies only the children were offered if they'd finished their meal. Folks in town speculated on how good they must be, and the kids practically licked their plates clean to earn one—but Lacey didn't let the adults have 'em. She declared it as a rule.

Only she'd set one on the ledge by the coal box for Jeff each time he made a delivery. A special one—extra big. Continuing to fan the door, he bit into the cookie. "Mmm."

"I've been meaning to speak with you about increasing the delivery of coal to every other day."

Jeff took another bite and waggled his brows. Mouth full of incredible taste, he suggested, "How about every day?"

Her gaze went from the remains of the cookie to his eyes, then back. "I wouldn't want to cast aspersions on your character or motives. Shall I presume the offer stems from the fact that winter is almost upon us?"

"Miss Mather." Jeff tucked the last portion of the cookie in his mouth, chewed and swallowed it with relish, then grinned. "I wouldn't take offense if you assumed my offer had anything to do with a tasty fringe benefit. No man in his right mind would pass up an opportunity to eat your cooking. As for winter—well, the weather's getting snappy."

She opened the cookie jar and held it out to him. "I've been thinking about that. Perhaps it's time to place an order with

Sanger's so the diner isn't without necessities. When do we expect the first snowfall?"

"Snow?" Millie let out a cackle and grabbed a cookie.

Jeff helped himself. "More often than not, it doesn't snow here until late, if at all."

A stricken expression crossed Lacey's pretty face. "You don't have snow for Christmas?"

"A few times we have." It hadn't ever mattered to him, but clearly the thought rocked Miss Mather to the core.

Millie dusted a cookie crumb from her lips. "A bigger mess you've never seen. Folks tracked slush and mud in here and never gave me a moment's rest. All they wanted was coffee, soup, and pie. Can't make much of a profit on that."

"With all the rain we've been getting, I thought—" Lacey let out a small self-conscious laugh. "I suppose it doesn't matter. You're both happy without the snow, and I'll be back in Boston up to my boots in snow for Christmas."

Suddenly the cookie tasted like sawdust. Jeff looked at Lacey and couldn't imagine her leaving. "You don't have to go."

Her eyes widened and glistened with sincerity. "But of course I shall. I've given my word."

"Frankly, I don't like the looks of this." Dr. Winston supported Aunt Millie's arm and carefully moved it. "It's healing more slowly than I'd hoped."

"Don't tell me you're going to splint me up again. I won't have it."

Lacey took corn bread from the oven and popped in pans of chocolate cake. "What do you recommend, Doctor?"

"Not another splint." Aunt Millie's repressive tone

matched her taut face.

"If we keep it heavily bandaged and in a sling, that ought to provide enough protection. You cannot use the arm yet for anything. Even lifting the lightest object might well snap the bone again."

"I don't need to be mollycoddled. Using the arm will strengthen it."

Doc folded his arms across his chest. "Millie, you're old, you're stubborn, and you're wrong."

"Two out of those three aren't flaws," she shot back.

"But that still means the doctor needs to bind up your arm," Lacey said.

"Not till after I eat a chunk of that corn bread. Doc, have a seat."

Lacey smiled at the physician. He'd about hit his limit in dealing with her aunt. "Please do sit down. Would you rather have vegetable barley soup or potato cheese?"

"Have the potato cheese. She wouldn't listen to me and add cinnamon or nutmeg to the vegetable barley." Aunt Millie shot Lacey a disgruntled look. "Everyone knows you add nutmeg and cinnamon to things with grains in them."

The doctor choked, coughed, then rasped, "I'd like the vegetable, please. And Miss Mather, you cannot possibly leave yet. At this point, your aunt still needs your assistance."

"I suspected as much. I'll send a telegram today." The thought of staying in Cut Corners awhile longer filled her with happiness.

The happiness lasted all through serving lunch, clear until she approached the telegraph office. Facing Ticks McGee after she'd turned down his marriage proposal qualified as more than a little awkward. In the time she'd been in Texas, there hadn't been a single day during which she hadn't received a gentleman's offer to take her out for a walk. . .and more than a few had actually embellished the invitation clear into a proposal that she walk down the aisle to him! Once she'd informed the populace that she'd be returning to Boston, Lacey presumed the nonsense would stop. On the contrary, it only got worse.

That scamp Jeff Wilson seemed to find the whole thing hilarious. Indeed, Lacey supposed it was. She tried to keep a sense of perspective. These men were lonely. And hungry. Madame said a man who had a full plate and a quiet woman who listened to him was a happy man. These men were seeking happiness. She oughtn't fault them for following their nature. Lacey just wished their nature would lead them to some other woman.

"Well, well! Miss Mather, what can I do for you?" Ticks perked up.

"Good afternoon, Mr. McGee. I'd like to send a telegram." She'd already composed it back at the diner, so she took the paper from her reticule and handed it across the counter.

"This is quite a lengthy one." He pulled the pencil from behind his ear and dabbed the lead on his tongue. "We could shave it down and save you a bundle."

Lacey suppressed a shudder at the fact that his hair oil slicked the pencil. "I appreciate the offer, sir, but that isn't necessary."

His brows scrunched into a deep V. "It costs a nickel per three words, Miss Mather."

"Yes, I know." She smiled. "I counted it at a hundred fifty-nine words. According to my arithmetic, it should total two dollars and sixty-five cents."

He tapped his pencil against her paper. "It goes against my

grain to take advantage of a lady. I'm sure I can help you out. You can't squander your money like that."

"My finances are not your concern, sir. The matter is important, and I'd appreciate you taking the utmost care in transmitting the letter precisely as I composed it." She set the exact cost of the telegram on the counter.

Muttering to himself, Ticks went over to the telegraph key. He settled into the oak chair, poised his finger over the apparatus, then squinted at the missive. His head shot up. "You're staying?"

"Only for a while longer."

"Why don't you have a seat? You can wait for a reply."

The last thing she wanted to do was spend more time in the stuffy office with a man far too eager to drag her to the altar. "Forgive me for asking you to deliver any reply to the diner. I have a few errands to run."

Exiting the office, she headed for Sanger's Mercantile. Perhaps if she and Vivian looked at what was in stock, they could concoct a softer, more comfortable bandage and sling for Aunt Millie.

Dear Aunt Millie. Lacey fretted over what to do about her relative. The old woman had plenty of spirit and a heart as big as the sky, but there didn't seem to be any reason behind some of her actions. *I'm sure it's the laudanum that makes her forgetful,* Lacey told herself. Then again, Chaps Smythe called her an "odd duck." The appellation did fit—after all, who else would think a roast beef ought to be topped with sugar? Well, regardless, Lacey loved her great-aunt. She wasn't in the least bit upset about extending her stay. What would Jeffrey Wilson say about it, though?

"Are you okay?" Jeff hovered in the doorway.

"Depends on who you're asking." Millie gave him a jaded look as she shuffled across the floor. "I say I'm fine. Doc still wants me trussed up like a coast-to-coast parcel."

He hadn't come to check on Millie's arm, but Jeff nodded. "You do what he wants. We need you completely healed."

"Yes, we do." Lacey stood by the sink dabbing peroxide onto a wad of cotton.

Jeff crossed over toward her and grabbed hold of her hand. Studying her slender fingers, he asked, "Did you cut yourself?" He'd heard she'd bought peroxide at the mercantile, and he'd hotfooted it over here to be sure she was all right. He'd heard other news about Lacey, too, that he wanted to confirm.

"No. I got some drippings on myself when I put the roast in the oven. Peroxide removes bloodstains." She slid her hand loose and continued to fiddle with the front of her too-fancy-for-the-wilds-of-Texas apron. What call did a woman have wearing anything that pristine and frilly when she stood in front of a stove?

"All those facts are a waste, what with you living at that school." Millie dumped sugar into her coffee and shook the spoon at Lacey. "Those girls won't use that knowledge a lick. They'll marry rich men and have maids and cooks to do the work for 'em."

He saw hurt darken Lacey's eyes. Clearly she felt she'd found what God intended her to do with her life. Having others disparage it upset her. Though he agreed with Millie's assessment, Jeff couldn't bring himself to say so aloud. Instead, he teased lightly, "According to Ticks, the girls will have to make do without you for some time yet."

Lacey nodded. "I'll be staying until just before Christmas.

That'll give Aunt Millie plenty of time to heal."

"I think I'll buy another fireplace poker from you, Jeff." Millie winced as she placed her arm on the table. "I'll use it to prod Ticks out of here. The man's making a pest of himself."

"Your niece has been good for business, Millie."

"Amazing what a pretty face'll do." Millie nodded. "Brings 'em all in, and they don't seem to mind that the food's seasoned all wrong. The girl cooks like an easterner."

"I've been able to thank God with a clear conscience for every last meal she's cooked."

Millie gave him a worldly-wise look. "Ecclesiastes 2:24: 'There is nothing better for a man, than that he should eat and drink, and that he should make his soul enjoy good in his labour. This also I saw, that it was from the hand of God.' That's you, Jeff Wilson. You're happy just to have a full belly and a hot forge."

"Contentment is a fine quality," Lacey said quietly. "Jeff works hard, and his heart belongs to God. In my estimation, that's more than admirable." She turned back to trying to remove the blot on her apron.

Jeff appreciated her compliment. Lacey wasn't one to pass out flattery. He patted the edge of her apron. "Well, you need to take a little credit for that contentment. I'm doing all of my eating here these days."

"You're always most welcome," Lacey said.

Most welcome. Was that just polite banter, or did she mean I'm more welcome than anyone else?

Peony took a sip of tea and gave Lacey a grateful smile. "It's helping. Thank you."

"Lemon's supposed to help, too. Here. I made lemon spritz

cookies for you." Lacey urged her friend to nibble. For the past week and a half, she'd been bringing little meals and treats to tempt Peony. Rafe took all his meals at the diner, and from the lines creasing his face, Lacey knew he was beside himself with worry.

"Dr. Winston says my tummy will settle down in another few weeks."

"Of course it will." Lacey smiled brightly. "In the meantime, since you don't have to worry about cooking, we need to plan your wardrobe for the *accouchement*."

Peony smiled. "Your propriety is so charming. How wonderful to grow up with such refinement."

Lacey urged her to nibble on a second cookie. "I'd scarcely call a school full of chattering girls refined. We were trained in all matters of conduct, but there weren't many opportunities to actually put the lessons into practice."

"I grew up with women, too—but not ones of respectability."

Reaching out, Lacey covered Peony's hand with hers. "Do you think such a thing matters to me? We have no say about the circumstances we're born into. It's what we do with ourselves that matters."

"I felt it only right to confess it. There are those who cannot—"

"Pardon me for interrupting you, Peony, but I cannot abide those with narrow minds and even narrower hearts. From the moment you stepped foot into the diner and offered to help wash up the breakfast dishes, you showed your true heart. God sent you to me as a friend, and I'm thankful. So now that we've settled that, why don't we design a dress for you to wear through Christmas? I'm sure with your clever sewing we could take deep seams to let out as your delicate condition progresses."

"I did order a length of beautiful green paisley."

Once she'd made sure Peony had finished the tea, cookies, and cheese, Lacey headed back to the diner. Aunt Millie was supposed to be placing an order over at Sanger's, and they'd already prepared the chicken pasties. Lacey would start popping them into the oven and have them ready just in time for the lunch crowd. She turned the corner and saw smoke billowing out of the diner window.

Chapter 6

W ell!" Millie plopped down in the chair and fanned herself with a damp, charred dishcloth.

Jeff stamped on another ember and poured one last bucket of water down the wall. The entire window frame looked like a chunk of charcoal, the panes were cracked, and what had once been curtains now made a sad pile of ashes on the floor.

"Aunt Millie!" Lacey barreled into the room.

"Over here. No use fussing."

"Are you well? Did either of you get burned?" Lacey's voice quavered as she made her way to her aunt.

"Wasn't nothing much. No real harm done." Millie shrugged. " 'Cept a couple of the pastries for lunch are singed."

"No one cares about that, Millie. We're just glad you didn't get hurt." Jeff set down the water bucket.

Lacey watched him solemnly. Her hazel eyes reflected a mix of horror and gratitude. One glance at the place told just how close this had come to being a disaster. "Thank you." She stumbled toward the other door and opened it wide. Smoke drafted on the breeze from the first door to the second.

"Smoke follows beauty." Jeff didn't intend to speak aloud. Once he realized he'd done so, he crooked her a grin. "I don't think there's much damage here. Nothing a little sanding, a few replacement boards, and glass won't solve."

"Erik Olson can handle that." Millie leaned back in her chair.

"I'll see him about it after lunch." Lacey stepped through the water puddles on the floor and opened the oven door.

"Careful!" Jeff cinched his arm about her waist and lifted her up and back. He'd barely managed in time. Gray water with gritty bits of soot and coal spilled from the appliance and splattered on the floor.

"Oh my."

Oh my. Jeff wanted to echo Lacey's words—but for an entirely different reason. He'd just grabbed an armful of woman, and he hadn't anticipated the effect. He didn't want to put her down. The sweet scent of her perfume engulfed him.

"The oven's stone-cold."

"Yep." He didn't tell her it took eight buckets of water before the dumb thing stopped steaming—all of course, after the half dozen he'd used on the wall and window. At the moment, he doubted she would accept that information with much poise.

Patting his arm, Lacey said, "You did a wonderful thing, Mr. Wilson. Heroic. There's no doubt you rescued my aunt and the diner."

From the way she twisted, he knew she wanted to be put down. Jeff took a few long strides and grudgingly set her on the dry patch of planks on the far side of the table. "I just happened along."

"Thank the Lord!" Lacey cast a glance at the shelves of towel-covered sheets. "You've already done so much. I do hate to impose, but would you mind awfully if I used your forge?"

"My forge?"

Twenty minutes later, Jeff stood beside Lacey at his forge. The crazy woman was dressed in her calico dress and a frilly white apron; she held a potholder in one slender hand and a long pair of tongs in the other. She'd dug out the biggest pot in the diner, given it to him, and now had lard melted and bubbling in it. "I'd far rather bake these. It's much more healthful," she said as she snagged the chicken pasties from the pot and replaced them with more.

"Smells great."

"Hey, there." Uncle Eb stood over at the rail. He shot Jeff a wily grin. "What's happening here?"

"Your nephew is saving the day." Lacey flashed Uncle Eb a smile. "He put out a fire at the diner, and he's letting me fix lunch here."

"What say, folks just drop by here to pick up their lunch? Looks like they can carry them meat pies."

"I don't know. . . ." Lacey looked up at Jeff. "What do you think?"

"After all the rain, it's a fair day. Ground's dry. We can stick out a bucket of apples and call it a picnic lunch."

"A picnic!" Her face lit up. "Oh, I love picnics. I know just what to do."

By the time lunch was scheduled, Jeff stood back and shook his head at the event. At Lacey's urging, he'd set out a pair of sawhorses and stretched a few solid planks across them. She'd covered them with a red-checkered tablecloth from the diner. A big vat of potato salad, a dish of pickle spears, slices of buttered bread, and a bucket of apples sat along it. Six more tablecloths lay on the ground, weighted by rocks and each holding one of the jars of flowers from the diner. She stepped back and sighed. "If only we had some music!"

"You could sing."

She turned the exact color red as the checkers in the table-cloth. "I'd scare away the diners. I confess, I cannot sing at all."

"No?" Her admission caught him off guard. "I thought those fancy girl schools turned you out with all sorts of musical accomplishments."

"They're supposed to. I failed abysmally. The music master despaired of teaching me to sing. I'm utterly and completely tone deaf. Even worse, I developed the revolting habit of getting hiccups whenever I attempted the flute." Her smile turned charmingly winsome. "It produces the oddest sounds."

"But you played the piano last week at church."

"Only because the pastor implored me to since no one else was more capable. I'm afraid the piano master pronounced my playing 'somewhere between painful and passable.'"

He scowled. "Was everyone there that cruel? I thought they pampered you at those places."

"Honesty is the best policy. How could I work on my shortcomings if no one pointed out the flaws? I do, however, hope to mention my impressions with a bit more tact when I'm overseeing the girls at my next post."

Her next post. She said it so blithely. What did she think she was doing, leaving a dotty aunt and a town full of people who cared for her, just to go back to an institution where truth wasn't tempered with compassion? Jeff wanted to roar. He wanted to rattle some sense into her. No way was he going to let her go.

Chapter 7

Erik Olson pounded in one last nail, then stood back to survey the repairs. "Ja. The window, bigger is nice."

"You outdid yourself," Aunt Millie declared. "I think the man deserves a cookie, don't you, Lacey?"

Lacey nodded. She didn't dare actually open her mouth to reply for fear that she'd start to giggle. The Swedish carpenter had been casting longing looks at the cookie jar from the moment he came over to assess the damage. To his credit, even when he'd been alone in the kitchen, he'd never sneaked a single crumb. His sense of honor touched Lacey. Then again, it didn't exactly surprise her. Erik was Jeff's friend—and as she'd been taught, a man could be judged by the company he kept.

"My niece made you a whole dozen of your own, Erik. You go ahead and enjoy 'em—every last one." Aunt Millie scooted a plate across the table.

Erik grinned and pulled out a chair. "Then I will eat them

here. My uncle and the other old men—they will gobble up the plate if I go outside."

"Milk, or coffee?" Lacey offered.

"Both." The carpenter gave her a boyish grin. "Milk for to dunk the cookies. Coffee to remind me I am no longer a boy, even though I enjoy the treat you keep for the children."

Lacey set the beverages before him, then turned back to the oven. She opened the door and pulled out the roaster just long enough to dump in the carrots and potatoes.

"Mmm, mmm, mmm. Something smells great."

She didn't even turn around. "Is there anything you don't like, Jeff?"

"Cranberries." His boots rang across the planks, and coal shuffled into the bin.

"Asparagus. He does not like that, either." Erik grinned. "He calls it 'ugly pencils.' "

Lacey wheeled around. "And I served you asparagus the first time you ate here!"

"Your asparagus is good. Millie, I still think you need to teach her chili doesn't take beans."

The older woman sighed theatrically. "You can lead a horse to water. . . ."

"Aunt Millie! Are you comparing me to a horse?"

"Don't get all het up and scandalized." Aunt Millie's face puckered. "Horses are fine creatures. Loyal. Hardworking."

Jeff shot a look at the new window ledge. "Good work, Erik."

"Thank you."

Lacey took the hint. She grabbed the cookie jar and held it out to him. He looked down at his sooty hands. "Here." Fishing out a pair of cookies, she slipped them into his hands.

"Much obliged." Jeff cast a look at Erik, who was plowing through the plate of cookies like a starving man. "If the old rangers catch wind of you eating those all by yourself, your days are numbered."

"You do not tell them. I will not tell them you eat a cookie each time you come to deliver coal." Erik bit off another chunk. "This is a good bargain. You come out better."

Jeff pounded his friend on the shoulder and belted out a chuckle.

The male camaraderie astonished Lacey. She'd never had an opportunity to watch men interact. The whole time Erik worked, Jeff had tracked in and out, lent a hand, and silently left. Neither of them ever said a word about the assistance. Rafe Wilson was the same way. He and Jeff were cousins, and they often seemed to carry on entire conversations over the dining table without saying more than a cryptic one- or two-word phrase apiece, grunt, nod, and grin.

Those masculine grins—Jeff's in particular—were oddly gratifying sights. Men, for being such odd, rough creatures, never looked very approachable. But when Jeff's mouth kicked up and his eyes sparkled with laughter, an odd sense of contentment washed over Lacey. Longing to keep him smiling, she said, "I've been thinking about Thanksgiving."

"Diner's closed Thanksgiving and Christmas. I made that mistake the first year. Worked myself silly, and all because everyone else was too lazy. Since then, I have a free pot roast luncheon for all the bachelors on Christmas Eve Day. That's as good as it's gonna get." Aunt Millie rapped the knuckles of her left hand on the table. "Let each of 'em cook their own turkey or goose."

"My goose is cooked, all right," Jeff muttered. He scowled.

"Come on, Millie. It's stupid for me to make a whole turkey just for myself."

"You got an uncle and a cousin and his wife. Your family'll take you in."

Lacey inhaled sharply. "Oh, but Peony can't cook. It's too hard for her."

"Good." Jeff's smile looked downright smug. "Then we'll all show up. You name the time."

"Ja, name the time." Erik bobbed his head.

"If you come, Swede will tag along," Aunt Millie groused.

"Of course they will," Lacey chirped. Excitement welled up inside. She'd always had to endure lonely holiday meals with the cook at the academy. This would be her first time to have a true holiday feast. "And so will Stone Creedon and Chaps Smythe. They sit and play dominoes and checkers with Swede and Ebenezer Wilson every day. I can't abide the thought that they'd feel left out."

"Child, you're talking yourself into a heap of work." Aunt Millie shook her head. "With my arm like it is, I'm barely helping out as is. You try cooking a whole fancy feast, and—"

"We'll all pitch in," Jeff said.

Flashing him a grateful smile, Lacey said, "So it's settled."

Jeff whistled under his breath. "Wow."

Lacey beamed. "Isn't this fun?"

"You outdid yourself." He stared at the dining room. She'd pushed two tables together to form a big square. A snowy tablecloth covered it, and she'd folded napkins on the plates to form fancy fan-shaped designs. Apples, nuts, and ribbons cascaded out of a pair of cornucopias as a centerpiece.

"I'll have to ask you to light the candles just before we

begin. I can't reach them."

"Sure." He'd come over early to help out—or as Millie put it, "rein her in." Lacey got some crazy notion that this was supposed to be a seven-course meal. For the past week, he and Millie kept cutting down Lacey's grand plan and nixed over half of the menu items.

It started when Lacey asked his preference between oyster bisque and some other fishy-sounding soup. "To be honest, I've got my mouth set for turkey."

"Naturally, we'll have turkey. I'm talking about the soup course, though."

Millie had chimed in. "Why waste time making that? They won't care. Give the men what they want."

"Very well." Lacey sighed, then brightened. "Then let's discuss appetizers. I was thinking how lovely it would be to have an assortment of—"

"Turkey, child. The men want turkey."

"And stuffing," Jeff had tacked on. "I couldn't care less about a bunch of little morsels. I'm saving all my room for the good stuff."

Good stuff. He hadn't known just what that meant to Lacey, but now he was finding out. "Did you sleep at all last night?"

"A little." She bustled toward the kitchen and over to the stove, where she lifted the lid on a pot and gave the contents a quick stir. "Aunt Millie, if you'd put the baskets of rolls on the table, I'd appreciate it. Jeff, would you please move this pot of potatoes onto the table so I can use the burner for something else?"

Hefting the pot, he asked, "Want me to drain the water?"

"Not just yet. It'll keep them hot until I mash them." She

set a coffeepot on to percolate, then opened the oven. The nearly overpowering aroma of turkey burst into the room, but Lacey reached beside the huge pan and pulled out another dish. She opened the lid, drizzled butter atop yams, and sprinkled brown sugar over it all.

Jeff's stomach rumbled. "I'm not going to be able to wait another half hour to eat."

"Yes, you will." She waggled her spoon at him. "I have this all scheduled, and no one is going to destroy my plan."

"Oh, give the man a cookie," Millie laughed as she came back in.

"It'll spoil his appetite."

"I'm not a child."

Lacey paused and looked up at him. Her lips parted, then closed. Though she'd already been rosy from the heat of the stove, her color heightened. "No one could mistake you for a child. Forgive me."

"It'll cost you a cookie." He winked. "You can buy me off cheaply."

"Spoken like a true friend," Millie said as she pulled butter from the icebox.

"Friends and family—that's what today's all about." Tears sheened Lacey's eyes, turning them into glistening pools of gold. "Being thankful to the Lord with those we love."

A knock sounded at the door. She smoothed her skirts and went to answer it. Millie watched her go, then murmured, "I didn't figure it out till last night. Did you know that gal hasn't had a family Thanksgiving since her mama passed on? She was only six. Ever since then, she's been stuck at that snooty school. It's why she's so dead set to make today perfect."

"Then let's make her dreams come true."

The turkey skidded off the platter and onto the table. Ebenezer Wilson growled, stabbed the bird with the carving fork and knife, and wrestled it back onto the platter, then proceeded to hack the beautiful golden brown bird into unidentifiable chunks.

"You made succotash!" Jeff shot Lacey a huge smile as he lifted the lid off the dish. "My favorite!"

"I'm glad." Well, at least that went well.

"What's this in the dressing?" Stone Creedon stabbed at something with his fork.

"Oysters," Lacey said as a sinking feeling swamped her. Didn't Texans use oysters in their stuffing?

"I say!" Chaps Smythe reached over, speared the oyster straight off Stone's plate, and gulped it down. "Excellent! I haven't had oyster stuffing in years." He then proved his liking for the dish by scooping almost a third of the bowl onto his plate.

Rafe kept trying to coax Peony to have a little taste of each item as the dishes were passed around the table. Lacey secretly thought it a marvel her friend wasn't abjectly ill just from the sight of her husband's heaping plate with gravy dripping off the edge. Lacey tried to distract herself by helping serve Aunt Millie.

Finally, everything had been around the table, and Lacey relaxed. She promised herself she was going to enjoy today. Picking up her knife and fork, she managed a smile. Everything wasn't exactly picture-perfect, but everyone seemed content.

Bang, bang, bang.

Chapter 8

L acey jumped at the sound, turned, and tamped down
a groan. Ticks McGee and Jay Harris both peered
through the window.

"I'll take care of this." Jeff rose and headed toward the door.
He opened it and said in a firm tone, "The diner's closed today."

"It can't be," Jay Harris said.

"Oh, I smell turkey." Ticks sounded somewhere between
heaven and torture.

Memories of lonely holiday meals washed over Lacey. She
rushed over to the door as tears filled her eyes. "Please join us.
I should have thought to invite you. I'm so sorry."

"You don't have to do this," Jeff said in a low tone. His
large body still blocked the door.

Lacey looked up at him. "I want to. Everyone deserves to
belong and be wanted."

"Okay." He brushed her tears away. "You men wipe your feet."

Rafe came over. "And go wash off that bay rum, McGee.

My wife can't take it."

Hours later, everyone wandered off. Lacey was up to her elbows in water, and Jeff dried the dishes. "We ran out of stuffing," she said.

"So what?" Aunt Millie awkwardly poured the last bit of cranberry jelly from a bowl into a Ball-Mason jar. "If you wanna squawk, then talk about what Eb did to the bird."

"No harm done," Jeff said blandly. "It still tasted great."

"I should have made another pie."

"There was plenty until we got company," Aunt Millie said in a wry tone.

Heavy-hearted, Lacey nodded. "I should have planned better. I should have invited them and made more." She glanced at Jeff. "I'm sorry you didn't get any pie."

"I had my dessert before supper—remember the cookies?"

"You're a gallant man, Jeffrey Wilson."

His big hands stopped drying a platter. Eyes steady as could be, he studied her and said, "You're every inch a fine lady, Lacey Mather—but more than that, you're a good woman. This Thanksgiving was unforgettable."

"Thank you. I've never received a sweeter compliment. I wanted to do something special so we could all look back fondly. Years from now, I know I'll always treasure this day that I spent with you."

"There can be more of them, you know." He reached over and brushed a bubble from her sleeve.

Her hands sank to the bottom of the sink, and her heart went right along with them. "No. I'll go back to Boston soon." Forcing a smile, she tacked on, "Where I'll even have a white Christmas."

"Stubborn woman." Jeff brought the hammer down again to punctuate his opinion. What was wrong with Lacey? Couldn't she see her life was here in Cut Corners?

"We came to talk sense into you," Uncle Eb said from beyond the rail.

Jeff glowered at him and the other three meddling men. "What now?"

"You can't let Lacey Mather go back East," Chaps declared. "It's simply unacceptable."

"You're thinking with your belly," Jeff said. It irritated him that these men only cared about Lacey because she could cook. Didn't they see past that? Couldn't they understand that she deserved to be loved and have a family surrounding her?

"Plenty of young bucks around Cut Corners. Every last one of 'em thinks she's a fine catch," Stone Creedon said.

"Better make a quick move," Swede advised.

"I think we've said enough," Uncle Eb declared. He nudged Chaps. "Let's get back to the game. I'm going to whup you like a rented mule."

"Pride goeth before destruction, and an haughty spirit before a fall." Chaps inspected him for a moment through his monocle—an action intended to lend impact to his words. The old ranger then straightened his shoulders and marched out with the others close on his tail.

Uncle Eb stuck his head back into the smithy. "Son, don't let pride keep you from love. She might well be a great cook, but the truth is, since she's come, you're a different man. Puts me of a mind on how I was once I met my wife. When God gives you that blessing, you have to accept it."

After he left, Jeff shoved the iron back into the fire. *Lord, I feel like that bar—You're going to have to heat me, bend me, and hammer me into the man Lacey needs. You're going to have to bend her spirit, too, because she's so dead set on taking a different path.*

Dear Mrs. Delphine,

I deeply regret to inform you that my great-aunt's health is still unstable. Her physician recommends that I remain with her until the New Year. Please forgive me for any inconveniences my absence causes you and the plans you've made for the holiday season.

Sincerely,
Lacey Marie Mather

Ticks read the telegraph and cleared his throat. "I'd be honored to have you sit with me for the Christmas Day service."

"Your offer is most kind, Mr. McGee, but I don't believe that would be wise." Lacey tried to speak gently. He was a nice man—but not the one for her. "When a reply comes, please give it to my aunt. I'll be out running errands."

"Sewing with Peony again?"

Lacey gasped. How did he know where she went and what she did? The very notion that he kept track of her made chills run down her spine. "Good day, Mr. McGee." She set payment for the telegram on the counter and left with what Madame termed "purposeful decorum."

Bless her, Peony had offered to have them sew back in Aunt Millie's parlor. After the fiery debacle the last time, Lacey knew nothing but relief that her friend understood the necessity of keeping close watch over the situation. Lacey stepped foot into Peony's place and asked, "What shall I carry?"

"Rafe already took it over. He refuses to let me lift a thing." She cast a look across the street. "Lionel Sager hired me to make a dress for Vivian for Christmas. Just wait until you see—it's a blue, button-down wool."

"What a wonderful surprise! I can't keep anything from Aunt Millie. She's more curious than any cat, so you know what I did?"

"No, what?"

"I sent away to Boston for Christmas gifts!"

"How clever of you!" They stepped out onto the boardwalk.

"She's a clever gal, all right," Swede declared as he hunkered over the checkerboard. "I'm thinking I ought to challenge her to a game."

Stone snorted. "You just want someone new to beat."

Peony dipped her head and kissed Ebenezer Wilson on his weathered cheek. "I'm going to Millie's to sew, Father. If anyone comes to the shop, you can tell them where I am."

"Okay, darlin'." The old man smiled at his daughter-in-law, then patted her hand. "Don't work too hard."

"I won't let her." Lacey held Peony's arm and led her down the boardwalk. The genuine affection between Peony and Eb never failed to touch her deeply. She couldn't recall a single time when her own father had given her the merest scrap of attention. "The Lord has blessed you so much," she said to her friend.

"Hasn't He?" Peony beamed. She glanced around and lowered her voice. "I confess to being selfish, though. I've been praying, Lacey. I've asked God to keep you here so I'll have a friend when my time comes."

Lacey's step faltered. "Now, Peony—"

"I put it in God's hands. Neither of us is going to snatch it back." She continued to sashay along the gritty boardwalk. "I do declare, I believe that you, Vivian, and I are the only ones who sweep in front of our establishments."

"You're trying to change the subject."

"And you'll humor me because you're such a dear." Peony's laughter tinkled on the crisp air.

"Ladies!" Ticks McGee looked like a crane as he lifted his knees high to pick his way across the rutted road. He waved a piece of paper. "Telegram!" Face flushed, he stood before them and straightened his shoulders. "Dear Miss Mather—"

"I'm able to read the telegram, Mr. McGee."

Ticks ignored Lacey and read, " 'I shall hold your aunt in my prayers. Please extend my wishes for complete recovery. Your loving care surely blesses her. I've arranged for someone to stay with those who are unable to go home for Christmas. Looking forward to seeing you in January. Sincerely, Amanda Delphine.' Isn't that the finest news? You'll be staying here in Cut Corners!"

"Only through Christmas, Mr. McGee." Lacey held out her hand.

Instead of giving her the telegram, he shook her hand!

Thunderstruck by his forward behavior, Lacey stood frozen to the planks beneath her feet.

"Miss Mather isn't a water pump, Ticks." Jeff sauntered over and slapped Ticks on the back in a friendly way.

"She's staying through Christmas!"

Jeff looked straight into Lacey's eyes. "That," he rumbled in a thrillingly deep tone, "is the best news of the year."

"What is that racket?" Jeff rolled out of bed and yanked on his jeans. Shrugging into his shirt, he headed toward the door. The instant he realized what and where the commotion came from, he jogged toward Millie's.

"Shoo fly, don't bother me," one of the cowhands from the Gustavson spread sang.

"Stop that caterwauling," Jeff snapped.

"Shoo fly, don't bother me." The cowboy took his hat from where he'd been holding it so earnestly over his heart and flapped it toward Jeff.

"Leave the man alone. He's shher–en–ading hishh lady love," one of the other cowboys slurred drunkenly.

Lacey Mather deserved far better than a penniless saddle tramp and his sotted sidekicks. Irritated, Jeff barked, "Hush. It's the middle of the night!"

"It's called a moonlight ser–a–nade. It's romantic." The cowboy glowered at him.

"That shhong didn't work. Try a differ'n one," one of his pals urged. "What 'bout 'The Bear Went Over the Mountain'?"

"I'm partial to 'Turkey in the Schtraw,'" another hiccupped.

"'Old Dan Tucker' or 'Little Brown Jug,'" a third suggested.

"Those ain't romantic," the suitor snapped.

"And 'Shoo Fly' was?" Jeff couldn't believe this ridiculous scene. "It's the middle of the night. Leave the poor girl alone."

"You just want the girl for yourself."

The accusation hung in the crisp air. Jeff widened his stance, stared at the men, and asked in a very still tone, "What if I do?"

Chapter 9

"hat if I do?" Jeff's words seeped into the room, and Lacey muffled her gasp. Awakening to the so-called serenade had been surprise enough for the night. An embarrassing surprise. Lacey hadn't opened the curtains or the door because she didn't want to encourage such nonsense. Aunt Millie slept through the whole thing, but Lacey didn't delude herself into believing that meant the rest of Cut Corners would do likewise. By tomorrow, she'd have to face all of the diners' smirks and teasing comments.

But now, Jeff put himself on the line. Of all the bachelors in this crazy town, only he hadn't pestered her. Oh, he'd definitely had his share of observations regarding her would-be suitors. Never once did he stoop to being cruel or unkind about those men, and he made it clear he found her worthy of such attention, however bumbling it might be. But he respected her ambition to go back to Boston and become a teacher. He alone hadn't asked her to change to suit his pleasure.

Such chivalry, she thought. *He's putting himself between those men and me. And honorable! He didn't tell a lie. They asked him, but he only responded back with a hypothetical question.*

Lacey leaned against the wall and drew her robe about herself more tightly. *It's all so confusing. I don't understand these men. I ought to be happy to go back to Boston, back to the company of genteel women whom I understand and young girls in need of guidance.*

I ought to, but I'm not sure I am.

"Come back in half an hour." Millie slammed the door in Jeff's face.

He stood out in the rain with a huge scuttle of coal. The last thing he wanted to do was traipse across the street again, then interrupt his morning's work to redeliver this fuel. Irritated, he booted the door open and groused, "I'm a busy man."

Feminine chatter suddenly stilled, save one high-pitched squeal.

Jeff stopped dead in his tracks.

Peony stood on crate, and Lacey knelt on the floor, pinning the hem of her dress. They'd stuffed a pillow or something under the skirt to allow for Peony's increasing size due to her delicate condition.

Peony let out a choked sob.

Lacey jumped to her feet and stood at an angle to block Jeff's view. "Why, Jeff. Yes, you are a busy man. No use in holding you back." Her voice stayed quite calm. All of those years of training served her well. "If you'll please fill the stove, I'd appreciate it. Oh, and I've been making gingerbread. It's not iced yet, but you're welcome to cut yourself a piece."

"Don't mind if I do." Given that reprieve, he hotfooted it

into the kitchen. It always struck him as silly for everyone to pretend to ignore the fact that the Lord was blessing a woman with a child. Nonetheless, Peony tried so hard to observe every societal dictate. Given her background, Jeff understood why it was so important to her. Lacey—well, she'd salvaged a bad situation with her smooth thinking.

Making it a point to be noisy so they'd be able to track his whereabouts, Jeff dumped the coal, clattered around to cut a huge chunk of the gingerbread, and shouted, "Thanks, Lacey." He strode through the diner and half slammed the door to reassure them he wasn't about to scandalize them with his presence again.

"What you got there?" Stone Creedon squinted at him.

"Gingerbread."

The old ranger spraddled closer and tore off a huge portion of the fragrant treat. "Guess it'll have to do. I was hopin' you'd bring out cookies."

"You know how Lacey is about those."

"She does?"

Jeff gave Stone a quizzical look. Given an opportunity, the old guy usually talked enough to explain his odd mishearings. Confronting him with them or asking him to use his ear horn only got him riled.

"Mayhap she oughtta git her some new shoes then. Or socks. Good cotton ones—not them silk kind."

"Jeff." Rafe sauntered up. He cocked his brow and grabbed for what little gingerbread remained. "We need to talk."

"Sure do. Jeff, tell Rafe all about it. He can talk sense into Peony, and then she can make Lacey see reason."

"What's happening with Lacey?"

Stone brushed crumbs from his droopy mustache. "She's

got bad toes." He perked up. "Tell you what. Me and the others, we'll come serve lunch and supper today. Thataway, Lacey can soak her feet."

"Great idea," Rafe said. He and Jeff watched as Stone headed toward his cronies. "Are you going to fetch Doc Winston?"

"I don't think there's any need. Stone just jumbled up what I said. So what do we need to talk about?"

"Word around town is you have Gustavson's cowboys sore at you. I saw the tail end of what happened last night, and I know you too well. If you were just trying to get rid of them, they'll be back and pester her half to death. If you're serious, then you need to make it clear to everyone that the little lady is yours."

Jeff leaned against the diner's wall. "Rafe, convincing them isn't going to be the hard part."

"Have you seen the sign-up list for the bachelors' dinner?" Peony asked Vivian as they decorated the church.

"No. Why?"

"Because I didn't know there were that many bachelors in Cut Corners. Gordon Brooks even signed up, so the Tankard will be closed!" Lacey tacked up a swag of pine. "I'll need to order more beef."

"Just tell me how much," Vivian murmured as she shoved her slipping spectacles higher on her nose. "I'll make sure we have it in the mercantile for you."

"That's not what I was talking about." Peony let out an exasperated sound. "Millie put out the list, and the page was almost full before lunch ended. Jeff wasn't at lunch, so when he caught wind of that list, he went and put his name at the very top in huge, bold letters."

Vivian clasped her hands over her heart. "Lacey, I'm sure the man has a tendresse for you."

If only he did. Lacey shook her head. "No, no. He's just being a very good friend. He's trying to shoo away all of those men so I don't have to deal with any more awkward proposals."

"I've never gotten a single proposal," Vivian said quietly as she lifted her hem and carefully got onto a stepladder.

"Neither had I until I came here," Lacey said crisply. "And I wouldn't consider any of the offers I've received as being serious. Those men want a cook. If I ever marry, it'll be because the man loves me, not because he loves my suppers."

Erik Olson entered the sanctuary. "But your cookies—they could win any man's heart." His light blue eyes danced with a teasing light. "I will settle, though, to have you as my sister in Christ."

"That's sweet, Erik," Peony said. "What do you have?"

"I heard you ladies were decorating the church, so I made this. It's the Advent wreath. Vivian, you have the right colors of the candles at the store, ja?"

"I'm sure we do." Vivian scrambled down the stepladder and over to him. "Wouldn't that look positively splendid in front of the pulpit?"

Erik smiled and turned to Lacey. "I am supposed to ask you a question. The bachelors' dinner—Ebenezer wishes to know if widowers are also invited."

"He never went before," Vivian said.

"Lacey was not doing the cooking then." Erik chuckled. "Please do not take this wrong, but Millie's cooking—it is bad. We all love her, so we took turns eating at the diner to make her feel good."

"She is lovable, isn't she?" Lacey looked at all of them. "So are you. What you all have here in Cut Corners is so special—you all care for one another."

"You could stay, you know," Peony said.

"Ja, you should stay." Erik nodded.

"Maybe she wants more adventure in her life," Vivian said. "Ticks told me a woman is a telephone operator in Boston now."

"Boston is altogether different from Cut Corners." Lacey dipped her head and pretended to concentrate on binding the pine boughs to form the next swag. The school in Boston had her pledge, but Cut Corners had her heart. *Lord Jesus, what am I to do? Please show me Your will.*

Jeff couldn't stand it anymore. He'd barely endured the bachelors' pot roast luncheon. Lacey turned the whole thing into a veritable feast. Oh, she'd gone way overboard—and though she'd had Mary Jo Heath, Vivian Sager, and even the young Widow Phelps there to help her serve, the men barely spared those single women a glance.

Every last one of those men fancied himself in love with Lacey. Jeff knew better. He alone suffered that particular malady. Lacey and the girls were picking up the dessert plates, but none of the men took the hint to leave.

Jeff wasn't about to depart until every last man had vacated the premises.

Lacey finally halted at the door to the kitchen and clasped her hands just below her bosom. The pose came naturally—it wasn't meant to be coy, but it drove Jeff daft. When she stood like that, it called his attention to her tiny waist.

"Gentlemen, you're all invited to return this evening at

seven. The whole community is welcome for a Christmas dessert reception."

The men all rumbled their delight.

Jeff stood up. "The lady's being polite, men. Now scat so she can get things ready." The guests trundled out, but Jeff's hackles rose when he spied Harold Myers slipping Lacey a note. Then and there, Jeff knew what he had to do.

Chapter 10

"Place looks awful fancy." Aunt Millie's grousing tone didn't sting one bit because of the wide smile she wore.

"So do we," Lacey said. "Your new dress is marvelous!"

Aunt Millie ran her left hand down the skirts of the blue delft print. "Never had someone give me a store-bought dress. It's like putting a wreath of flowers on a mule."

"Nonsense!" Lacey pulled her Sunday-best apron over her new Christmas gown. For tonight, she'd attached a collar with little green sprigs embroidered along the edge and added a wide green sash. The festive look matched her mood. "I hope we have enough food."

"As much as the men ate today at lunch, they shouldn't be able to wedge another bite in sideways for three days," Aunt Millie said. She sighed. "I may as well confess, I don't blame 'em. I guess we've all grown accustomed to your eastern recipes. My pot roast never tasted like that."

"Her recipes aren't all she brought with her from Boston,"

Jeff said as he let himself in. He held the door wide open. "Take a look."

Lacey tilted her head to look around him. "Snow!"

"Yup." He grinned. "Merry Christmas."

"Oh, snow!" She dashed past him and out into the gently falling flakes and turned her face upward. "Thank You, Jesus! Now it really feels like Christmas!"

"Here." Jeff wrapped something around her.

Lacey glanced down at the soft white merino wool shawl and gasped. "This is beautiful, Jeff."

"Merry Christmas. I figured if we didn't get snow, you'd still have something white falling onto your hair and shoulders."

"That's the most thoughtful thing anyone has ever done for me."

"Lacey. . ." Jeff turned her toward himself.

"Hoo–oo–ey! It's snowing!" Stone Creedon shouted as he and the other old rangers ambled up. "Hope you got lotsa hot coffee on the stove, missy."

"I do. Please, come in." Lacey wished Jeff hadn't been interrupted. He'd looked very intent. Then, too, she'd wanted to tell him her news. Would it make him half as happy as it made her?

"I'm gonna drink a pot all of my own," Stone continued to ramble.

Lacey cast Jeff an apologetic look. She needed to assume her duties as a hostess.

He heaved a sigh. "Go on."

All of Cut Corners turned out for the Christmas Eve dessert reception. Lacey wove in and out of the crowd, chatting with her friends and neighbors while setting out more pies, tarts, cakes, and cookies.

Happiness bubbled in her like the coffee perking on the stove. She'd asked God for direction, and He'd been faithful. The letter from Amanda Delphine today released her from her commitment to the Ladies Academie. From now on, she'd have a home—here, with Aunt Millie.

Jeff followed her into the kitchen. "Want me to take that cake there on into the other room?"

"Oh no." She smiled. "Tomorrow is Rafe's birthday. I made that cake so we could celebrate."

"Come here." Jeff dragged her from the kitchen to the parlor.

"But everyone—"

"Everyone can wait." He cupped her face in his rough hands. "Lacey, I've tried my best to respect your wishes. I know you want to go back to that fancy school, but I can't let you go. I want you to stay here. With me. Lacey, I'm not good with words. What I'm trying to say is, I love you. I want you to marry me."

"This is all so sudden." Madame drilled all of her young ladies to stall for a moment with that phrase so they could gather their thoughts. Lacey laughed. She didn't want to pause. "Oh, Jeffrey. How can you say you're not good with words? Those are the best words I've ever heard. Nothing would make me happier than to stay in Cut Corners and be your wife."

His eyes lit with joy.

"I received a letter from Mrs. Delphine today. She said the other woman is working out well, and if I didn't mind, she'd like to allow her to keep the position. I'm free to stay here, with you."

"And I'm not going to let you go." He pressed a swift kiss on her cheek, then grabbed her wrist and dragged her back into the diner. "I have an announcement! Lacey's going to marry me!"

Everyone cheered.

Old Ebenezer Wilson slapped him on the back. "No time like the present. What do you say, Parson Clune?"

"It's a fine time to be married."

Everyone hastened across to the church. Peony quickly untied Lacey's apron and removed the green-trimmed collar. Vivian pulled a length of elegant white lace from her pocket. "Here. And I have a bouquet, too."

"You do?" Lacey stared at her in amazement.

"Of course I do. Jeff came to the mercantile today to buy your ring. I thought you'd probably get married after church tomorrow, but I brought everything over to the sanctuary tonight before your party."

The sanctuary was nearly freezing, but the crispness in the air made the pine boughs more fragrant. "It's too cold to sit in the pews," Parson Clune decided. "Everyone stand around the edges in a big circle."

In a matter of minutes, everyone held a bayberry candle. By that glow, Uncle Eb escorted Lacey to the altar.

Solemn vows, a kiss, and then Jeff swept Lacey into his arms. "This is the merriest Christmas since Christ came!"

"And there's a wedding cake back at the diner," Aunt Millie declared. "It's Rafe's gift to the bride and groom."

Jeff carried Lacey outside and halted as snowflakes danced about them. She snuggled close. "I love you."

"Now that's an even bigger miracle than snow for Christmas."

"Hundreds of years ago, God touched our souls with the gift of His Son. Tonight He touched our hearts again with

His gift of love for one another. I'm in your arms, Jeffrey. I'm home."

"Welcome home." He dipped his head and sealed his greeting with a kiss.

Brown Sugar Cookies

2 cups light brown sugar
1 cup melted butter
3 eggs
¼ cup milk
1 tbsp. vanilla
1 tsp. baking soda
5–5½ cups flour

Mix ingredients in order given. Add just enough flour to make dough firm enough to roll. Cut into shapes as desired. Decorate with raisins or brown sugar, bake at 350° for 8–10 minutes or until edges are lightly browned.

CATHY MARIE HAKE

Cathy Marie Hake is a Southern California native who loves her work as a nurse and Lamaze teacher. She and her husband have a daughter, a son, and two dogs, so life is never dull or quiet. Cathy Marie considers herself a sentimental packrat, collecting antiques and Hummel figurines. She otherwise keeps busy with reading, writing, and bargain hunting. Cathy Marie's first book was published by Heartsong Presents in 2000 and earned her a spot as one of the readers' favorite new authors. Since then, she's written several other novels, novellas, and gift books. You can visit her online at www.CathyMarieHake.com.

Unexpected Blessings

by Vickie McDonough

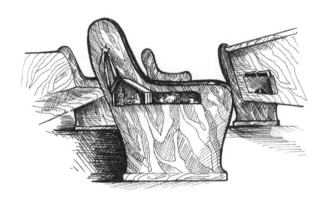

Dedication

To my four sons, Brian, Adam, Eric, and Sean, who have been a source of many blessings in my life.

And to Meridith, my beautiful daughter-in-law, who has added a fun and interesting dimension to our family—and has given me someone to go shopping with.

And to my husband, Robert, whose encouragement and prayers have kept me writing when I've gotten discouraged.

Of his fulness have all we received,
and grace for grace.
JOHN 1:16 KJV

Chapter 1

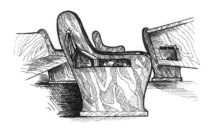

Near Cut Corners, Texas
December 1880

Anna Campbell yawned and glanced again at the cameo watch pinned to her blouse. Twenty more minutes, and the life she'd known for the past two years would change forever. How could she give up the two young children she'd come to love as her own? Closing her eyes, she thought back to all the fun times she'd had with Mark and Molly.

The train's gentle rocking tempted her to lay her head back and rest. It had been months since she'd had a decent night's sleep. Before the children's parents had died. . .

"Listen up, folks."

The loud voice jerked Anna from her dozing. She glanced around, confused about where she was at first.

"We'll be arrivin' in Cut Corners in about five minutes," the conductor yelled over the loud *clackety-clack* of the train.

Anna's heart quickened. Only a few more minutes until

she had to turn Mark and Molly over to a stranger. The time she'd dreaded for months was finally at hand. She turned her head, working the kinks out of her neck, and looked to the left, checking on her two young wards. Molly lay slouched against the side of the train, arms hugging her dolly, while Mark slept with his head in his sister's lap, his thumb only a half inch from his open mouth.

Anna swallowed. How could she bear to do this task that was set before her?

"We've a mess of coal to unload for the blacksmith," the conductor shouted, "so y'all are free to disembark, if you've a mind to. Ain't much of a town, but Lacey's Diner is a right fine eatery. You've got one hour. Not a minute more." The odd little man dressed in a stiff white shirt with black pants and a matching vest eyed everyone as if looking for disagreement. When no one commented, he tipped his cap and headed down the aisle.

Ain't much of a town. His words made Anna's stomach churn. She'd had her fill of small-town life—with its gossiping busybodies and lack of amenities. When she'd left her home of Persimmon Gulch, Arkansas, and moved to Dallas, she had vowed never to step into another small town. Well, maybe the ticket taker was underestimating things.

"Never heard of Cut Corners before," the thin man sitting across the aisle said as he twirled one end of his handlebar moustache between his fingers.

"Ain't even a flyspeck on a map." His rotund partner spat out a brown projectile of tobacco juice into the pathway between the seats.

Anna gasped and jerked her long black skirt out of the aisle. How uncouth! As she examined her hem, she leaned toward the men to better hear their conversation. This was the first information she had been able to garner about the town of Cut Corners. None of her friends in Dallas had even heard of the place. She needed to know what she'd soon be facing.

"Yeah, four ex-Texas Rangers started the town a decade or so back. The railroad came through, but the town never grew all that much. I suppose you'll see for yourself. Looks like we're pulling in now." The man lifted his derby hat off the seat and set it on his bald head.

Anna looked past the two men, trying to see through the grimy windows. The rains they'd passed through earlier had dampened the panes, and now coal dust from the engine clung to the glass, obscuring her view. The train's perpetual rocking finally ceased as the big machine glided to a stop at a small wooden depot and gave a loud shuddering hiss.

Leaning back in her seat, Anna closed her eyes and willed her frantic heart to calm. How could she turn Mark and Molly over to a stranger? How could she leave them behind and return to her life in Dallas? But what choice did she have?

All her life she'd dreamed of playing the piano on stage, and now that dream was within her grasp. All she had to do was get past this little bump in the road. Mark and Molly belonged with the only family they had left, not with a nanny who had cared for them for two short years. She might love them, but she wasn't family.

And her future employer had made it clear that Anna couldn't work for her at the beginning of next year if she was still caring for Mark and Molly. Oh, if only she were married, but even then the children weren't hers to keep. The Olsons' attorney had made that clear enough.

Heaving a sigh of resignation, Anna turned and gave Mark a gentle shake. "Wake up, sweetie. We're here."

The boy shot up like a cannonball, looking both excited and wary. "Unca Erik lives here?" He scrambled off the seat and moved to the window, pressing his face against a clean spot in the glass. "Ain't nothin' but a field out there."

Anna smiled. "Try looking out the other side of the train. And don't say 'ain't.'"

Four-year-old Mark scurried across the aisle, clambered onto an empty seat, and plastered his face against the window. Molly sat up and rubbed her eyes. "What's wrong?"

"We've arrived in Cut Corners."

Six-year-old Molly's pale blue eyes took on a frantic look. She glanced around, watching the other passengers depart. Her trembling lower lip cut Anna to the core. Molly looked back at her with tears shining in her eyes. "I—I don't want you to leave us, Anna."

In a quick second, the girl was in her arms, clinging to her, the child's tears moistening the front of Anna's dress. Ever since they'd lost their parents in a tragic accident two months ago, Anna had prepared the children for the moment when she'd deliver them to their uncle Erik. Still, she never dreamed how heart wrenching it would be. She had pushed the uncomfortable thoughts away, just as she had when she'd left her own family back in Persimmon Gulch. But she couldn't avoid them any longer.

Mark shuffled back across the aisle. "Cain't see nothin'. Can we go now?"

Anna smoothed down the boy's white blond hair, tucked in his rumpled shirt, and smiled. Mark had enjoyed his first train ride. Leaving the urban comforts of Dallas and stepping out into what he thought was the Wild West was a great adventure for him. He'd been talking for a month about seeing real live cowboys and outlaws instead of businessmen in suits.

After hearing what the two travelers had said about the town being started by four ex-Texas Rangers, Anna couldn't help but wonder if Mark wasn't right in his expectations. She wouldn't mind seeing a few rugged cowboys, but outlaws were a different story.

Taking a deep breath, she stood, dusted off her dress, and then donned her long, navy traveling coat. She helped the children into their jackets and picked up the carpetbag that held her only change of clothes. Planning on a quick trip, she'd only brought the necessities.

Molly wiped off her pinafore, just as Anna had done, then she brushed off her dolly's dress. A melancholy smile tugged at Anna's lips. The young girl mimicked almost everything Anna did. Her eyes blurred. How could she get past this moment without her heart breaking? Without crying?

Sucking in a shuddering breath, she hiked her chin, resolving to be strong for the children.

Ten minutes later, with their luggage left with the depot clerk, she stood in the middle of the road, looking out on the puny two-street town. Bile burned her throat. She knew the children would grow up without their privacy. That was life in Small Town, Texas. Everybody knew everything.

At least they didn't have to fight the weather today. The morning's December chill had soared to a pleasantly warm afternoon. And with the rolling hills and screen of trees surrounding Cut Corners, the wind wasn't nearly as fierce here as it was in the flatlands of Dallas.

Ranger Street ran parallel to the railroad tracks, and off to her right she could see the blacksmith shop, a livery, and the saloon. Straight ahead was Main Street. Seeing the church across the tracks brought little comfort, but the fragrant odors emanating from the nearby diner made her tummy fuss. A home-cooked meal would help comfort the children and give her time to figure out how best to locate and approach Erik Olson.

Crossing the tracks, she noticed a group of old men circled around a barrel on the boardwalk in front of the mercantile. They looked to be engrossed in some sort of game.

"Where's all the cowboys?" Mark asked.

"This town only has two streets?" Molly looked up, confusion and anxiety filling her gaze.

For a child who had lived her whole life in Dallas, this place must seem rugged. Anna counted the buildings, her heart sinking further. Barely a dozen structures lined the two streets. Cut Corners made Persimmon Gulch look huge.

With Christmas just a few weeks away, maybe she should have waited until after the holidays to bring the children to their uncle. Maybe she should just turn around and take them back to Dallas with her.

But she couldn't. She had her dreams—and a new job waiting. Plus, Hans and Jessica Olson's last will and testament had stated that in the event of their deaths, the children were to be delivered to their uncle, Erik Olson. The small stipend the will granted to Anna would keep her until she started her new job, but it wasn't enough to support her *and* two children. Besides, she had no legal grounds on which to keep them; only their uncle did.

Not for the first time, Anna voiced a prayer to the God she no longer believed in. Just in case He was real, she pleaded that Erik Olson was an honorable man, one who'd love the children, treat them kindly, and not steal the money left to them.

"I'm hungry." Mark stared up at her with a hopeful gaze. Both children had the same blue eyes and towheaded blond hair—characteristic of their father's Swedish heritage.

"Me, too." Molly tugged on Anna's hand then pointed to Lacey's Diner. "Can we eat there? It smells good."

Anna smiled and nodded just as two men stopped in front of her.

"Whoo-wee! Would you look at that?" The man standing in the middle of the dirt street nudged his friend in the side.

"She's got young'uns." He rubbed his whiskery chin, wiped his hand over oily, slicked-back hair, and eyed her like a rancher inspecting a new cow. "You think she's married?"

Chills charged up Anna's back. She glanced past the two strangers and saw the four old men straighten and turn in her direction. Would they be of any help if she needed it? She tightened her grip on the children's hands. Her heart pounded like Indian war drums.

"Don't rightly know, Ticks. Why don't you ask her?"

The man named Ticks took a step toward her then looked down at his clothes. "Reckon I could do with a bath before I approach such a pretty little filly." He glanced at his friend. "You don't look so fine yourself, Brooks."

Anna stepped back and smacked into something solid. Two large, warm hands on her shoulders steadied her. The men looked past her, their expressions curious but wary.

"I hope you two weren't bothering this woman." The big man behind her replaced his *w*'s with a *v* sound and spoke in a singsong cadence. Anna swirled around at the sound of the familiar Swedish accent. She stared straight into a blue plaid shirt sprinkled with sawdust and smelling of fresh-cut pine. She tilted her head up. Her heart stampeded, and her throat nearly strangled her breath when she recognized the man's face. He looked so much like Hans Olson that he must be his brother, Erik. The very man she was looking for.

"Aw, we didn't mean her any harm," one of the men behind her said. "We're just surprised to find such a pretty gal standin' in the middle of the street looking so lost."

"Yeah, that's right. We're just headin' over to the barbershop to see if Jay could give us a shave and haircut."

Anna couldn't move. The children pressed against the back of her skirt, and Erik Olson's big, solid body blocked her in front. Though he was taller than his older brother and much wider in the shoulders, he sported the same fair hair that was the Olson trademark. Icy blue eyes glared at the two men behind her. She didn't think she'd like to be on this man's bad side. *Please let him be kind to the children.*

She heard the two men behind her shuffle off. As if just realizing how close he stood to her, the children's uncle stepped back.

"Poppa?" Suddenly Mark charged forward and locked his arms around Erik Olson's leg.

The man stared down in shock then glanced back at her. Gently, he unlocked Mark's arms and nudged him back toward her. "I am not this boy's *fader*. And you should not be standing in the middle of the street. It is dangerous for the *barnen*." He tipped his cap and turned, striding toward the diner.

Dangerous for the children? Anna looked around, trying to imagine how standing in a completely empty street could be dangerous. Without thinking, she reached down and patted Mark, who now clung to her skirts. "That's not Poppa. That man is lots bigger." Molly pivoted around from watching the man enter the diner.

"He's got hair like us. And he talked Swedish like Poppa. Is he our Uncle Erik?"

"I don't know, sweetie, but I'm going to find out." Anna stooped down, embracing her wards in a hug. Her heart ached for them. Had Mark already forgotten what his father looked like? If only she had been born into a wealthy family, then she'd have the funds to fight to keep the children. How could she hand them over to this curt stranger?

Erik felt like a louse as he pulled out a diner chair and dropped into it. Why did that boy think he was his fader? He should have been kinder to the child, but he'd been taken by surprise and had been embarrassed standing so close to that woman. One look into those doe-like eyes, and his mind was as mixed up as if someone had dropped a case of nails into a barrel of screws and bolts. Had he actually lectured her not to stand in the road, as if Cut Corners had any real activity worth mentioning?

Lacey Wilson hurried across the room. "Good evening, Erik. What would you like for supper tonight?"

Heat charged up Erik's neck and into his ears as he tried to avoid staring at the diner owner's bulging belly. The woman had married the blacksmith last Christmas and was now carrying her first child. Shouldn't a woman in her condition stay home?

"Uh—*pannkakan*."

She blinked. "You want pancakes for supper?"

"Ja." He nodded to Lacey, and she turned toward the kitchen with an odd look on her face. What he really wanted was a big, fat steak, but between the two women he was so befuddled that he'd said the first thing that popped into his mind.

Remembering the less-than-desirable food he'd eaten when Lacey's great-aunt had owned the diner, he breathed a prayer of thanks to God for bringing Lacey to town. Erik was certain that Jeff Wilson, the blacksmith, was also glad Lacey had come to Cut Corners, considering she was his wife now.

For the past two years, a lucky couple in Cut Corners had found love at Christmastime. First it was Sheriff Rafe Wilson and the prissy dressmaker, Peony. Then last year, the sheriff's cousin and town blacksmith had the good fortune of winning Lacey's heart. A pang of jealousy charged through him at the thought of how well Jeff Wilson ate these days.

Erik had long ago given up hope of finding a wife in such a small town, but he couldn't help wondering if this yuletide season would bring about another wedding.

The door squealed, and *that* woman walked in, carrying the boy and holding the little girl's hand. She looked around the room, caught his gaze, and then ducked her head and moved toward the only empty table. With the travelers from the train availing themselves of the services of the small diner, it was filled to capacity. Both children stared at Erik from across the room with a mixture of curiosity and something else that he couldn't quite put his finger on.

He thought it odd that the woman was so dark and the children so fair. Why, the barnen actually looked more like him than they did her. Erik winced as a pain nailed him deep in his heart. He rarely thought about having a family of his own, but when he did, that longing pierced his being. With no single women in Cut Corners except for older widows and a couple of young girls, there wasn't much chance of finding a wife. Course, there was always Lionel Sager's clumsy sister, Vivian, but most of the bachelors stayed clear of her, having been the victim of her bumbling ways in one manner or another. The knot on the back of his head was finally disappearing after she accidentally beaned him with a shovel she was selling to another customer in the mercantile.

Besides, he was a carpenter, like his Savior, and was happy being unmarried, just like Jesus had been. His life was rich and full. God enabled him to use his talents to create furniture that the women in town raved over. He had a small shop of his own, and recently he'd been contracted to build new pews for the church, which also served as the school. That was a privilege he took very seriously.

He looked across the room, and his gaze smacked straight into that woman's again. Her cheeks flushed a becoming red shade as she turned away. Why was she so interested in him? He peeked down at his shirt. No varnish stained this one, and it was properly buttoned. He glanced at his reflection in the window. His hair wasn't sticking up.

Staring back at the woman, he saw her lovingly hug the boy, then reach across the table and pat the girl's hand. She obviously cared deeply for her children.

He tore his gaze from her thick mass of dark brown hair, reached in his pocket, and pulled out a piece of paper and a stub of a pencil. Licking the lead, he began working on the engraving design for the sides of the church pews. Better to concentrate on work than think about a pretty woman.

Chapter 2

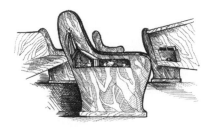

Anna watched the man she believed to be the children's uncle plod out of the diner after he'd eaten a huge stack of pancakes drenched in maple syrup for supper. She desperately needed to talk to him alone, providing he *was* Erik Olson. She had to verify that fact, but what could she do with the children? Glancing around the room, she realized only two tables were still occupied now that the train passengers had departed.

The kind waitress sat at a table talking with a burly man, who'd just come into the diner. She looked relieved to be off her feet. Anna wanted to ask her some questions, but she hated to disturb her. As if she felt Anna's stare, the woman pushed up from her chair and ambled toward her.

"Have you finished your meal?"

Anna shook her head. "No, Mark seems to be having trouble finishing his supper tonight."

The woman straightened and pressed her fists against her back. "I'm Lacey Wilson."

"Anna Campbell."

"That big, handsome man decimating the apple cobbler is Cut Corners' blacksmith and my husband, Jeff Wilson." Lacey turned and gave the nice-looking man a heart-tugging smile and a little wave. He winked at her then went back to devouring his dessert.

A pang of jealousy pierced Anna's heart. Would she ever have a husband of her own?

Lacey turned back to face them. "You know, Mark, we have a policy here that any child who eats all his food gets a free cookie. We've got oatmeal raisin or ginger cookies today."

The boy's eyes widened. He looked at Anna then back to his plate. She knew his brief encounter with his uncle had sorely disappointed him, but the child had a passion for ginger cookies. He picked up his fork, stabbed a carrot slice, and shoved it into his mouth.

"I ate all *my* food. May I please have a cookie?" Molly pushed back her plate and set her hands in her lap.

"My, my! Any young lady with such nice manners deserves a treat in my book, as long as it's okay with your mother." Lacey lifted an eyebrow and looked at Anna.

Anna's heart jumped. Though it wasn't the first time someone had mistaken her for the children's mother, it always surprised her. She stood to her feet. "Might I have a look at those cookies?"

Confusion etched Lacey's pretty face for a moment, but then she glanced at the children, and understanding dawned in her eyes. "Why, certainly. Just follow me."

"Finish your food, Mark." Anna glanced at Molly. "I'll be right back with your treat, sweetie." The girl smiled, revealing the gap where her front tooth had been only last week. Regret that Molly's parents hadn't lived long enough to see their daughter lose her first tooth tightened Anna's chest as she followed Mrs. Wilson into the kitchen.

Lacey pulled out a chair at what looked to be her worktable and slid a partially sliced apple pie out of their way. "Please have a seat. These days I take every chance I can to sit down."

Anna slid into the chair. "I need to ask you a question about that tall blond man who just left, Mrs. Wilson."

"Erik Olson?" Lacey's eyebrows lifted. "What about him? And please, call me Lacey."

Relief flooded her that she'd found the children's uncle so easily. "What can you tell me about him?"

An ornery smile tilted Lacey's lips. "He's quite handsome, isn't he? And, oh, so talented. He made that lovely hutch in the dining room."

Anna's cheeks warmed at the woman's insinuation that she was interested in Mr. Olson because of his looks. Not that she hadn't noticed how nice his pale hair and eyes looked against the golden tan of his skin. And those broad shoulders. She'd always thought Hans Olson was a nice-looking man, but he was lithe and fair skinned—a result of working in a bank instead of outside like his brother obviously did.

"I. . .uh, yes. I noticed the fine woodwork on your hutch. Very nice, indeed."

Lacey's knowing smile told Anna she knew exactly where her thoughts had been. Best she put an end to those shenanigans right away. "Erik Olson is Mark and Molly's uncle."

Instantly Lacey's smile died, and confusion tilted her bow. "Everyone know one of the town's founding fathers is Erik's uncle Lars, or Swede, as he's called around here, but I didn't realize that Erik had any other relatives. It doesn't surprise me, though; he's a rather private person. Quiet. Keeps to himself."

Stunned at the declaration that the children had another relative still living, Anna remained silent. How would this affect them? If Erik Olson were a reputable member of the town, then he most likely would welcome having more of his kin around. "I need to talk to Erik. Could you please tell me where I can find him?"

"His shop's at the end of town. It's not far. So I gather you aren't the children's mother?"

Anna shook her head and smoothed a crease in her skirt. "Their parents died in a carriage accident in October. It's all very sad. Besides being my employers, they were also my friends. I've been the children's nanny for more than two years. The Olsons' will left orders for me to deliver the children to their uncle in the event of their deaths."

Lacey reached across the narrow table and touched Anna's arm. "I'm sorry for your loss. Would you like me to watch the children so you can talk with Erik privately?"

Anna glanced up, grateful for Lacey's offer. She blinked away the tears blurring her vision. Talking about Hans and Jessica Olson had been harder than she imagined. Though she'd never left Mark and Molly in a stranger's care, somehow she knew Lacey Wilson was someone who could be trusted.

"I need all the experience with children I can get."

"I'm sure you'll be a fine mother. At least your child will be well fed. That supper was delicious."

Lacey laughed and eased out of her chair. She took a plate off a shelf and placed two oversized cookies on it. "Thank you for your kind words. I truly appreciate them. Why don't we take your youngsters these cookies so you can go talk with Erik. I even have a checkerboard in case you're gone awhile. You just take your time."

Erik sat on the porch in front of his carpentry shop in one of the two rocking chairs that he'd made the past summer. On most evenings, if his uncle Lars, or Swede, as the townsfolk called him, wasn't with one of the other Meddlin' Men—as he and the other three ex-Texas Rangers were called because of their fervent matchmaking ploys—he and Erik sat on the porch playing dominoes or checkers.

He adjusted the lantern that sat on the small table between the two chairs to give him better lighting. Using his pocket-knife, he strategically carved away chips of oak until the beginnings of a camel's head emerged. A soothing warmth settled in his chest. The camel was the final piece of the nativity set that he was carving as a surprise Christmas gift for Parson Clune and his wife.

Erik put his best effort into each item he made—whether for pay or for pleasure, whether a fine piece of furniture or a simple child's toy. God had blessed him with a talent to create beauty out of wood, and when he stood back and surveyed each finished item, he could feel God's smile.

As he shaped the tip of the camel's ear, he heard footsteps coming his way, echoing across the boardwalk. A woman, he'd guess by the short, clipped sound. Working on the tedious section, he couldn't look away, lest he hack off the ear as well as a chunk of his finger. Most likely, whoever it was would turn into Doc's place anyhow. The only other building this far down on his side of the street was the barbershop, and it was closed.

Erik stuck his tongue in the corner of his mouth as he whittled the point of the ear. He had to get it just right.

The footsteps continued his way. Maybe someone's wife had seen him outside his shop and decided to sneak out after dinner to do a little Christmas shopping. All the women in town loved his furniture, and he even had customers from other nearby towns. He could barely keep a few items in his store because they sold almost as fast as he could make them. In fact, after he sold a large dining table and chairs to a local rancher and the hutch to Jeff and Lacey, he had to bring the handcrafted casket he'd just finished into his shop to fill up the big empty space.

A smile tugged at his lips. Whenever a lady entered his shop, her eyes would go wide as saucers once she saw a casket sitting next to his fine crafted furniture. He chuckled aloud at the memory.

"You must take great pleasure in your work to find it so satisfying."

He glanced up at the sound of the feminine voice he recognized from earlier. His knife slipped and came to rest with a burning sting in the meat of his hand, just below his thumb. Hissing from pain, he looked down at the earless camel.

"Oh! Oh! I—I didn't mean to startle you."

Standing, he closed his knife and yanked his bandanna from his back pocket. He wrapped it around his bleeding hand, ignoring the stinging pain.

"Oh, my, I'm so sorry. Let me help. Please." The woman he'd seen earlier from the street and diner rushed forward, wrapping her soft hand around his wrist. His heart thumped at her touch, and he noted how white her skin looked next to his sun-bronzed arm. "I thought for sure you heard me. I mean, I sounded like a herd of buffalo clomping across the boardwalk."

"It vill be fine. It is yust a little scrape." He'd cut himself so many times over the years that one more nick wouldn't matter.

She studied his hand as if she didn't believe him, then finally looked up. "I wonder if I might have a word with you?"

A tingle tickled his chest. Her dark brown eyes and long lashes were the prettiest he'd ever seen. He shook his head. This woman was a stranger. "Yust who are you?"

"Oh, um. . .I'm Anna Campbell."

"What business do you have vith—?" He shook his head. Whenever he was upset or angry, his Swedish accent thickened. "What business do you have with me? Perhaps you wish to purchase some furniture for a Christmas gift?"

"What? Uh. . .no." Her gaze darted across the road, as if she were checking to see if other people were around. "I have business of a particularly private nature, Mr. Olson."

Curiosity seeped through him like a sponge absorbing water. "Please have a seat. We can talk here without being disturbed." As he sat down, he peeked under his bandanna, relieved to see the bleeding had already stopped. The camel's ear was another thing. He'd have to find a new piece of wood and start from scratch. With Christmas only a few weeks away and several unfinished orders to be completed, not to mention working on the church pews, he didn't have a lot of extra time.

He pulled his chair around so he could have a better look at Mrs. Campbell, but for the life of him, he couldn't figure out what kind of private business she had with him. She made a pretty picture sitting there in her dark blue traveling coat with her thick hair piled up on her head in a beguiling way. Some man was mighty lucky to have such a lovely wife.

"I'm sure you've probably realized the children traveling with me aren't my own. After all, they don't resemble me in the least. Not that I don't wish they were mine, but I'm not even married. They're very sweet children, mind you."

Erik smiled at her ramblings. She seemed as nervous as he was curious. For the first time, he glanced at her left hand. The fact that she wasn't wearing a ring confirmed her statement about being unmarried. He was trying to ignore how his heart had skipped when she'd said that.

"I suppose you've received the letter from the Dallas attorney, informing you about the children."

Erik narrowed his eyes and shook his head. He had no idea what she was talking about.

Her eyes widened. "You didn't get the letter? Oh, my. I knew that attorney wasn't dependable." Her gaze took on a faraway look for a moment, and then she turned back to him.

"I truly don't know how to tell you this." She studied her hands in her lap, which were practically twisting her coat in half; then she looked at him with sad, sympathetic eyes. "Your brother and his wife recently died in a carriage accident. I'm very sorry for your loss, Mr. Olson." She reached out and touched his arm.

"According to their last will and testament, you have been granted guardianship of Mark and Molly Olson, your niece and nephew."

Miss Campbell's words pierced his heart deeper than the knife that had cut his hand. What kind of cruel joke was this woman playing? And for what purpose?

Erik lurched to his feet, his anger mounting. His brother had been dead at least eight years. He still remembered the day his father had broken the news to him. There was no way this side of heaven that those children could be related to him, even if they did resemble his family. "What you say is impossible."

"What?" The woman frowned in confusion and stood. The

top of her head barely reached the bottom of his nose. "I don't understand."

"My brother has been dead for eight years. He cannot be the fader of those barnen."

Eyes wide, Miss Campbell clutched her handbag to her chest. "You *are* Erik Olson, correct?"

He nodded, still wondering if she was trying to swindle him somehow.

"Your brother's name was Hans?"

His heart clenched. It had been years since he'd heard his brother's name voiced out loud. "That is correct. How vould you know that?" Erik clung to the beam supporting the porch's roof. How could this woman know his brother? She couldn't be any older than her early twenties. That would have made her very young when his brother was alive.

She dropped into the rocker then bolted back to her feet, her skirts swishing. "I worked for your brother and his wife, Jessica, in Dallas until their accident in October. I've been Mark and Molly's nanny for more than two years." Her eyes pleaded with him to believe her.

Sure enough, this woman trickster was mighty convincing.

"The Olsons' will stated that in the event of their deaths, I was to bring the children to you. I've done that. Now if you'll be so kind as to follow me, I'd like to introduce you to your niece and nephew. We've had a long trip from Dallas, and we're all quite tired and in no mood for games." Turning, she marched back toward the diner.

Confusion, hurt, and anger surged through Erik. How could such a sweet-looking woman be so cruel as to taunt him with something that was impossible? His brother was dead, and he'd lost his fader five years earlier. His only living relative was his uncle Lars, who lived in the area above his shop with him.

His uncle and the other Meddlin' Men often teased Erik for being so calm. Nothing ever riled him. Well, they'd be interested in seeing him right now. He was good and riled.

"Miss Campbell."

She stopped in front of the lighted window of the barbershop and pivoted, her dark brows lifting. "Yes?"

"My brother Hans died eight years ago. I don't know what kind of trickery you're involved in, but I vill not be a part of it. Good evening." He tipped his cap and turned down his lantern, ignoring her stunned expression. After entering his shop, he turned the lock on the door—a lock he'd never used until today.

"Mr. Olson? Wait! I can assure you I'm not playing games. I'm very serious." Her fervent knocks on the glass window reverberated across the room as he marched into the back area and upstairs. Even so far away, he could hear her steady pounding and hollering. Finally after several minutes, silence reigned.

Erik slumped into a chair, tired and confused. What had she hoped to gain from him? Money? He had a fair amount in the bank, but she had no way of knowing that. To be rid of two children that she seemed to care deeply about? It didn't make any sense.

"Fader God, what is the meaning of all this?"

Erik rested his head on the tall back of the chair. If the woman was still in town in the morning, he'd have no recourse but to talk to the sheriff. He couldn't let any of his friends get taken in by her swindler's game.

Chapter 3

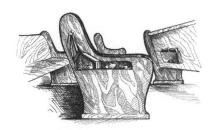

Anna stomped back toward the diner, tears of anger dripping down her cheeks. *Of all the nerve. Accusing me of deception. What kind of man is this Erik Olson?*

Stopping in front of the entrance, she brushed her tears away. It wouldn't do to upset the children. After taking several deep breaths, she opened the door and walked in.

Mark sat on his knees, leaning over a checkerboard, so totally engrossed in his game with Jeff Wilson that he didn't even realize she'd returned. Molly smiled up at her and waved a damp cloth, then returned to washing off the tables.

"I hope you don't mind that I put Molly to work. She begged to help me." Lacey followed behind the girl, wiping down the sugar containers and collecting the salt dishes and their tiny silver spoons onto a tray. The diner was completely empty except for the Wilsons and Anna and the children.

Lacey laid her cloth on the table and crossed the room, setting the tray on the hutch. "So, how did it go?" she asked, keeping her voice low.

Anna shook her head and motioned toward the back. Nodding, Lacey turned and ambled toward the kitchen. After Anna entered, Lacey dropped down the curtain over the doorway, giving them some privacy.

"Not good. Horrible, actually. He accused me of trying to swindle him."

Lacey spun around. "I don't believe that. Erik Olson is the kindest, gentlest man in this town."

Anna hiked up her chin. "Well, I assure you it's the truth. He said his brother died eight years ago and that Mark and Molly can't possibly be related to him."

The diner owner sat and motioned for Anna to join her. Placing her reticule on the table, Anna dropped into the chair. Exhaustion washed over her like a flash flood. She had dreaded saying good-bye and turning the children over to their uncle. She had imagined all sorts of things, but never once had this scenario popped into her mind.

"I don't know what to do. The will states Erik Olson is now the children's legal guardian. If I had some way to support them and the right by law to do so, I'd gladly keep them myself. They're very precious to me."

Lacey straightened and kneaded her fist in the small of her back. "I just can't imagine Erik reacting that way. He's a big puppy dog. Gentle. Sweet."

"More like a wolverine."

"I do recall having heard that Erik's brother died a long time ago, so I can see why he'd be confused when you showed up saying these children are his brother's."

Anna glared at Lacey. "Well, I certainly didn't make up the story. What would I hope to gain? In truth, I'm the one who's losing the children I love."

Lacey held up her hand, and her gentle expression was like throwing a bucket of ice water on Anna's anger. "Yes, I can see that's the case. I think the best thing to do would be for you to take a room at the boardinghouse for the night and get a good rest. Things will look better in the morning when you aren't so exhausted."

Anna looked down, chastising herself for taking her anger out on this woman who'd been nothing but kind to her. "I suppose you're right. At least it will give me a little more time with the children. If only the attorney had given me a copy of the will, but he refused since I wasn't family."

Lacey pushed up from the table, came around to Anna's side, and reached for her hand. "Erik Olson is a man of God. He will do the right thing, but he can't be rushed into anything. He's a perfectionist and takes his time to do things right. Let's pray on this matter tonight and see if God won't soften Erik's heart so he can see the truth."

Anna nodded, grateful for the woman's kind, encouraging words, though she seriously doubted prayer would help the situation. As they entered the dining room again, Mark looked up with smiling eyes. "Anna, I ated all my food, and Mrs. Wilson gave me *two* cookies."

"How nice! Are you ready to go?"

Molly hugged Anna around the waist. "Are we going to Uncle Erik's? Is he happy to see us?"

Anna's gaze darted to Lacey's. She read the sympathy in the woman's hazel eyes. "Um, no, sweetie, I thought we'd stay in the boardinghouse tonight. It's too late for your uncle to make arrangements for you to stay with him."

"Oh."

Anna's heart plummeted at the disappointment in that

single word. Mark yawned as Molly laid her head against Anna's stomach. Fighting back tears, Anna mentally lashed out at God. *How could You put me in this situation?*

Her strict, Bible-thumping father said God was a cruel taskmaster, taking what He chose and pouring out where He pleased. The only true love Anna had ever known had been in the Olsons' home. And now, two by two, God was taking the Olsons away.

"Thank you for your kindness. I appreciate all your help, Lacey."

"Think nothing of it. We're happy to have you in Cut Corners, no matter what the circumstances." Lacey squeezed Anna's shoulder and gave her a smile of encouragement.

Jeff Wilson lumbered to his feet. "I noticed your trunks at the depot when I signed for my load of coal. I'll head over there and carry them to the boardinghouse for you."

"Why, that's very kind of you. Thank you so much."

An hour later, after being mothered half to death by the kind but talkative Lula Chamberlain, owner of the boardinghouse, Anna had put Mark and Molly to bed in their room. Mark slept on the settee while Molly dozed in the double bed that she and Anna would share. True to his word, Mr. Wilson had hauled both of the children's trunks from the depot. She breathed a sigh of relief, knowing that the two containers holding all the children's worldly belongings were safe and secure.

Peering out the dark window, Anna thought back to her conversation with Erik Olson. Had she relayed all the important information? Could she have broken the news more gently?

She stared up at the three-quarter moon illuminating the outline of the town. What would she do now? Expecting to return to Dallas tomorrow, she had only brought one change of clothing. The small stipend she had received from the Olsons' will wouldn't keep her for long, especially if she had to continue providing for the children.

If she didn't have commitments in Dallas to play the piano for several Christmas functions, she might be able to stay in Cut Corners until the idea that he was now a guardian to two small children had sunk into the man's thick skull. It was crucial that she practice her songs so she'd be ready for her musical events. Playing for the three engagements was her only way to make money until she started her new nanny job at the first of the year. And she couldn't do that if she was still responsible for Mark and Molly. No matter how much she loved them, they were better off with their uncle, who could provide for them. At least he'd have the money that Hans and Jessica had left, plus he seemed quite capable of providing by his own means. She simply had to make Erik Olson see reason, and she had to do it tomorrow.

Erik inhaled the fresh scent of oak as he sanded the top of the dresser he was making for James Heath to give to his wife, Arlene, for Christmas. The near-freezing morning temperatures had given way to a warm, sunny day. He loved working outside, where the breeze could cool his sweat-soaked body and the sun provided plenty of light.

The covered porch he'd built on the back of his shop had cabinets where he stored his tools and smaller projects. When the weather turned too cold to work outdoors, he cleared a corner of his shop.

Running his hand across the dresser's top, he reveled in its smooth texture. All he had left to do was to varnish it and attach the knobs, and it would be finished.

"Um. . .excuse me."

Erik spun around at the sound of the soft, feminine voice. He rubbed his fingertips across the scab where he'd cut himself the previous night when Anna Campbell had surprised him. What could she want now?

Her gaze darted from his to the chest of drawers and instantly sparked with admiration. Stepping forward, she ran her hand along the top of the dresser's beveled edge. "You do such nice work. That hutch you made for Lacey is beautiful. It must give you great satisfaction to create something so lovely from a rough piece of wood."

His chest swelled with pride but immediately deflated, knowing that his skill was a gift from God and nothing he could personally take credit for. "Thank you. So how can I be of help?"

Her gaze turned pleading. "I wondered if we could talk about the children again."

"What is left to say? They are very nice barnen. . . children, but they cannot be my brother's."

"How can you say that? They greatly resemble you. All three of you have nearly the same color hair and light blue eyes. You and Mark even have similar dimples in your left cheek like H–Hans had."

She choked on Hans's name, sending a shaft of regret straight to Erik's heart. If only his brother *had* lived long enough to have children, Erik would welcome them with open arms, even though he knew nothing about raising youngsters. He wiped his sweaty forehead with his sleeve.

"I do not know what else to say. When my fader, brother, and I first come to America, Hans and Fader had an argument over where we would live. Fader had told us we go to Texas, and Hans was all excited that we would live with the cowboys. Ja, he always had a fascination with the cowboys. When Fader told us he had decided to join his sister in Minnesota rather than following Uncle Lars to Texas, Hans got very angry."

Erik winced at the memory of their argument. He hadn't wanted to lose his brother when he'd just gotten used to his mother being gone. But that's exactly what had happened. "Hans was twenty and already a man. He took his trunk of clothing and set off on foot." Miss Campbell had to understand the truth. Swallowing hard, he forced himself to continue. "That was more than ten years ago. I never see Hans again."

"But you finally got to Texas."

"Ja, that we did. Uncle Lars had written to us after he left the Rangers and told us of the town he and his friends had started. Fader liked the idea of helping to birth a town, and his aching bones did not like the cold Minnesota winters, so we come here."

Miss Campbell twisted the string handle of her reticule in her hands. "But that still doesn't explain why you thought your brother died years ago."

"Fader told me about two years after Hans left that he had received a letter from Texas saying that Hans had died in a fire."

"But who sent the letter? It doesn't make sense. Why would the Hans Olson I knew leave his children to you if you weren't his true brother?"

Erik straightened. He could tell by her confusion that Miss Campbell honestly believed he was the children's uncle. Instant remorse flooded over him for accusing her of being a trickster. She was just trying to find the children's family. "Perhaps there is another Erik Olson in Texas?"

She shook her head. "In Cut Corners? Hans stated in his will that his brother lived in Cut Corners, Texas."

Sucking in a short breath at her comment, hands on hips, Erik turned and walked a few paces away. He had to escape those pleading brown eyes. They made the woman look vulnerable and needy. And though he wouldn't admit it, Anna Campbell had managed to instill a measure of doubt in him. Could Hans have been alive and living less than a day's train ride away all these years? If he had known where Erik lived, why hadn't he contacted him before? It was more than he could handle—to think that the brother he'd loved and mourned had perhaps played a cruel joke on him.

Even if the children were his relatives, he knew nothing about caring for them. But in his heart of hearts, he knew his brother hadn't deceived him. Anna Campbell was misinformed. Besides, the children knew and loved her. They were far better off with her than him. He turned back to face her. "I am sorry, but I cannot take those children."

Anna closed her eyes, making him wish there was another solution to the problem. "Even though I'd love to keep them, I don't have the means to support them or the legal right to keep them. Besides, I have obligations in Dallas—Christmas programs where I'm supposed to play piano. I need to get back to Dallas and practice. And the first of the year, I have a new job as a nanny. It's impossible for me to keep Mark and Molly, no matter how much I want to."

"I am sure you will work it all out. You are a resourceful woman."

Her eyes hardened and her brows dipped. "And just maybe you should own up to your responsibility to your brother's children." She spun around and marched past his shop toward Main Street.

Heaving a sigh, he yanked off his cap and ran his fingers through his hair. His uncle Lars lifted his hat as Anna scurried past him; then he turned his twinkling gaze on Erik. The old man hustled toward him, and Erik could almost see his uncle matching up him and Anna. Picking up his sandpaper, Erik returned to his work, hoping his uncle wouldn't make a mountain out of a molehill because he was talking alone with a pretty woman.

"Well now, what was that lovely woman doing here?"

Erik sighed. Ever since Uncle Lars and the other Meddlin' Men had succeeded in matchmaking couples the past two years, he'd known it was only a matter of time before they tried to find him a mate.

"She claims the barnen she has with her are Hans's children and that Hans and his wife died in October in an accident." He watched his uncle's gray eyebrows lift higher with each sentence he related.

"Ja, I noticed they favored the Olson family the first time I saw them, but Hans has been dead a long time, so they can't be his. Hmph! That pretty young woman is not the children's mother?" Uncle Lars rubbed his stubbly chin. Erik didn't like that ornery twinkle in his pale eyes.

"Do not make any plans to marry her off. Miss Campbell is going back to Dallas. She has obligations."

"Ja, and yust maybe she vould stay right here vith the proper motivation."

Erik gawked at his uncle, who easily slipped from the normal Texas twang he'd taken on in the decades that he'd lived in the state back to his Swedish cadence to emphasize his point.

"I do not intend to motivate her, so you and your cronies vill yust have to find another bachelor to fix her up vith. I am happy being single."

"Harrumph." Swede stroked his chin as if in deep thought. "I bet that Ticks McGee or that saloon owner, Brooks, would be interested in her by the way they acted when she first arrived."

Erik straightened and impaled his uncle with a scowl. Swede knew just which apple to pull from the barrel to motivate him. Erik wouldn't wish Ticks or Brooks on any decent woman, much less one as passionate and beautiful as Anna Campbell.

Chapter 4

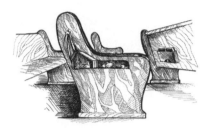

The next morning, Anna counted the pittance in her reticule and heaved a sigh of resignation. Two nights at the boardinghouse had used up most of her money. If she were going to stay in Cut Corners until the children's uncle came to his senses, she'd have to find some kind of work. She'd been prepared for Erik Olson to embrace his wards and happily take possession of them, not to reject them.

Yesterday's dress and undergarments hung drying on a borrowed rope tied to the bedpost and wall lantern. She'd planned on making this a one-day trip, not a weeklong stay.

Lacey would know if anyone needed help. Anna could cook, clean, sew, and even play piano—not that anyone in this tiny town had need for that. They most likely didn't have a piano. She'd not even heard one in the saloon the evening she had arrived in town.

She pulled the blanket up around Mark's neck and pushed back his straight bangs. Though a rooster somewhere nearby had alerted her that morning had dawned, the children slept soundly. They always had been late risers.

Leaving word with Miss Chamberlain to keep an eye on them, she hurried out the boardinghouse entryway to Lacey's Diner next door. Her stomach grumbled at the fragrant odors wafting on the cool morning breeze. At the diner's entrance, she hesitated. During the breakfast rush probably wasn't the best time to talk with Lacey.

A tall, thin man she hadn't seen before crossed the dirt road and headed in her direction. He tipped his hat and smiled, then held the door open for her. "After you, ma'am."

What else could she do but go in? As she looked around, her gaze landed on Erik Olson's broad back. His long, white blond hair glistened in the morning sunlight streaming in the window near his table. An older man sat with him, both eating a huge stack of pancakes. The man stopped eating with his fork halfway to his mouth and peered at her. Erik obviously thought he was missing something because he turned around.

The pleasant smile in his eyes darkened, and he turned back to his food. Anna noticed that most of the people in the diner were men, and they were all staring at her. Looking at the floor, she headed straight to Lacey's back room, knowing her cheeks must be flaming.

Her friend glanced up from the plate of cinnamon rolls dripping with creamy white icing that she was dishing up and smiled when Anna entered the kitchen. "Anna. Good morning."

"Morning. I don't suppose you'd have time for me to ask you a question, do you?"

Lacey wiped her hands on her apron. "Sure. Just let me

deliver this to the sheriff. He has a passion for my cinnamon rolls. Sometimes he slips over after eating breakfast at home just so he can have one. Don't tell his wife." Wearing a conspiratorial grin, she lifted the plate and entered the dining room.

Anna smiled, knowing the secret was safe with her since she'd never even met the sheriff's wife. Course, in a small town like this, the woman was probably fully aware of what her husband did. Anna knew well how fast gossip traveled on the human telegraph of a little town. And she never wanted to live in one again.

Lacey bustled back into the room. "What can I help you with? Erik still holding out?"

Nodding, she watched Lacey hurry to the table and flop down. She pulled over a bowl of puffy bread dough, pinched off a wad and patted it into a ball, probably for rolls for the midday meal. The busy woman reminded Anna of a hummingbird, flitting from one thing to the next. Pulling out the other chair, Anna sat. "I don't suppose you need any help here or know of someone else who does."

Lacey's blond brows wrinkled. "I'm not all that busy here, except when the train comes in. My aunt Millie helps me when she's feeling up to it, but she's been feeling poorly the past week. This used to be her diner. I wish I could offer you a job. I'd love the company."

"It's hard enough to find work in Dallas, but I can't imagine there being anything for a woman in a town this small."

Lacey finished filling one pan of rolls and started another. Suddenly a spark lit her eyes. "I know. Vivian Sager works in the mercantile that her brother, Lionel Sager, owns. Yesterday Vivian twisted her ankle severely and almost broke it. She's supposed to stay off it for a week or two, so maybe Lionel could use your help for a while. At least until Erik comes through."

"I'm not so sure he will come through. He seems determined that there's no way the children could be his brother's. It's truly sad. I don't know what to do. Legally, I'm not allowed to keep them myself, even if I had a way of supporting them."

Lacey laid a flour-coated hand on Anna's arm and gave a gentle squeeze. "I'm praying about it. God will work things out the way He thinks is best for us. He loves us and can see the whole picture while we only get a small glimpse. We just have to be pliant, like this bread dough, and allow the Master to shape and mold us however He wants."

Anna wished she could believe Lacey. Hans and Jessica had believed in a loving God, too, but the thought was so contrary to the way she'd been raised. If only she knew which was the real God, the One who loved His children and wanted only good for them, or the domineering, controlling One her father had shoved down her throat all her life.

She sighed and stood. "I'd better get back to the children. They've been rather clingy since their parents died. I'll go over to the mercantile later on."

"Let me know if Lionel hires you. I'll try to think of another position in case that doesn't work out." Lacey smiled and set her empty bread bowl on the counter, then headed out to check on her customers.

Not wanting to face Erik again, Anna let herself out the back exit. Just maybe God would smile down on her today and she'd get that job.

With his belly full, Erik knew he couldn't put off the task he'd been avoiding any longer. Two nights ago, a sudden thunderstorm had blown through, and a large branch had knocked a hole in the roof of his outhouse. With a bandanna secured over his nose and mouth and his tool belt around his waist, he stepped into the small, pungent-smelling structure.

He tested the wooden platform, making sure it would hold his full weight, then stepped up and used his hammer to tear out the damaged boards. The open door, along with the hole in the roof, allowed just enough light so that he could see clearly.

Thinking back to breakfast, he'd been surprised to see Anna Campbell up so early this morning. For some reason he figured a city gal like her would most likely sleep till noon. But then again, the children probably didn't let her sleep late very often.

Another shaft of longing coursed through him. If Mark and Molly were truly Hans's children, then he would do right by them and embrace them with open arms. It baffled him how Miss Campbell knew so much about his brother. Where had she gotten her information? And what did she hope to gain by pushing the children on him?

A scuffling sound drew him back to the job at hand. Erik peered through a slit between two wooden planks to see who was in his yard. He stiffened as Mark and Molly entered his line of sight.

"He's not here," the young boy said.

"Yeah, he's probably working somewhere." Molly spun around, her long braids sailing in a wide circle around her.

Erik leaned his head to the side so he could keep the children in view. He had plenty of tools and equipment that could harm them, but he wasn't quite ready to show himself. He wasn't sure if he was up to facing these two youngsters alone.

"Why don't he like us?" Mark flopped down on the edge of the back porch, his short legs kicking back and forth.

Molly heaved a sigh and sat beside her brother. "I don't know."

"Anna said he'd wuv us."

"Love. Not wuv."

Erik had to smile at Molly's firm correction. She sounded like a miniature schoolteacher. As Mark's words soaked in, guilt pierced him. For the first time, he considered what these children must be going through. Had they come here hoping to find family, only to be rejected? From the looks of their clothing, they'd been well cared for. They weren't urchins begging for a handout. And if they'd really lost their parents recently. . .

A loud metallic clatter drew his attention back to the children. His heart raced. What happened?

"Ma—ark!" Molly's voice rang out, strong with admonition.

"It was an ax—dent."

Erik took a step to his left, trying to get a better view of the kids. When his foot dangled in midair instead of hitting solid wood, he suddenly remembered just where he was. Losing his balance, he flung out his left arm, and his hand banged against the back of the privy. He regained his balance and carefully set his foot down on solid wood, heaving a sigh of relief. Between his near miss and his concern for the children, his heart was stampeding faster than a herd of mustangs.

He readjusted his bandanna over his nose as a shadow

darkened the front of the privy, and he looked down. Molly peeked around the edge of the outhouse door, eyes wide. Mark looked around her, his little mouth hanging open. They must have heard him clambering around.

"A wobber!"

Molly's eyes widened until Erik thought they'd pop. Suddenly her face turned white, her eyes closed, and she exhaled an ear-splitting scream. She slammed the privy door shut. He heard a rustling sound and then the pounding of feet running away.

Lowering himself to the ground, Erik couldn't hold in his laughter. They'd thought he was a robber. He tugged his bandanna off his face, wondering just what mayhem the children had caused to his tools. He pushed against the privy door, but it wouldn't budge. His heart skidded to a halt in disbelief. Peering through a crack, he saw that his broken shovel handle was wedged against the door. Those pint-sized mischief-makers had barricaded him in his own outhouse!

<hr>

"Why, yes, Miss Campbell. I certainly could use your help for a few days." Lionel Sager smiled, revealing his large buckteeth. "With Christmas just around the corner, I'm expecting a big shipment of supplies to arrive any day. Vivian's accident left me shorthanded. When can you start?"

Relief and anxiety battled within Anna—relief to have a way of making some money and anxiety because she'd never worked in a store before. "Well, there's the matter of the children. I don't know anyone in town whom I could leave them with."

Lionel waved his hand in the air. "I don't reckon it would hurt to have them around the store for a few days, as long as they don't get into things. Maybe we could even give them some little jobs to do, so they could earn a penny or some stick candy."

Anna smiled at the man's kindness to her. "That's very generous of you. I can assure you they're very well-behaved children."

Suddenly, the mercantile door slammed open and Mark and Molly charged in, both talking at once.

"A wobber." Mark's chest heaved.

Molly bounced up and down. "Anna! Anna! There's a man with a mask in Uncle Erik's outhouse."

Anna glanced at Mr. Sager, hoping the children's unusual outburst didn't make him change his mind. Instead of being angry, the tall man looked genuinely concerned. She turned her attention to the children.

"Now, what's this all about?"

The children finally caught their breath. "We went looking for Uncle Erik but found a robber in his outhouse."

If the children hadn't been so serious and she hadn't been so concerned for their safety, Anna might have laughed. Why would an outlaw hide in a privy? A slow tremble journeyed up her spine. Had the children actually come face-to-face with a real, live outlaw?

"He's still there," Mark offered.

"What?" Anna stooped down to his eye level.

"Molly locked him in."

Anna turned her gaze on the girl. Molly nodded her head so hard that her long braids bounced up and down. "I slammed the door and stuck a big stick against it."

Anna glanced at Mr. Sager, who lifted his eyebrows. A sudden commotion drew her attention to the doorway. The four old men whom she'd passed on her way into the mercantile stood just inside the door, listening.

They were an odd quartet. Anna was certain one of the two taller men was Erik's uncle. He was the man Erik had been eating breakfast with. His hair was more white than blond, but he had those familiar blue eyes. The other tall man was a bit thinner than Swede, as Lacey had called him, and had salt-and-pepper hair. Between them stood a man of medium height, dressed immaculately in fine-tailored clothing. He stood polishing a monocle with his pure white hankie and looked out of place with the other men. The fourth man was shorter than the rest and lifted an ear horn to his ear. "Did that boy say there's a rabbit in an outhouse somewheres?"

Anna bit back a smile and shook her head. "He said there's a robber in Erik Olson's outhouse."

The old man's eyebrows lifted. "That's a right odd place for a robber to be. Ain't nothing in there to steal."

"Ja, we should go check it out," Swede said, his tone serious. "Lionel, can we borrow your shotgun?"

Mr. Sager nodded, ducked under the counter for a moment, and then stood with a rifle in his hand. He passed it over the counter to Swede.

"Much obliged."

Swede grabbed the weapon, then squeezed past his friends and hurried out the door. The other three men shuffled outside, with Mark right behind them. Anna grabbed at the back of his jacket, but the child was too quick for her. She hadn't wanted him anywhere near the scene in case the robber started shooting, but now she had no choice except to follow.

"Molly, you stay here with Mr. Sager. I'll be back as soon as I get Mark."

Molly's eyes widened as she looked at the mercantile owner.

He smiled at her. "I'll let you help me, if you'd like to."

Anna knew Molly loved going shopping. Working in a store was just the thing for her. The child smiled and nodded, then turned her gaze on Anna. "You promise you won't be gone long?"

Anna gave her a hug. "I promise, sweetie."

She hurried out the door, her concern for Mark growing with each step she took. It wasn't ladylike to run, but she couldn't slow her feet, especially when her heart raced ahead of them, knowing if there were gunfire, Mark could get caught in the middle.

As she rounded the back corner of Erik's shop, she heard a gale of masculine laughter. Mark stood in the middle of the group of men, smiling like she hadn't seen him do since his parents had died. What in the world was going on?

She glanced at Erik, and an odd feeling tickled her stomach. What was it about the man that intrigued her? He stood outside the circle. A red bandanna hung around his neck and matched the color of his cheeks.

"Just imagine, our quiet Erik a robber," Swede said. The group erupted in another round of guffaws.

"Yeah, and he was hog-tied by a couple of young'uns. Don't that beat all." The tall man next to Swede slapped his thigh and laughed.

"What about tying up hogs?" The man with the ear horn yelled. "James Heath's got hogs on his ranch."

At the man's error, the other three old men roared with laughter. Mark grinned right along with them, warming her heart. But what had happened to the robber? Had he gotten away?

Anna cleared her throat. "Um. . .excuse me, gentlemen.

Could someone please tell me what's going on? Where's the robber?"

The old men straightened, and Anna could tell they were trying hard to curb their mirth. Almost in unison, they turned toward Erik. His ears turned a deep scarlet.

"I'll let my nephew explain that one," Swede said with a grin.

Erik held his uncle's gaze for a moment then glanced at her. He ducked his head and stared at the ground. "There was no robber. The barnen locked *me* in the privy. I had my kerchief on my face because I was working inside, and they mistook me for a bandit." His ears looked even redder than before.

The old men snickered and chuckled as if it were the funniest thing to happen in years. Smiling, Mark came over and wrapped his arms around her skirt in a sweet hug. Anna saw the humor in the situation with Erik, but in her heart, she knew the truth. Now that the children had caused him such embarrassment and made him the laughingstock of the town, Erik Olson had one more reason not to accept them as his own.

Chapter 5

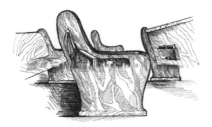

Erik looked over his wood-carving tools, making sure each knife, gouge, and chisel was in its slot, then rolled up the leather pouch and tied it shut. The church was the best place he could think to hide until the hullabaloo about his being locked in the privy died down. He'd made the mistake of going to Lacey's Diner for lunch. It seemed the whole town had heard about the incident—and wanted to tease him.

Erik hated being the center of attention; he much preferred blending into the background. Besides, he'd heard enough jokes about his being whipped by those two youngsters to last a century. And his sides actually ached from being elbowed so many times.

Thankfully, he hadn't seen Miss Campbell or the children since morning. It had taken him half an hour to pick up all the nails that Mark had spilled in the dirt when the boy knocked over the bucket that Erik stored them in. He didn't blame the children. Accidents happened. And if truth be told, when people weren't ribbing him about the privy incident, he couldn't help chuckling himself.

As he crossed the street, he could see the Meddlin' Men in front of the store, playing dominoes. Instead of walking down the boardwalk to the church, Erik decided to take the scenic route. He strolled past the sheriff's office, which sat across the street from his shop, then turned left and passed behind the bank and mercantile until he came to the church. At least he avoided more of the townsfolk's humorous comments that way.

Nearing the church, he caught the sound of piano music drifting on the mild afternoon breeze. The tinkling sound of "Silent Night" drew him to the church door. He didn't realize how much he'd missed hearing music until just now.

Quietly, he pushed down on the handle and opened the door of the church. Slipping inside, he removed his cap and stood there leaning against the wall, eyes shut, traveling back in time—back to Sweden when he was a young boy and his mother would play the piano in their modest home. Back to a time when his family was still alive and he knew no troubles.

All too soon, the music stopped. Opening his eyes, Erik looked at the front of the small building where the upright piano sat in the corner. His heart leaped when he realized Anna Campbell was the pianist. The afternoon sunlight illuminated her from behind, giving her an angelic appearance. She stretched her arms, then looked down at the keyboard and started playing "O Come, All Ye Faithful."

Erik stood there mesmerized. Finally, he realized he wasn't getting any work done, and even though he hated to disturb Miss Campbell, he needed to get busy while he still had sunlight to work by. As she played the final chord, Erik stepped forward, clearing his throat. She looked up, eyes wide, and her hand flew to her chest.

"I am sorry to bother you, Miss Campbell, but I must work on the church pews."

She glanced at the benches then back to him. "Pastor Clune assured me I wouldn't be bothering anyone if I practiced piano in the afternoons while the children rested. It's important that I keep my fingers limber."

"You are not bothering me, but I fear that I will disturb your lovely playing."

She lowered her gaze, and her cheeks turned a be-coming pink. "You're replacing the benches?"

"Ja." He moved down the center aisle. "I have finished the first two but still need to work on engraving the designs on the ends."

Standing, she strolled over to the front bench and ran her hand along the shiny wood. "You made this? I was admiring the new pews when I first came in. Your work is exquisite."

"Thank you." Erik's chest swelled with delight at her comment. "I still have eight pews more to make."

"I wish I could see them when they're finished."

Anna looked up at him, and he couldn't tear his gaze away. She was more beautiful than a vibrant sunset. Soft tendrils of coffee brown hair framed her oval face. Her dark eyes stood out against her pale skin. Erik blinked, pulling himself away from the enchanting picture she made. He should be thinking about his work, not about Anna Campbell.

She cleared her throat and brushed a strand of hair from her face. "If you're sure my playing won't bother you, I'll continue. I only have a couple more songs to practice, and then

I'll be finished for today."

"Ja, sure. You go right ahead, and I vill yust work on my carving." Erik stuffed his cap into his back pocket, ambled down the aisle, and sat on the floor between the front two benches. He turned to the one with the sunshine illuminating it, then unwrapped his tools and laid them on the floor. Using a straight gouge, he carefully chiseled out the hillside background of the shepherds in the field gazing up at the angel of God. Each engraving on the side of the benches depicted a different scene from Jesus' life. The first few would illustrate the story of Christ's birth—the shepherds, wise men, and the manger.

He'd only been contracted to make the benches; the engravings were his offering to God for blessing him with his talent. It would take a long time to complete the designs, but he didn't mind. They would be his legacy.

All too soon, Miss Campbell played the final notes to "The First Noel." He had been singing the words in his mind as he chiseled out the angel with a brilliant spray of light around it. How appropriate to sing of the shepherds as he worked on their scene.

Miss Campbell gathered up her music papers, and the piano bench squealed as she slid it back so she could stand. When a shadow darkened his work area, he realized she was standing at his side, watching him. His chisel slipped and cut the angel's glow in half. Letting out a sigh, he stood and turned to her.

Just as when he had first met her in the street, she stood right in front of him. Her head tilted up to see his face. At this close range, he noticed a few soft freckles dotting the bridge of her petite nose like the gentle spots on a fawn's back. A sweet floral scent wafted off her, stirring his senses. His heart pounded a ferocious rhythm. Her perfect pink lips separated, and he wanted nothing more than to lean down and kiss them.

"You're an artist. Did you know that?"

Her soft words touched a cold, lonely place in his heart that he hadn't known existed. "You are, also."

She blinked, and her thin brows lifted in surprise. "Me?"

"Ja. God has gifted you to play the piano more lovely than anyone I have ever heard." He pressed his hand to his chest, hoping she wouldn't hear his rebellious heart.

She shook her head. "I don't know how much God had to do with it. I've practiced very hard. It's been a dream of mine to play piano for people for as long as I can remember. My mother taught me, and then I moved to Dallas so I could study with someone more skilled."

Hearing her lack of gratitude to God for her talent made his heart ache. "You have learned very well, but do not discredit God. All good things are from Him."

Scowling, she backed away. "That's not what my father said. He taught me that God is a hard God. He takes what He wants and blesses whom He chooses. The only chance we have to please Him is to work hard."

Erik shook his head, grieving over her words. "That is not true. God is a God of love. It is not by works that we are saved but rather faith. We are His children, and He loves us with all His heart. His very own Son died that we might be reconciled with God and know His peace in our hearts."

"You sound just like your brother."

Erik sucked in a sharp breath at her unexpected comment.

"Hans had only been a Christian a short while. Jessica was the one who helped him get over his anger at your father. She told me that when she and Hans first met, he was like a raging bull whenever she mentioned his family. He never told her what happened, but she knew he and his father had had a parting of ways."

Shoving his hands in his pockets to keep them from shaking, Erik had to ask what was on his heart. "If what you say is true, and my brother became a Christian, then why did he not contact me and let me know he was alive, especially if he knew where I was living? It seems a cruel joke to play on someone you are supposed to love."

She held her papers against her chest like a shield and shook her head. "I don't know. I guess maybe he was still afraid of facing your father. Or maybe he was ashamed of his part in the argument and hadn't yet gotten up his courage to apologize."

Stepping forward, she reached out and touched his arm. "I'm truly sorry for how things have turned out. I know what it's like to lose a family. Mine aren't dead, but I'm dead to them. Father told me that if I left Persimmon Gulch to never come back. I'll probably never see my little sister again."

"I am sorry." Erik pulled his hand out of his pocket and laid it on top of hers. "It is sad that fathers and children are so often at odds with each other. I wish I could help you with the children, Miss Campbell, but I just cannot believe in my heart that my brother was alive all these years and never sought me out. We were very close."

She pulled her hand from his. "I'm sorry you feel that way. You put me in a difficult spot. The Olsons' will appointed you as guardian to the children and the family finances. I have no legal right to keep them. What am I supposed to do?"

Feeling caught in the middle, Erik shrugged. "I do not know."

Miss Campbell backed away. "I was just about ready to believe in Jessica's loving God when she and Hans died. If your God is so caring, why would He take the parents of two innocent children?" She heaved a deep sigh; her anguished expression tore at Eric's heart. "Why would He separate me from the children I love and leave them with an oaf of an uncle who doesn't even want them?"

She spun around so fast that her swirling skirts almost tripped her. Grabbing hold of the back of the pew, she steadied herself, then marched to the side of the church, down the aisle, and out the door. With a loud bang, it slammed shut behind her and bounced open again.

Erik slumped down onto the floor. The questions she raised were good ones. Oh, he didn't doubt that God knew what He was doing. God could have protected Mark and Molly's parents, but for some reason He had chosen not to. He knew that even when things were their darkest, God had a plan. And His plans far outweighed Erik's. Still, he could not for the life of him figure out what God had intended in this situation.

Even if he accepted the children, they still needed a mother. He ran his hands through his hair. He needed to pray. Needed to hear from God. Everything Anna Campbell had said about his brother and his father rang true. How could she know all of that unless the Hans she knew really was his brother? But if that were true, why had Hans never contacted him? Erik leaned his head against the pew behind him and stared out the window, eyes blurring with tears.

"God, what would You have me do?"

Erik stared at the piece of paper. How did one draw the likeness of Christ, the Son of God, on paper? He was determined to finish drawing the designs for the pew engravings before Christmas, but this one had been giving him trouble for days. The designs focusing on Jesus' birth were finished, and now he was working on the ones representing Christ's life.

If he drew a picture of Jesus teaching on the hillside, he'd have to draw the faces of the many people in the crowd unless he drew Jesus' face and showed the crowd from behind. Thus his problem—how to draw the face of his Savior.

As a carpenter, Jesus most likely would have been muscular from hard work, so recreating His body wouldn't be too difficult. Erik licked the end of his pencil and drew his Lord's hair. Another fairly easy part.

An hour later, as the afternoon sun dipped lower in the sky, Erik studied his drawing. A deep satisfaction warmed his chest. The face he peered into was both strong and gentle, compelling but enigmatic.

He set the drawing beside him on the small porch table that sat between the two rocking chairs. Tomorrow he'd finish engraving the shepherds' scene and start working on the wise men design. By Christmas, he should have the first four pews finished and in place.

Lacing his hands behind his head, he smiled at the memory of the schoolmarm's pleased expression when he had shown her how the fold-down desks all but disappeared into the back of the benches. Students could drop down the desks to write on them or fold them up when not needed.

Soft footsteps and quiet giggling drew his attention to his left. On the boardwalk in front of the barbershop, he could see Mark and Molly making their way toward him. The little girl looked to be hiding something behind her. Behind them, he could see Anna leaning against the front of the boardinghouse, watching the children.

All too soon, the tiny duo stood in front of him, shy smiles gracing their cherubic faces. What could they be up to?

"Anna said we could bring you a surprise." Molly looked down at the floor then over at her brother. The little boy's bright eyes twinkled with excitement. Mark moved closer and leaned on Erik's knee.

"Yeah, we brunged you a cookie."

"Ma—ark. It's s'posed to be a surprise." From behind her back, Molly retrieved something rolled up in one of Lacey's blue-checked cloth napkins. She unfolded the fabric, revealing bits and pieces of a crumbled sugar cookie.

Their generosity and kindness overwhelmed Erik. How long had it been since someone had done something so nice for him? He glanced down the street at Miss Campbell, who was still visible in the afternoon shadows. Could she be trying to sway him over to her way of thinking by encouraging the children to give him a gift?

"Anna says we have to hurry back 'cause it'll be dark soon."

Mark leaned against Erik's knee. "Them's yummy cookies, but they make me thirsty."

Erik accepted the treat from Molly. "I thank you for your kindness." Even if Miss Campbell was behind the ploy, he didn't want to disappoint the children, who looked so eager to please him.

"I love sugar cookies. And I already have a tin of water right here," he said, motioning toward the metal cup on the table.

"I'll get it." Mark pushed away from Erik's knee like he'd been shot from a cannon. Hurrying past his sister, he reached for the cup. Erik noticed the boy's untied shoestring at the same second Mark stumbled on it, falling across the table. The oil lamp and tin of water tumbled sideways as the table flipped under Mark's weight.

Erik reached for the child and caught him, saving him from injury. Mark grabbed him around the neck, obviously a bit shaken at his near miss and the sound of shattering glass.

"Mark?" Anna called. Erik heard quick footsteps as she hurried toward them.

"You are all right." Erik patted the boy's back then set the child down and turned to upright his table. His heart leaped to his throat as he stared at his ruined drawing. All his hard work had been destroyed in an instant. Water and lamp oil saturated the paper, blurring the lines of Christ's face. As he picked up the drawing, it fell into soggy pieces in his hand.

Miss Campbell stopped behind Molly, putting her hands on the girl's shoulders.

Molly's lower lip trembled. "You dropped your cookie." Tears coursed down her cheeks, and she turned suddenly, burying her face in Miss Campbell's skirt. Mark scowled at Erik then ran down the boardwalk.

He knew exactly how the children felt, but it wouldn't do to lash out in anger for something that was an obvious accident. Mark had only meant to do him a kindness. Pressing his lips together, Erik struggled to get a grip on his emotions.

His evening's work was destroyed, as well as the cookie he'd wanted to eat. Were children always this much trouble?

Chapter 6

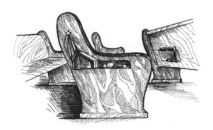

Erik stood with his fist on his hips, looking at his work area. Someone had been messing with his tools again. His best hammer lay in the dirt, next to five bent-in-half nails that someone had attempted to pound into a scrap of wood. On the ground beside the wood lay several more of his valuable tools.

Heaving a sigh, he strode over to his worktable and noticed the characters he'd carved for the nativity set had all been moved. The pieces looked no worse for wear. At least the bees-wax shine he had rubbed into the wooden people and animals hadn't been dulled by the handling. In all the years he'd had his workshop set up in back of his little building, nobody had ever bothered a thing. Why now?

Suddenly, he heard a giggle coming from behind his privy. He straightened and looked behind the outhouse, spying a blond head. Another childish giggled followed. *Hmm.* Perhaps he had found the troublemakers already. It seemed they couldn't stay away from him—or his tools.

Was this mischief their own doing, or were they under orders from Miss Campbell?

Erik picked up the tools and board with the nails, then sat down on the edge of his back porch, hoping to make himself less intimidating. He hadn't talked to Mark and Molly since the evening when they'd brought him the cookie, three days earlier.

Maybe he could gather some information on their parents if he could get them talking. He yanked the crooked nails free of the wood and peeked up to see the two children slinking toward him. Smiling, he looked up. They stopped dead in their tracks.

"Welcome." He motioned the children forward. "Come and sit with me."

The two youngsters looked at each other then back at him. They seemed drawn to him yet cautious at the same time. Molly hiked her chin and glared back. "You don't like us."

He blinked. Why would they think that? He liked all children, even ornery ones; he just didn't want to be forced into being responsible for children who weren't related to him. "That is not the truth. I do like you."

"You don't want to keep us." Mark stuck out his bottom lip and leaned against his sister, who immediately wrapped her arm around him.

Remorse flooded through Erik. In his battle with Anna Campbell, he'd forgotten about the two innocents caught in the middle. He softened his expression, hoping to make them understand. "Please, come sit with me." He patted the porch. After a moment of indecision, the children inched forward. How could he make them understand?

Finally they sat, one on either side of him. "First off, you must know that I do like you both. Very much." He smiled into the pale blue eyes so much like his, and a desire deep inside him flickered to life.

"Your Anna believes that I am the brother of your fader."

Mark shook his head. "Nuh-uh, you're our unca."

Erik bit back a smile but shook his head. "I am not so sure of that. You see, I only had one brother, and he has been dead a long time."

Molly scowled. "Nuh-uh, he only died in Optober."

"No, sweet thing, that was your fader but not my brother." Trembling with the delicate nature of his job, he breathed a prayer for God's guidance. Maybe he shouldn't even be having this talk, but they needed to know the truth. Why hadn't Anna told them?

He knew in his heart that she still held out hope that he'd take the children. "I do not believe that I am your uncle. My fader told me many years ago that my brother had died."

"Poppa wanted to come see you." Molly looked up with wide, innocent eyes. "I heard him tell Momma. But he said he couldn't take off work."

A sudden lump filled Erik's throat. Anna hadn't told him that. Still, his mind couldn't reconcile the situation with what he knew was the truth.

"We had to move."

Erik looked at Mark. Tears blurred the boy's eyes, making Erik want to pull him onto his lap. Overcoming his discomfort, he wrapped his arm around the boy. Mark scooted closer and rested his head against Erik's chest. A fatherly desire flamed to life within him.

"The lawya man is selling our house." Molly offered. "We moved to a boardinghouse with Anna. I get to sleep in her bed."

"I don't." Mark stuck his lip out again. "I sweep in the chair."

Compassion warred with sensibility. He had no place to put two children. Sure, he planned to build a house someday, but he had never quite gotten around to it since his place above the store was adequate enough for him and his uncle.

Erik shook his head. How could he even be considering taking in these children? He couldn't care for them. Cook or sew for them. They needed to be with Miss Campbell.

"So tell me what you were making with my tools."

He glanced down at Mark. The boy pushed away and wiped his eyes with his coat sleeve. "A Christmas present. For Anna."

"We don't got any money." Molly leaned on Erik's thigh and looked up. "Anna likes music boxes. She looks at them in the store, but she never buys one. We wanted to make one for her."

Their unselfish desire to please Miss Campbell touched Erik deeply. Maybe he couldn't be the uncle they wanted, but this was something he could help them do. "I can help you make a music box for your Anna."

"Weally?" Mark's eyes danced with the same excitement that ignited Erik's insides.

"Ja. But we have to find a very special piece of wood. And you must promise me that you won't bother any of my tools again. Some of them are dangerous and could hurt you."

Both children smiled and bobbed their heads in agreement.

"C'mon." Both Mark and Molly jumped to their feet. Mark grabbed Erik's hand and pulled him up.

"First we have to ask your Anna if you can work here with me." Standing, Erik pulled his cap from his back pocket and

set it on his head.

"C'mon. She won't care. She's working at the mercantile."

Erik's heart warmed as Molly slipped her tiny hand into his, but the words she shared were like throwing cold water onto him. "Why is Anna working at the mercantile?"

"She needs money." Mark said. "To feed us."

"Yeah." Molly's expression changed instantly. "She cries at night. And I heard her tell Mrs. Wilson she needed to work to get money."

Gently tightening his grip on the children, Erik glanced heavenward as they crossed the street. Had his refusal to accept them put Anna in such a bind that she had to take a job?

Still, the children weren't his responsibility.

So why did he feel so guilty?

Anna pressed down her apron, ever so grateful to Lionel Sager for allowing her to work a few days in the mercantile. She peeked out the window to see if the children were still in view. They'd been content this morning to help out in the store but had eventually grown restless. She'd bundled them up and sent them outside to play on the boardwalk in front of the mercantile but told them to stay nearby.

As soon as she finished unpacking the crate filled with bolts of cloth, she'd go check on them again. She admired the shimmering green fabric that she had just unpacked. If she weren't leaving town so soon, she could make the material into a lovely Christmas dress for Molly. Heaving a sigh, she checked off the item on the freight receipt and reached for the next bolt.

"That's beautiful fabric you have there."

Swirling around, Anna smiled at Matilda Phelps, who rubbed her hand along the green cloth. A shy smile creased the

woman's face as she looked around the store.

"Is. . .uh, is Mr. Sager here?"

"No, he had to go to the train depot to pick up some more orders that arrived today. Is there something I can help you with?" Anna knew the answer to that question before she asked it.

"Oh, no, thank you. Maybe I'll come back later." The young widow Phelps nodded and slipped out the front door.

Anna heard the Meddlin' Men chuckling from their corner. When the weather turned colder yesterday, they'd come inside to play their games and to talk.

"That Matilda's sweet on Lionel," Stone Creedon said, his bushy eyebrows lifted high. He raised his ear horn, as if expecting a reaction to his comment.

Chaps Smythe, the mayor, lifted his monocle to his eye and studied the checkerboard. "I say, ole chap, you might be on to something there."

Eb Wilson leaned over Mr. Creedon's shoulder and watched the game. "Lionel don't pay her no never mind. She's a wastin' her time."

"No. No, I say she just needs a helping hand. Perhaps there will be another Christmas wedding this year." Mr. Smythe jumped his man over two of Mr. Creedon's. "King me, Stone."

Stone Creedon grumbled but placed a red circle over his friend's game piece.

Biting back a smile, Anna pulled the next bolt of cloth from the crate and checked it off the list. Everything she had heard about the four ex-Texas Rangers was true. The sweet but ornery old men were the town matchmakers.

A noise drew her attention to the back of the store. Vivian Sager hobbled in using her crutches and stopped in front of

the rack that held the dime novels. She adjusted her glasses and straightened a few novels, casting shy glances at Anna. Suddenly, several of the small books slid out of her hands.

"I'll get them." Anna slipped from behind the counter and picked up the three booklets from the floor. "Here you go."

"Thank you." Vivian struggled with her crutches but managed to slip the books back into their rack. "I guess I'm not used to being idle."

Anna smiled. "I know what you mean, but your brother told me you were supposed to stay off that ankle."

"I know." The tall, thin woman heaved a sigh. "Guess I'll head back to my cot."

Anna felt sorry for Vivian, who seemed so lonely. "I could visit you later, maybe bring you something from Lacey's Diner."

For a moment, Anna thought she saw hope brighten the woman's blue eyes behind her spectacles, but she must have been mistaken because Vivian shook her head. "I appreciate the offer," she said quietly, "but please don't feel beholden to it. I know you must be busy, what with your new job here and taking care of those two children."

Before Anna could reply, Vivian awkwardly turned on her crutches and hobbled out of the room. Yes, she was busy, but she wouldn't mind getting to know Lionel's sister better. However, the woman seemed bent on rejecting her every advance at friendship.

The front door squeaked open, and Anna spun around to see a woman she hadn't met before. She flipped back a stylish wool cape, revealing a cute toddler clinging to her neck. Her eyes scanned the room and landed on the crate of cloth. A smile tilted the woman's lips, and she made a beeline for the fabric.

"Mornin', Peony," several of the old men called in unison from their corner.

"Good morning, gentlemen." She waved at them but turned back toward the crate. The cute, wide-eyed girl chewed on the end of her mother's scarf.

Anna hurried back to the counter, not wanting the woman to mix up the unpacked items with the ones Anna hadn't yet checked off her list. The woman fingered the green fabric then glanced up when Anna stepped behind the counter. Her eyebrows tilted in confusion, and she looked around the store.

"I'm Anna Campbell."

"Peony Wilson," she said, still looking a bit confused. "Where's Lionel and Vivian?"

"Lionel's at the train depot, collecting his latest shipment, and Vivian is on bed rest until her ankle heals. I'm just filling in for a few days."

"Oh, yes, I heard about Vivian. How is she doing?"

"Restless." Anna and Peony shared a chuckle.

"I should probably make dinner for her and Lionel one evening." Her gaze shifted back to the bolt of cloth. Peony fingered the dark green fabric. "This is beautiful. I normally order my own fabrics, but I got busy with Christmas orders and somehow overlooked it. I can't believe I did that."

"Things do get hectic at Christmastime. They're especially busy this year." Anna lifted out the next bolt of fabric, checked the number, and marked it off the freight list. She had a feeling Mrs. Wilson would want to see all the way to the bottom of the crate.

"I just have to have ten yards of that green fabric." Ignoring the everyday calicos Anna had just unpacked, the woman leaned over, peeking into the crate. "What else do you have in there?"

Anna quickly inventoried the rest of the order while Peony watched. After a few moments, she sat the toddler at her feet. "Don't worry; she's not walking yet. I'll sure be glad when she does. She's a hefty little tyke. I heard you had two children."

"No." Anna shook her head, not sure how to explain the situation without encroaching on Erik Olson's privacy and wondering at the same time just where her two wards had sneaked off to. "I'm their nanny."

Peony's eyebrows lifted. "So, what brings you to Cut Corners? It's not exactly a major destination. Few strangers come here except to trade and get supplies."

Anna had taken Lacey Wilson into her confidence because she needed help, but she didn't want the children's situation gossiped about to the whole town, at least not until Erik had been swayed to take them in. "So, are you related to Jeff and Lacey Wilson?" Anna asked, hoping to distract the woman.

"Yes, my husband, Rafe, the town's sheriff, is Jeff's cousin."

"It must be nice to have family nearby. By the way, your dress is lovely. Did you make it yourself?"

Mrs. Wilson smiled broadly. "Yes, I'm the town's dress-maker. That's my shop across the street."

"Oh, that's right. I remember seeing it. That wedding dress in the window is exquisite." Anna looked out the store window and across the street to see the front of Peony's small shop. Just then, Erik Olson entered the shop with Mark and Molly in tow.

Chapter 7

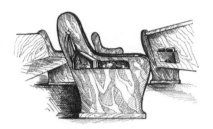

Anna swallowed the lump in her throat as she wondered what kind of trouble the children had gotten into now. If they kept pestering their uncle, he'd never agree to keep them. Though he hadn't said anything about it, Anna had seen Erik Olson's destroyed drawing the night the children had taken him the cookie.

He'd had every right to lash out in anger, but he hadn't. In fact, he'd seemed more concerned about the children being upset over their spoiled surprise than he had over the detailed drawing that he'd obviously labored on a long time. If that had been her father. . .no, she wouldn't think about him. Those awful days were over. She'd never again have to face her father's uncontrollable rage.

As Erik entered the shop right behind Mark and Molly, his gaze darted over to where the Meddlin' Men played their game. Anna was sure his ears turned red. Of course, maybe it was just from the chilly air outside.

Walking toward her, Erik removed his cap and cleared his

throat. Both children plowed past Mrs. Wilson and grabbed Anna's skirt, looking up with excited, hopeful eyes. "Can we help Uncle Erik?" Molly asked.

"Yeah, can we?" Mark's eyes twinkled in a way she hadn't seen since October. "Please?"

Erik shuffled closer to her, wringing his hat in his hands. Anna bit back a smile at seeing the big man so nervous. "I was. . .uh. . ." He glanced at the old men in the corner, and Anna followed his gaze. The men had halted their game, and all four sets of eyes were on her and Erik.

Mr. Creedon lifted his ear horn. "Somebody tell me what they're saying. I cain't hear a thing."

Obviously not wanting his uncle and friends to overhear them, Erik leaned closer. Anna's heart rate took off like a racehorse galloping down the lane. He was so close that she could see the faint stubble of golden hair on his jaw. The odor of fresh wood mixed with his manly scent, drawing Anna closer.

"I was wondering if the children could help me with a project I am starting."

Mark bounced up and down, while Molly yanked on Anna's apron. "Please, can we?" they cried in unison.

Anna took a moment to grasp what Mr. Olson was asking. He wasn't there to complain about the children, but rather he wanted to spend time with them. Her heart soared, and she couldn't hold back her smile. Maybe he was finally softening.

"Um. . .sure. I have to work another two hours. If you finish before then, just bring them back to me."

"Ja, sure. I will do that."

"Goodie!" Molly clapped her hands.

"You'll make sure they stay with you and keep their coats on?"

"Ja, I will, though it is not so cold out now as it was this morning."

Erik smiled, revealing the dimple in his cheek. Anna was sure that if he didn't leave soon, she would faint from lack of breath. What was wrong with her?

She watched the trio exit the store, the children giggling and skipping as they followed close on Erik's heels. Mrs. Wilson left with her youngster in tow shortly after purchasing several selections of fabric and some thread.

Anna reached into her pocket and pulled out a scrap of paper. She scanned the telegraph message, wishing more than anything that she didn't have to send it:

Hildegard Beaumont
    Deepest regrets. Unforeseen circumstances. Cannot perform at Christmas party.

                                                    Anna Campbell

Canceling such a prestigious event would surely hurt her reputation and make it harder for her to obtain opportunities to perform in the future. Still, she had two more Christmas parties that would allow her to demonstrate her abilities. Certainly those in attendance would want to hire her if she did well.

"Uh-hem."

Anna looked up to see Lars Olson standing in front of her. She crumpled the message and stuck it back in her pocket.

"It seems you and my nephew are working things out." Erik's uncle lifted one white eyebrow as if daring her to disagree.

And disagree she would. "I've yet to make him believe that he's related to those children."

"Erik never moves quickly. He's like the Bible verse in James about being slow to speak and slow to anger. Just like with his woodworking, he takes his time with everything. You must be patient with him and pray. God will speak to his heart."

"Do you truly believe that, Mr. Olson? The part about God speaking to his heart?" So many people in this town believed in a loving God that Anna was beginning to think her father had been completely wrong about Him.

"Ja." He nodded his shaggy head. "I do. Erik listens to our Lord, and he will do what God tells him."

Anna nibbled the inside of her lip, unsure if she should voice her thoughts. Sucking in a deep breath of courage, she plowed ahead. "Do you believe that Mark and Molly's father was Erik's brother?"

When he nodded his head, an overwhelming sense of relief soared through her.

"Ja, I do. After everything Erik has told me that you've said about Hans, I have to believe it's true. You know things no one could know unless they knew Hans." He laid his tanned, calloused hand on hers. "Erik is hurting because the brother he so admired knew where he was all these years but didn't contact him."

"I wish I knew what to do to help him. I didn't mean to cause trouble." Anna swiped at a tear tickling her cheek. "I don't want to leave the children here, but legally I have to, Mr. Olson."

Patting her hand, he smiled. "You will call me Swede, like everyone else. And we will pray for God to open Erik's eyes and to work things out. Ja?"

Nodding, Anna squeezed his hand, knowing in her heart that this man could be a good friend.

Anna shivered, not from cold but from the deed she'd just finished. A telegram canceling what would have been her third performance was on its way to Dallas. All her dreams had been shattered. And her funds were again running low after spending more than two weeks in Cut Corners. She heaved a sigh of resignation and headed back to the boardinghouse.

If she hadn't had to put aside the money for three train tickets back to Dallas, she'd be all right. Christmas was only three days away, and she had nothing to give the children. At least she was still able to work in the mercantile and might be able to barter with Mr. Sager to get them something small.

And she'd made a decision.

She would approach Erik Olson a final time about the children, and if he still refused to accept responsibility, she'd take them back to Dallas with the ticket money she'd saved and she'd shake the dust of Cut Corners off her feet. Somehow she'd fight the legal system for Mark and Molly. And just maybe God would help her.

She entered Lacey's Diner and walked to the kitchen. For the past few days after Anna had gotten off work, she had visited the diner, and Lacey had shared verses with her from the Bible. The words the wise woman shared had lowered Anna's defenses and made her see that God was truly a God of love.

Easing down in the chair, Anna stared across the worktable at Lacey. "I'm ready."

Lacey's smile could have brightened the whole town. "You're ready to give your heart to God?"

Anna nodded.

Lacey laid aside the apple she was peeling. She wiped her hands on her apron, reached across the table, and took Anna's hand. "I'm so happy for you. As you get to know God, you'll see how much He loves us."

They bowed their heads, and Lacey led Anna in a prayer of salvation. Anna's heart felt light and warm in a way she'd never before experienced. Her father's portrayal of a mean, cruel God didn't line up with what she'd read in the New Testament. God loved her—and the children. She knew that now. He would provide for them.

Erik blew the shavings off the top of the music box that he was engraving for Anna. Would she like the angel he'd carved on the lid?

All that was left now was to varnish the wood and install the music box kit that he'd had Lionel order for him. The children had enjoyed sanding the wood and helping assemble the small box.

His hours with them had turned out to be some of the most enjoyable he had experienced lately. After working with Mark and Molly, he'd played chase and hide-and-seek with them, just as he had as a child. God was surely softening his heart and drawing them together.

What would You have me do, Lord?

How many times had he asked God that question?

Now he knew the answer in his heart. He would tell Anna that he would keep the children, even though he still didn't believe they were his brother's. It no longer mattered. His chest warmed with the thought of raising the youngsters.

He loved hearing them call him Uncle Erik—or Unca Airwick, in Mark's case.

There was just one problem. The children still needed a mother. And not just any mother. They needed Anna. *He* needed Anna.

Erik couldn't pinpoint when he had started caring for her, but care he did. Never having been in love before, it took him some time to understand what was happening to him. Instead of avoiding Anna as he had been, he was ready to do as the Meddlin' Men had suggested—to take the initiative and get to know her. The fact that he was actually listening to the old matchmakers' advice surprised him because, in the past, he'd staunchly refused to have anything to do with their ploys to pair him up.

But with Anna it was different. Whenever she was near, he got all mushy inside like a bowl of Lacey's creamy mashed potatoes. His heart raced, and his hands sweated. He loved those dark brown eyes of hers. But would Anna even give him the time of day after the way he'd treated her and hadn't believed her?

Erik picked up a small brush from off his workbench and wiped away the remaining wood shavings covering the angel. Would Anna realize that it resembled her?

He opened a cabinet door and placed the music box out of sight until he could help the children varnish it. Suddenly, he heard the pounding of feet running toward him. He turned and saw Anna, with skirts held high, racing around the side of his building.

"Please, Erik, tell me the children are here." Her frantic gaze darted everywhere. Her bosom rose and fell from her exertion. "Where are they?"

Erik shook his head and hurried down the porch steps. She must be terribly upset because she'd never called him by his first name before. "I have not seen them today."

Anna grabbed onto his arm. "Are you certain? I can't find them anywhere."

"When did you see them last?"

"I had to send a telegram, so I told them they could play outside while I did that. I left them playing ball in front of the boardinghouse and Lacey's Diner. I was only gone a few minutes." Her face flushed with a hint of anger as her brows dipped low. "Well, I would have been if that Ticks McGee hadn't tried to convince me to have dinner with him."

Erik fought back a surge of jealousy that Ticks was crowding in on his woman. He shook his head. Anna wasn't *his* woman. She probably didn't even like him.

"Please, can you help me find the children?"

The anguish on Anna's face pierced his heart, and he tugged her to his chest. She came willingly. "Ja," he said, leaning his chin against her soft hair. "I vill help you."

He wanted to relish the feel of Anna in his arms, but that would have to wait. Mark and Molly might be in danger, and he had to find them. "Tell me where you have looked."

Anna didn't push away as he expected but held on to his waist. "I looked in the boardinghouse, at Lacey's, and the mercantile. I thought for sure they'd be here when I didn't find them. They love spending time with you."

"And I enjoy spending time with them."

At that, she pushed back, wiping a tear with the back of her hand. "Truly?"

"Ja." He reached out and brushed some sawdust from her head, enjoying the silky texture of her thick hair.

"You smell like fresh-cut wood."

Erik tightened his lips. "I am sorry."

Anna touched her hand to his chest. "No, don't be sorry. I like it." Her delicate smile made his belly feel as if a hundred butterflies were dancing in it. Her eyes, though still filled with worry, contained a hint of something else. Could she have feelings for him, also?

"So where should we look next?" she asked.

Shaking away thoughts of Anna, he focused on the children. "We will check inside my shop, just to make sure they are not there. They like sitting in the child-sized rocking chairs I made for Pastor Clune's children."

Without asking her permission, Erik took Anna's hand and helped her up the porch steps, through his back room, and into his shop. The small rockers were empty, and there was no sign of the children. He turned to see disappointment lace Anna's pretty face.

She ducked her head and ran her hand over the top of a small dining table, then looked up and caught sight of the casket covering the north wall. Her eyes widened, and she looked back at him. "Why do you have a casket in your shop?"

He shrugged and grinned. Reaching down, he righted a chair that had somehow fallen on its side. "Somebody has to make them. Plus, I have sold so much furniture that I needed something to fill the empty space in here. But we should not be concerned about that. We must find the children."

He tugged her outside and headed for the train depot. As a child, that's where he would have gone. They searched the whole depot area, then headed for the livery. Next they stopped at the blacksmith shop and talked with Jeff Wilson.

In spite of the cool day, the brawny man swiped the sweat off his forehead. "No, I haven't seen hide nor hair of them two young'uns. Soon as I finish shoeing this horse for Gus Gustafson, I'll help you look for them. Have you asked anyone else to help search?"

Erik shook his head. He hadn't asked for help because he

felt certain that he and Anna could locate the children. They headed back to the mercantile to get Swede but met a crowd congregating in the street. Swede hurried toward them with the other Meddlin' Men close behind.

"We just heard the children are missing. What can we do to help?"

After several minutes of discussion, the crowd split up into small groups and set out in different directions to search the whole town. It would be dark in a few hours, and though the day had been fairly nice, the temperature would plummet with nightfall. It was agreed that when the children were found, the church bell would be rung.

At Swede's insistence, Erik and Anna headed back to his shop in case the children showed up there. Erik would much rather be out searching, but he couldn't leave Anna to wait and worry alone.

She blotted at the tears running down her face as she shuffled toward the shop. Erik's heart nearly broke seeing the feisty Anna Campbell in tears. He wrapped his arm around her shoulders and pulled her against him. When they reached his shop, she turned and looked up. "This is all my fault."

"I do not understand."

Anna wrung her hands and stared at the ground. "I told them I would take them back to Dallas with me."

Erik's heart clenched as if it were locked in a vise. Anna was leaving—and taking the children with her?

"No! I do not want you to take Mark and Molly away. I have decided I will keep them."

Anna blinked. Surprise and confusion played across her face. "You want to keep them? Even though you don't believe they're your brother's children? Why?" The last word came out as a whisper.

He shrugged. "I have grown to care for them. Even to love them, I think. And God spoke to me that this is His will."

"I can't believe it."

"It is true. But there is just one problem."

Her brows crinkled. "What?" Wariness darkened her eyes.

"The children need a mother, too."

"So you're getting married?" She looked down at the ground again but not before he saw her eyes tear up.

Excitement and concern that she'd refuse him made his knees weak and his hands tremble. "Perhaps I will marry you, if you will have a stubborn old carpenter."

Chapter 8

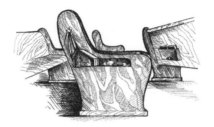

Anna's head darted upward. "You want to marry *me*?" A shy smile tilted her lips. "You certainly have odd timing."

Behind him, Erik could hear the many voices of his friends and neighbors calling for Mark and Molly. "Ja. But you just informed me you are leaving, so I am running out of time."

"You don't even know me, Erik."

He loved the sound of his name on her lips. The only thing more pleasing would be his lips on hers, but this wasn't the time for kissing. "I do know you. You are a persistent woman who goes after what she wants, even if she must sacrifice to get it. You are beautiful, inside and out. And God has blessed you with a talent many only dream of."

Blushing, Anna laid her hand on his arm. "I will consider your offer—once we find the children. All right?"

Erik nodded, knowing he never should have broached the subject of marriage at such a time. It wasn't like him to be impulsive, but where Anna was concerned, nothing was normal.

Anna shivered in the fading sunlight.

"We should go inside," he said, taking her by the elbow. "It will only get colder out here."

She hesitated and looked down the street.

"Everyone knows we are here. They will come to my shop when they find the barnen."

Anna nodded and followed him inside. She strolled over to the woodstove in the back corner and lifted her hands, while Erik lit the lantern on the wall. "I want you to know that I gave my heart to God yesterday. Lacey helped me."

Erik strode up behind her, laying his hands on her shoulders. "Anna, that is wonderful! I know it was hard for you because of your fader, but I am very happy. You will see that God is a God of love, not hate."

She spun around, surprising him with her expression laced with hurt and anger. "Then why are the children missing? Doesn't God care?"

He ran the back of his finger down her cheek. "Of course, He does. He cares more for the children than we ever could. We should pray for them. Will you pray with me, Anna?"

She stared at him for a moment. Her features softened; then she nodded and bowed her head.

Holding both her hands, Erik poured out his heart to God, knowing that finding the children safe could make a difference in Anna's faith. She was an infant Christian. If Mark and Molly were not found safe, could her new faith survive?

"Thank you for that prayer, Erik." Anna leaned toward him, and he wrapped his arms around her.

"You are welcome." He laid his cheek against her head, finding needed comfort in her embrace. He couldn't let her see how worried he was because it would only cause her more concern.

A scuffling sound near the casket snagged his attention. Anna jumped in his arms and turned her head toward the noise. "What was that?"

"Rats, probably."

She shivered. "Must be awfully big rats."

Erik stared at the casket. Something wasn't right.

Again he heard a scraping sound, and he was certain he saw the casket lid move. Suddenly, he knew what was wrong. He always left the hinged casket lid open. Who could have closed it?

Gently setting Anna aside, he hurried across the room.

"What's wrong?" she asked.

Slowly, Erik lifted the hinged lid of the casket and a small hand popped out.

Anna screamed. Molly screamed in response and rubbed her eyes, blinking at the light in the room.

"Molly!" Anna crossed the room in an instant and picked up the girl. "We've been looking everywhere for you! I was so worried. What in the world are you doing in Erik's casket?"

Mark, just waking up, rubbed his eyes, then stretched and yawned. "We wanted to sleep in a manger like baby Jesus did."

Erik looked at Anna. He could see the relief in her eyes.

"Yeah. Just like the story you read us, Anna." Molly shook her messed-up tresses. "We climbed in, but the chair fell over, and we couldn't get out."

"And then the lid shutted." Mark grinned. "It was weal dark inside. I wasn't scared, but Molly cwied." Mark held out his arms, and Erik picked up the boy and hugged him tight.

"You were too scared. You yelled and yelled for Uncle Erik."

"I am sorry I did not hear you. I was outside working."

Erik patted Mark's back and the child looked up, his bottom lip sticking out.

"Anna says we have to go back to Dallas."

Erik and Anna exchanged glances. Her dark eyes sparkled with promise, sending Erik's heart into a frenzy. "We will talk about that later. First, we must let the town know you are found safe. Then we will eat dinner at Lacey's. Ja, Anna?"

A smile danced on Anna's pretty lips. "Ja, Erik."

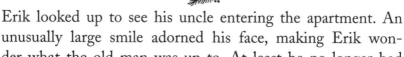

Erik looked up to see his uncle entering the apartment. An unusually large smile adorned his face, making Erik wonder what the old man was up to. At least he no longer had to worry about being a victim of the Meddlin' Men's matchmaking schemes, now that Anna had agreed to marry him.

He still couldn't believe he was getting married. He, who had never done anything hastily his whole life, was marrying a woman he'd only known a few weeks. Yet he knew in his heart it was God's will.

It was the perfect solution. The children would have two people who loved them to raise them and care for them. And Anna wouldn't have to leave or worry about working to support herself.

And he loved her. Oh, how he loved her.

"A-hem."

Erik glanced up, realizing he'd been daydreaming.

"You'll never believe what I've got."

"I do not know."

Eyes sparkling with delight, Swede pulled a battered envelope from his pocket. "I have an early Christmas present for you."

Erik had no idea who could be writing him a letter —unless

it was the one from the attorney. He took the envelope and stared at his father's name and his own on the front. Flipping it over, his heart nearly stopped beating. The name on back read Hans Olson.

His gaze darted to his uncle's. Swede smiled and shrugged his shoulders, probably wondering, just like Erik was, how a letter eight years old could have found its way to him.

Shaking, Erik slumped into a nearby rocker and wiped his sweaty palms on his pants. He ripped open the envelope and pulled out a crumpled letter. Unfolding it, he began reading out loud:

> *October 10, 1880*
> *Dear Fader and Erik,*
> *I am much too late in writing to you both. It has taken many years for me to get over my anger. Too many. Please forgive me. I have been so wrong. I am very sorry so many years have been wasted.*
> *You'll be happy to know that I am married and living near you in Dallas. I have a beautiful wife, Jessica, and two charming children, Molly and Mark.*

Stunned, Erik looked up. "The barnen. They truly are Hans's children. Our niece and nephew." He shook his head, realizing how close he had come to letting Anna leave with them.

He finished reading the letter, rejoicing that his brother had given his heart to God. Nothing could please him more. Hans went on to say how he hoped to visit at Christmas.

Erik heaved a sigh. If only he had known Hans was in Dallas, he would have gone to his brother. But it was too late for what-ifs.

Rising from his chair, with tears in his eyes, he hugged his uncle, wondering how his brother's letter had managed to get lost in the mail for so long.

But then, wasn't this God's perfect timing?

Knowing that he'd come to love Mark and Molly before he knew they were blood relatives warmed his soul. Yes, God's timing was perfect.

"Why wait to be married?" Swede had said when he told Erik he had decided to move to the boardinghouse until Erik could build a house for his new family. Things would be a bit crowded for a while with a wife and two children living in his small upstairs area, but they'd be happy times.

The kettle of water he was heating for his bath hissed on the stove. "Time to get ready," Erik told his uncle.

"Ja. I'm looking forward to hearing our Anna play piano."

"Ja. Me, too." Erik placed the cherished letter in his Bible and shrugged off his shirt. First, he would attend his last bachelors' Christmas Eve pot roast luncheon at the diner; then he would listen to his beautiful beloved's exquisite piano playing; and finally, he would shock the town with his announcement.

Anna's fingers flew over the ivory keys as the people in the crowded church belted out "O Come, All Ye Faithful." Pine fragrance scented the air from the lovely decorations that Lacey and Peony had put up.

Anna had been so honored when Pastor Clune had asked her to play for the Christmas Eve service. Playing in a church on the eve of Christ's birth brought so much more satisfaction than playing for her wealthy clients at their parties, thrown mostly to impress their peers, would have.

It was a miracle that Erik had received his brother's letter.

What a blessing! She peeked at Erik and the children sitting on the front row and hit a wrong note. Erik's eyebrow lifted, and Anna winced; then she eased into the correct note, admonishing herself to keep focused on the job at hand.

When Erik had asked her to marry him, she'd been completely taken off guard. She hadn't even thought he liked her, though she had to admit, his gaze tended to linger whenever he looked at her.

And when exactly had she started having feelings for him? All she knew was that going back to Dallas no longer interested her. Everything she loved was in this small town. The children. Erik's ornery Uncle Lars and the other Meddlin' Men. The townsfolk, who were quickly becoming her friends. And Erik.

She played the final note then folded her hands in her lap, waiting to see if Pastor Clune would start another off-key carol. He stood from his spot between his wife and Erik and walked to the front. Anna's heart was still warm from the touching Christmas message the pastor had shared earlier. For a moment, he stared at the faces in the crowd.

"Thank you all for coming out in the cold to attend our Christmas Eve service. I know you're all anxious to attend the dessert reception at Lacey's Diner, but first, let's show our appreciation to Miss Anna Campbell, who graciously agreed to play piano for us tonight."

All eyes turned toward Anna as cheers erupted and the room resounded with fervent clapping. She smiled to the crowd, then ducked her head, never quite comfortable with compliments.

"Anna, would you come here, please?"

Blinking in surprise, she glanced up at the pastor's outstretched hand. The piano bench squeaked as she slid it back and stood. From the second row, Lacey Wilson, sitting next to her husband, smiled, giving her courage. Mark and Molly sat next to Erik with grins that warmed her heart. Moving to the front, she took the pastor's hand.

"This is from Mrs. Clune and myself." The kind pastor squeezed her hand, then handed her a beautifully monogrammed handkerchief with lace trim. Anna didn't miss the significance of the initials Mrs. Clune had skillfully stitched.

"Erik Olson, would you also come up here?"

Tingles dashed from Anna's heart down to her toes as Erik stood and came to stand beside her.

"I'm sure you all have noticed the four new pews Erik made and installed up front. They're much nicer than the church board could ever have hoped for when we hired him to do the job. And his engravings are magnificent."

The crowd again erupted in clapping and loud comments of "well done" and "good job." Anna peeked up at Erik then smiled when she saw his ears turning red. He was even more uncomfortable with public attention than she.

Pastor Clune held up his hand. "I believe Erik has something to say."

Erik looked at Anna with a smile that turned her insides to cornmeal mush. The dimple she loved seemed to wink at her with a promise of what was to come.

He cleared his throat, as if working up the nerve to speak to the crowd. Anna slipped her hand into his and squeezed.

"I'd like to invite all of you to attend our wedding—mine and Anna's. Here, in the church, next Saturday at two."

A few people, Anna noted, looked genuinely surprised. Perhaps the gossip mill in Cut Corners wasn't quite as rampant as in Persimmon Gulch.

Again the small building was filled with the cheers of their friends and neighbors rejoicing that another Christmas wedding would occur this year. The Meddlin' Men pounded each other on the back as if the wedding was all their idea. She could hear Stone Creedon's gravelly voice about the din. "What's all the excitement about?"

And for once, Anna didn't care. The man she loved would always be beside her, along with Mark and Molly, and maybe even one day soon, she would bear children of her own—hers and Erik's.

"Kiss her," someone in the crowd yelled.

Ignoring Pastor Clune's surprised expression, Erik pulled Anna into his arms, and his lips met hers in a wonderful promise of more to come.

Anna knew this would be a Christmas she would never forget—a Christmas filled with so many unexpected blessings.

Soft Ginger Cookies

1 cup molasses
2 tablespoons warm milk
1 tablespoon ginger
1 teaspoon cinnamon
½ cup soft butter
1 teaspoon baking soda
Enough flour to mix soft as can be handled
on the board, about 2½ cups

Dissolve soda in the milk; then mix ingredients in order given. Shape into balls the size of a hickory nut on a floured board. Press ball to ½-inch thick with a flat-bottomed glass dipped in cold water or lightly dusted with flour. Place on greased cookie sheet, about 1½ inches apart, and cook at 350° for ten minutes. Makes three to four dozen cookies.

VICKIE MCDONOUGH

Award-winning author Vickie McDonough has lived in Oklahoma all her life, except for a year when she and her husband lived on a kibbutz in Israel. Her inspirational romance credits include novellas in *A Stitch in Time, Brides O' the Emerald Isle, Texas Christmas Grooms* and *Lone Star Christmas. Sooner or Later* is her first novel and will be released by Heartsong Presents in November 2005. Her second Heartsong, *Spinning Out of Control*, is due out next year.

Vickie also writes articles and has written over 450 book reviews. She is a member of numerous writing groups and was awarded the 2004 Tulsa Nightwriter of the Year award by a local writers' group. Vickie is a wife of thirty years and mother to four sons. When she's not writing, she enjoys reading, gardening, watching movies, and traveling. Visit www.vickiemcdonough.com to learn more about Vickie's books.

A Christmas Chronicle

by Pamela Griffin

Dedication

A big, Texas-sized thank you to all my crit partners and writer friends who helped on this project. And to Jon Jones, Linda Rondeau, and Calvin Wood, a special thanks for info regarding the square dance and calls.

As always, I dedicate this book to my patient, sweet Lord, who taught me what it really means to please Him, yet accepted me just as I was.

For do I now persuade men, or God?
or do I seek to please men?
for if I yet pleased men,
I should not be the servant of Christ.

GALATIANS 1:10 KJV

Prologue

Cut Corners, Texas
1881

Stone Creedon eyed the checkerboard with unsuppressed glee. Victory over Swede would finally be his. "I got ya now, you old goat. Take a long, hard look at Cut Corners' new champion." He cackled out a laugh.

Swede only harrumphed a couple of times. Watching from nearby, Mayor Chaps Smythe brought his monocle to his eye to peer more closely at the board, while Eb Wilson shook his head slowly in amazement. Trim and tall, he was the only one of the four who hadn't changed all that much since their younger days as Texas Rangers.

"Mark Olson, you get that overgrown puppy out of the store this instant! You know my brother doesn't allow animals inside." Vivian Sager's words to the boy were so high-pitched, even Stone could hear them, and he winced when her shoes clomped his way. "Why, he's tracked muddy paw prints all over my clean floor!"

Quick as greased lightning, Vivian swished past, her elbow knocking into Stone's head and her ungainly skirts knocking board and checkers off the barrel and onto the oak planks. Swede roared with mirth and slapped his knee. Stone seethed words not fit to be aired under his breath, as the board—and his sure victory—clattered to the floor while the wooden disks rolled and landed with ricocheting spins and plops even a partially deaf man could hear.

"Oh, Mr. Creedon, Mr. Olson, I'm so sorry." Vivian raised long fingers to both cheeks, which were flushed beneath her round spectacles. "Did I hurt your bad ear, Mr. Creedon? Are you alright?"

"Stop your fussin' gal, I'm fine."

"I certainly didn't mean to. . .well, I hope you know I never would have. . ." Appearing to be plumb out of words, she colored as red as a ripe persimmon, picked up her skirts, and hastened to the back storage room as if a fire had been set beneath her heels.

Stone blew out a disgusted breath and bent to help Swede and the others pick up the checkers. "You know," he said, "I think it's time we get her hitched."

Swede straightened in surprise. "Who? Vivian?"

"See any other woman round here?"

"That's a pretty tall order, don't you think?" Eb asked.

Stone scratched his whiskered jaw. "I reckon us four could do it. We got the other three hitched, didn't we? And who woulda thought Erik would stop bein' so mule-headed and finally marry up with Anna?"

"Ja, but Vivian?" Swede dumped the checkers on the board he'd replaced atop the barrel.

"Swede's right," Eb put in. "Rob Baxter was the only man to show interest in Vivian, you'll recall. Interest he lost directly after that little accident when she waited on him. Doc says he'll most likely never walk right again."

"All the more reason why we need to get her married up," Stone stressed, "so she can stay home like most womenfolk and raise young'uns. It's time she was put in her place. Her brother'll probably thank us for gettin' her out from underfoot."

"Hmm, I am not so sure." Swede studied Stone with narrowed eyes.

"I say," Chaps inserted in his very British way, "have you someone in mind, Stone?"

"Matter of fact, I do. When that last mail delivery batch came through, a letter from my nephew Travis was in it—he's one of them chroniclers that gallivant throughout the West, totin' a camera. Takes pictures for some fancy magazine back East."

Swede nodded. "I heared of them, these chroniclers."

"Well, he wrote that he'll be ridin' through Cut Corners nigh unto three weeks."

Grinning at the idea that now filled his head, Stone settled back in his chair and eyed his three matchmaking partners. Their present work was a far cry from the old glory days of bringing law and order to the Wild West, but attempting to bring order to these youngsters' lives by trying to find them lifelong companions was just about as important, he reckoned. Besides, once the couples were hitched, they tended to stop interfering in his affairs. Ever since that dunk in a frozen river years ago, when he'd rescued a lad from being swept away by the current and had consequently caught a high fever, losing most all his hearing in his right ear, the women had been fussing over him like he was a little boy in britches. Especially that old gossip, the widow Chamberlain, though he figured nothing could be done about pairing her up with anyone.

"Yep." He laced his hands across his thick paunch. "I reckon Travis'll do just fine."

Chapter 1

Almost one month later

Travis McCoy settled his shoulder blades comfortably against the wooden chair and rubbed his stomach. "I declare, Mrs. Chamberlain, that was by far one of the best meals I've had in weeks. Make that months. One doesn't get fare like this while traveling the plains. Hardtack and beans are my usual diet."

As if waiting for such approval, Lula Chamberlain, the fiftyish owner of the boardinghouse, hovered beside the table where Travis and his uncle Clive "Stone" Creedon were eating. She beamed a gap-toothed smile at Travis then looked at Stone. He didn't say a word.

"Thank you for speaking your mind, Mr. McCoy. My pecan pie is some of the finest in all of Cut Corners, as my dear deceased husband Roderick Chamberlain III used to claim, may he rest in peace. Now that young Lacey Wilson who runs the diner? I heard tell she uses white sugar in her pies, though she's tight-lipped when it comes to revealin' her recipes to any-one but family, so I can't be certain. But that fancy white sugar is something which I just don't abide. You can't get the right texture and flavor when you use white sugar for the filling, but will she listen? Not a whit. It's like trying to talk sense into a flea."

His uncle raised his cup. "I'll take more tea."

"Not tea," she said more loudly. "Flea."

"You got fleas?" he shot back.

"Oh, never mind." Exasperated, she swung her hands into the air. "Whyever don't you use that ear trumpet of yours?" She scooped tea leaves into Stone's cup and poured steaming water over them.

"Cain't stand the thing." His gray mustache twitched as he gave a sniff. "Fool thing don't work right, nohow."

She blew out a breath, causing the straggle of silvering hair that had escaped her bun to fly upward. Again, she turned her gaze toward Travis and smiled. "You do have such an interest-ing occupation, Mr. McCoy, in using your cameras to take pho-tographs of the landscape and such. I have a brother who's also lived quite the adventurous life. He was a Pony Express rider, but then he took himself an Indian wife, and now he lives like a savage, wild on the prairie. . . ." She tsk-tsked, gossiping on as she'd done nonstop since Travis had arrived in Cut Corners hours ago.

"Well, my occupation does fill a need," Travis replied when he could get a word in edgewise. Yet his thoughts were any-thing but modest. He loved his work and knew he was good at what he did, striving to be the best. His was a lonely job, but lack of companionship was a sacrifice he was willing to make. Truth be told, if the good Lord didn't want him to continue in his pursuit of chronicling the West, it would probably take a knock upside his noggin for him to get the picture.

"You'll be staying in town for the harvest dance next week, won't you?" Mrs. Chamberlain loudly inquired. "I imagine a number of young ladies from these parts will have quite a hankering to meet you. Ranchers' families come from miles around for the occasion."

Stone abruptly cleared his throat, stood, and stared at him. "How about we step outside for some air?"

"Alright." Travis pulled his napkin from his collar, sensing his uncle wanted to talk.

"What about your tea?" Mrs. Chamberlain asked.

"It'll keep." Stone shuffled outside onto the porch, and Travis followed.

Due to the sharp wind that blew from the north, Travis was glad he still wore his coat. He would have preferred the warmth of the cozy parlor he'd glimpsed upon his arrival but kept his thoughts to himself. Glancing to his left, he caught sight of two young boys approaching his wagon. They poked at the tarpaulin covering the back, as if hoping to get a peek at what lay underneath.

"You there," he called. "Get away from that wagon!" His livelihood was inside, and suddenly he questioned the safety of leaving his conveyance there. Maybe he should camp in the rear of the wagon, crowded though it was, rather than partake of the luxury of a room at the boardinghouse.

"Don't worry about them two," his uncle said with a dry chuckle as they watched the lads skitter down Main Street and head toward Ranger Road, the only two streets the town possessed. The wind blew orange red dust in a swirl around the boys' legs. "They're curious as young chickens in a new barnyard, but they know better than to fiddle with the equipment in your What-izzit Wagon."

At that, Travis grinned. When he'd first stopped in front of the boardinghouse, people drifted across the street from the mercantile, clustering around as he pulled back the tarp to show his uncle the wagon's contents. Someone asked the inevitable question, "What-izzit?"

Travis had joked that Matthew Brady, the famous Civil War photographer he so admired, had soldiers who posed that very question upon seeing his array of boxlike cameras and other equipment. And so Mr. Brady's wagon had been dubbed "what-izzit" from that point on. Now Travis's wagon bore the honor of that same title.

"Remember that young gal you met at the mercantile?" his uncle asked casually, tucking the fingers of his gnarled hands in his suspenders.

Travis drew his brows together. "I can't say as I recall any girl."

"Well then, you must be losin' your eyesight, since it was a woman who waited on you when you bought them groomin' tools of yours."

Travis wiped a hand across his smooth jaw, feeling civilized again. It was a relief to have gotten rid of the scratchy beard, though he'd kept the mustache. He'd learned that the town had a barber, but Travis preferred to groom his own face. Something about allowing a stranger to put a blade to his throat didn't sit well with him. "You mean the woman who knocked over the stand of shaving brushes when she collected one for me?"

"Yep, that's the one."

While he stared at the weathered board walls of the mercantile directly across the street, Travis tried to form a mental picture. An image of a woman almost as tall as he, gangly, and skinny as a post came to mind. Spectacles. A thick cloud of dark hair. He shrugged, setting his sights on the wooded bluffs beyond the store. The setting sun filled the sky with a blaze of orange, and purple shadows buried deep into the hills. He longed to find the perfect spot, set up his camera, and get started.

"Well, I'd consider it a favor if you'd ask her to the harvest dance."

"What?" Stone's words knocked Travis from his mental photograph. "You can't be serious."

"Sure am. She's decent folk, goes to church. Helps her brother run the mercantile."

"That's all well and good, but I'm not looking for a companion. Besides, I'm not even sure I'll be here next week to attend any dance."

"Well, that's another thing," Stone said quickly. "I talked to Chaps—the town's mayor—before your arrival, and we'd like to requisition your services to take us a photograph of everyone in this here town. It'd be nice to frame and keep for posterity's sake." He sounded as if he were parroting the Englishman, whom Travis had met that afternoon. "We figure sometime in mid-November would be best."

"Why so late? Why not now?"

"Well. . ." Stone shuffled his feet, his gaze going to the glimpse of railroad tracks near the church. "Fact is, there's a few citizens who got business outta town and won't be back till then. Chaps wants them in the shot. They're important to the town, you see."

Why did Travis get the feeling his uncle was making this up as he went along?

"Mrs. Chamberlain said you're welcome to stay here at the boardinghouse as long as you like. Her fees are purty reasonable." Stone cleared his throat. "Anyhow, Chaps asked me to talk the matter over with you, bein' as you're my nephew and all. I'll make sure you get a handsome price for your troubles."

Travis pondered the idea. "I suppose I could put off leaving till then."

"Good. Then there'll be no problem about the dance. If I was you, I'd ask Miss Sager soon—tonight even. A lady likes to have enough time to get herself a purty dress and all them doodads."

"Whoa there, back up a minute." Travis lifted his hands out to his sides. "I never said I was going to any town dance. And how would you know what a lady likes? You've never been married."

"Spending time at the mercantile every day, a man hears women chattering about all sorts o' things he has no business knowin'." Stone scratched his gray-whiskered jaw. "It's just a dance. I ain't askin' you to court her or nothin'."

Travis thought a moment. "One thing isn't exactly clear to me. Why would this be a favor to you?"

"I told her brother I'd ask. Lionel's a right nice young man—plays a mean game of checkers—and his sister's a sweet little gal. So I'd go if I was you. Cain't hurt nothin'."

Narrowing his eyes, Travis surveyed his uncle. He stood a good foot shorter and stouter, his straight hair unkempt, his clothes clean but well-worn. Travis had a feeling that Mrs. Chamberlain was responsible for any cleanliness concerning the man's garments. An idea came to Travis, one that made him fight back a smile. Triumphant, he played what he was sure was his trump card.

"Alright, tell you what, Uncle. I'll go to your town's shindig and ask—what was her name again?"

"Vivian. Vivian Sager."

"I'll ask Miss Sager to accompany me—but on one condition."

The zeal ebbed out of Stone's eyes. "What condition?"

"That you do exactly the same. You ask to escort Mrs. Chamberlain to the harvest dance."

"What? That old gossip?" Stone scoffed and shook his head. "Nothin' doin'."

Travis allowed the smile to spread across his mouth. He was glad he remembered what his mother had said about her brother Clive being a confirmed bachelor. The ex-Texas Ranger claimed in a former letter to his sister that he wanted "nothing to do with womenfolk cluttering up his personal lifestyle." The nickname of "Stone" fit him well. And with the kind of existence Travis led as a nomad photographer on the plains, he was destined for a life of bachelorhood like his uncle.

His gaze going to the hills, Stone grumbled loudly to himself, pulling down hard on his suspenders until Travis thought they might be in danger of popping undone. The wind picked up as twilight descended. Travis was just about to seek the warmth of the front parlor, and a second slab of pie, when Stone turned.

"Alright, Nephew, you got yourself a deal. I'll ask that woman to be her escort—and you'd better do the same and ask Miss Sager first thing after sunup tomorrow."

At a sudden loss for words, Travis only stared, caught in his own trap.

Vivian swept the spilled sugar into her cupped hand, disposing of the grains into a nearby bucket set on the floor expressly for refuse, then once more carefully went about measuring the sugar Anna Olson wanted. The two fair-haired children, Mark and Molly, longingly eyed the candy jars along the counter. Lacey Wilson slowly paced, smoothing the back of her baby daughter whose rosy cheek lay upon her shoulder. Peony Wilson, the sheriff's wife, waddled into the shop, her extended stomach evidence that her second child would soon be born, only a month after Anna's was due. Peony's little girl, Lynn, smiled widely when she caught sight of the Olson children and toddled their way, her dark ringlets bouncing.

"Good morning, Anna, Vivian." Peony nodded toward each woman, then caught sight of Lacey near the pickle barrel. "Oh, there's the little one! Why, hello there, Mercy Mae." She headed that direction and began cooing baby talk.

Vivian went about her work, preparing Anna's order, her ears attuned to the three women visiting and chattering away, happily content in their roles as wives and mothers.

She had never fit in with those women. They'd never treated her rudely, though they rarely sought her company. But maybe that was partially her fault. Being around them made Vivian all the more aware that she would never have what they did. They were all beauties with engaging personalities; she was plain with the social skills of a turtle—and just as awkward. In the past three years, all three of those women had found love during the Christmas season, each of them receiving proposals during that month of goodwill and cheer. A few of the local yokels joked that Cut Corners at Christmastime always brought Cupid in for a spell. Of course, the four ex-Texas Rangers, who'd been dubbed the Meddlin' Men, had had a lot to do with pairing off those couples.

Vivian doubted that either Cupid or the four match-makers could help her find a husband. Not that she would ask any of those aged gentlemen for assistance. No, sir. She didn't get along well with people; they always seemed to be watching her, as if waiting for her to trip over her huge feet. Besides, she wanted more to life than just getting married and raising babies, though she did love children. She wanted adventure, as well. Doubtless, she would be denied both.

Sighing, with her face poised toward the front of the store, Vivian stilled as she recalled those fantastic stories from the dime novels she kept hidden beneath her bed. She wouldn't wish any of their maladies upon herself, of course, but those stories were always full of excitement—spinning yarns of gamblers on steamboats, sharp detectives donning disguises and solving impossible mysteries, cowboys chased by war-painted Indians—and many contained braver-than-life heroes rescuing fair damsels in distress. . . .

The door to the mercantile swung open, and Vivian watched as a tall, handsome stranger strode inside, his mink dark eyes focused on her. She blinked, lowering the scoop from where she'd held it in midair.

"Good morning, sir," she managed, her voice crackling hoarse. She cleared her throat and shook from her mind images of heroes. "How can I be of service to you today?"

"I understand there's a dance in town next week."

Vivian raised her brows, not fully comprehending. "Yes?"

"My uncle mentioned it last night, and. . ." He shuffled his feet, looking discomfited. He smoothed his palms along his trouser legs. "I was wondering. . . ."

The three women ceased talking with one another, their

curious gazes darting back and forth from Vivian to the stranger. He glanced their way then blurted, "Give me a penny's worth of those."

"You want lemon drops?" Vivian asked, uncertain.

"Uh, yeah."

A lengthy silence followed as she collected the sugar candy from the jar.

"Well, I suppose it's high time I return to the diner," Lacey said slowly, as if she'd rather not go. "I don't know what possessed me to come here this time of morning. Aunt Millie must be wondering where I am. Lovely to see you ladies. Vivian, I'll return this afternoon after the lunch crowd thins and tend to my shopping then."

She breezed through the door, baby over her shoulder. Anna and Peony glanced at the silent man then at each other. Peony grabbed her little girl's hand as both women made their excuses. "Come along, Molly and Mark," Anna said.

"Can't we have a piece of candy, too?" the boy asked.

"Not today. But remember, if you do as you're told and clean your plate at the diner, Miss Lacey will give you each a cookie."

Mark and Molly shot for the door. "We'll be good, Auntie Anna!" Molly cried. "Bye, Miss Vivian!"

"Good-bye." Smiling, Vivian glanced at the children as they and the women left the store. She recalled how after she'd sprained her ankle last year and was laid up on a cot that Lionel had placed in the storage room—since she couldn't maneuver the stairs—the children had often come to visit her while Anna worked in the mercantile. Mark had played with her crutches, pretending to be a wounded cowboy, while Molly perched on Vivian's cot and kept her informed about the music box they were helping their Uncle Erik make for Anna. She hadn't invited the children's company, but when they were gone, she'd found she missed it.

Vivian wrapped the candy in parcel paper and handed it to the stranger. He gave her a penny, which she put in the till, and then she replaced the glass lid on the jar.

"Miss Sager." He cleared his throat. "W–would you accompany me to the dance next week?"

It was a good thing Vivian had replaced the lid, because she would have dropped it if she hadn't. She felt as if she'd turned hard as rock candy, unable to move.

"Pardon?" She must have misunderstood.

The paper parcel rustled in his grasp. "The dance. The harvest one. Would you accompany me to it?" This time the offer came out hurried, clipped, almost as though he would rather she decline.

Incredulity warred with indignation. "Sir, I don't even know your name. If this is your idea of a prank, I consider it to be in poor taste. Now, if you require no further assistance, I have other business to attend to."

Surprise made his features slacken. "But we have met— well, not formally. You sold me the shaving brush yesterday and a clean shirt. My uncle is Stone Creedon."

"You're Mr. McCoy?" Incredulity made her eyes widen as she spouted the awed words. She adjusted her glasses, pushing them higher.

The shaving kit, not to mention a haircut and good cleansing, had done wonders for this man. The scruffy beard had concealed the strong lines of his well-shaped jaw and firm chin. Without that brown curly fuzz covering his cheeks, his cheekbones were more defined, and his dark eyes stood out even more, especially with the way his shiny, thick hair curled at the temples. A closely trimmed mustache slanted down both sides of his thin upper lip and curled a bit at the corners of his fuller bottom one. Suddenly she felt somewhat light-headed and clutched the countertop between them with her fingertips in an unobtrusive manner. "And you wish to take me to the dance."

"Yes. That is, if you haven't any other plans."

"I. . ." Her brain suddenly quit, as if a mental candle had been snuffed out. She couldn't string two words together.

Lionel picked that moment to amble in from the storage room. "Well, howdy, Mr. McCoy. I couldn't help but overhear your offer, as I was in the back doin' book work. And as Vivian's guardian, I just want to say that I heartily approve of you taking my sister to the harvest dance." Almost as tall as Mr. McCoy, he shook Travis's hand. Both men smiled at one another.

"Well, alright then. What time should I come by and pick her up?"

"Seven o'clock is fine."

"I'll be here." Without even so much as a farewell nod to Vivian, Travis left the store.

Vivian's rock candy blood simmered to boiling sugar as she frowned at her brother and crossed her arms over her chest. "Honestly, Lionel. I can't believe you would just grant permission like that without seeking my opinion on the matter."

He raised thick skeptical brows. "You would have refused him?"

"No. Perhaps. I don't know. I simply would have preferred the pleasure to make my own choice since it wholly concerns me."

"Really?" Her brother's level look made her uncomfortable, underlining what she already knew.

Vivian twisted around and busied herself tidying shelves with a feather duster. As one of the clumsiest old maids in Cut Corners, her marriage prospects were slim pickings. Only one man had ever proposed, and it hadn't been out of burgeoning love but rather the desire for a woman to cook for him and his brother and run his home. After Rob Baxter's clumsy proposal while she waited on him as he bought hunting supplies, shock had made her drop the cask of gunpowder on his foot, breaking his toe. Since that day, he'd hobbled clear of her.

Vivian had passed the old maid marker years ago and was fast approaching her twenty-fifth birthday. She had resigned herself to the fact that she would always live under her brother's roof. Mr. McCoy's invitation had shocked her speechless, especially since she hardly knew the man. One meeting, exchanging items for cash, could hardly be construed as an introduction.

Yet it was evidently enough for her brother, who'd started courting the widow Matilda Phelps this past summer. Perhaps neither of them wanted two women running Lionel's household, since Vivian was sure a proposal to Matilda was forthcoming; and out of desperation, Lionel was trying to match her up with the first available stranger who moseyed into the store.

Also knowing that Stone Creedon was Mr. McCoy's uncle, Vivian felt positive that the Meddlin' Men were up to their tricks again. Why else would the newcomer ask her—a stranger—to the dance, unless egged on by his uncle? She should be upset, but that emotion was absent for some reason.

Remembering Travis's good looks and his exciting, adventurous profession, Vivian decided that one arranged evening with the man—even without her consent—could be managed.

Vivian turned to face her brother. "Very well. I'll go."

She wished she could take her duster and erase that knowing grin right off his face.

Chapter 2

S orry," Vivian muttered as she lagged behind Travis.

While the ring of men and women joined hands and traveled in a wide circle south, Vivian worked to get her feet to go the right way on the elevated oak-board dance floor built just for the occasion.

"Possum on a post, rooster on a rail, swing your honey round, and everybody sail!" the caller yelled in a singsong voice from his place near the lively fiddle players.

"Oof!" Seth Baxter exclaimed from behind when Vivian barreled into him.

"Pardon," she murmured as Travis brought her round again.

The rest of the caller's instruction she should be able to manage fairly well, as long as Travis didn't go too fast.

Travis was going too fast.

Vivian cringed as she almost ran down the couple in front of her while everyone returned to their starting positions. It was a wonder she didn't have them all catapulting off the foot-high stage Erik Olson had built. The caller shouted another direction, placing her among the three women of her square to form a ring. They joined hands and traveled in a circle north a few times; then she returned to Travis to be swung around in the opposite direction. Travis and the other three men formed their own circle, each putting a hand out to form a wheel and going round and round, south.

Dizzily, she watched them, clapping and trying to keep time to the music, as everyone else did, though her clapping seemed off by a mile. The call came for Travis to return to her side.

"All jump up and when you come down, swing your honey, go round and round."

They gave a little hop—then Travis linked elbows with her, swinging her around again and again. Vivian lost all balance and fell into him, her big foot clomping down squarely on his.

He winced.

"Sorry." She gave him a sheepish smile.

Four more calls followed, including an allemande—the men going one way, the women the other in the same circle, interweaving and clasping hands as they did. Then came a promenade, with Vivian paired off with Travis, and again stumbling in her large boots—and the square dance was thankfully over. They bowed to each other, then to those at their sides.

The fiddles picked up another lively tune. At Travis's rapid-fire suggestion that they sit this one out, Vivian heartily agreed.

Although the night air was chilly, she was perspiring. Travis offered to retrieve some refreshment, and she thanked him. She wished for a fan to cool herself such as some of the women had, but she never carried such trifles. Plucking at the damp pouf of curls stuck to her forehead, she vainly tried to fluff them back into shape, then slid her hands to the back of her upswept hair to make sure none of it had come unfastened.

As long as Travis was gone—two songs worth—Vivian wondered if he was ever coming back or if he'd fled the dance. She wouldn't blame him if he had.

After a moment, she spotted him talking with his uncle in a golden circle of torchlight. The two seemed to be in disagreement. She wondered what topic of conversation would have both men frowning at one another and talking so fast.

Vivian's gaze wandered back to the dancing. Her lips tipped upward in a smile when she caught sight of Mark and Molly off to the side of the stage, spying on the adults and giggling behind their hands. Mark bowed to Molly, and she curtseyed. Then the children linked elbows and attempted their own dance in the calf-high grass, awkwardly skipping round and round till Molly's white blond braids were bouncing. On them, "awkward" looked adorable.

Travis finally returned and handed Vivian a mug of cool cider. The tart taste of apples teased her tongue and refreshed her. Travis sat stiffly beside her on the boardwalk, his focus nailed to the dancers.

Vivian cleared her throat. "I do apologize for that fiasco out there, but dancing was a pastime my brother never thought important enough to teach me."

That seemed to snag his attention a bit. He gave a nod, angling a glance in her direction. "I suppose I'm as much to blame. I'm out of practice. You mentioned your brother. Are your parents still living?" As he spoke, his gaze drifted back to the dancers and to one young couple in particular. Red-haired, blue-eyed Mary Jo Heath, her laughing smile wide, kicked up her skirts as she expertly danced with Ned Turner.

"They died of cholera when I was a child," Vivian said a little more loudly. "Lionel raised me."

He gave a half nod in reply.

At least he didn't watch her with eagle eyes, as many of the townsfolk frequently did, seeming to anticipate her next graceless move. Vivian sipped her cider before trying again. "I have a question that's been puzzling me, Mr. McCoy. Lionel told me about your What-izzit Wagon and all the cameras you keep inside. But why keep so many? Why not just one?"

That fully sparked his attention. "The size of the negative I wish to make has a huge bearing upon the camera size. For a wide panorama, I need a bigger camera. And of course, a smaller camera captures miniature photographs. Head shots, for instance."

"Then you take photographs of people, too? I wondered, since your uncle formerly mentioned that you captured scenic views of the West."

"Yes, I've captured images of cowboys on a cattle drive, workers on a railroad in progress, and a wagon train party I tagged along with for a few hundred miles. I even obtained permission to photograph residents on an Indian reservation on the other side of the Red River." His dark eyes fairly blazed with excitement.

"Oh? And did you happen to see Mrs. Chamberlain's erstwhile brother there?" As soon as the flippant words left her mouth, she regretted them. "I do apologize; I shouldn't have spoken so. I simply don't understand why she's so bothered about him taking an Indian for a wife. The woman converted to the faith, after all. Oh, dear, now I sound like a gossip. Forgive me. Perhaps I should drown my tongue in this cider."

She took a sip, embarrassed. Honestly. She wasn't accustomed to making social conversation, and she feared she was failing at this as miserably as she did at dancing.

He chuckled, a light in his eyes as he studied her. "I can't say that I've had the pleasure of meeting the couple. But many of the tribe I met—the Tonkawas—were friendly and amiable about having their photograph taken. Only a few of the elderly held themselves in reserve and refused. Of course, I respected their wishes." He fully twisted his body in her direction so that he faced her. "I have wonderful images of the experience that I held back from those photographs I sent to the magazine. I'm forming my own private picture collection of life in the West."

"Really? How interesting. I'd love to see them."

"Would you?" His gaze grew thoughtful.

"Yes, I think your profession is so exciting, and I just love adventure." She almost admitted to being a dime novel enthusiast but, since some frowned upon a lady partaking of such a reading pastime, decided not to. "Please tell me more." Turning toward him, she perched on the edge of the boardwalk so that their knees were only inches apart.

The rest of the evening flew by. Vivian found herself caught up in his tales—some humorous, some dangerous, all of them riveting—and it wasn't until the fiddlers stopped playing that she looked around the area to see that only a few people remained. She watched as men began to douse the torches that had provided light.

"I wonder how late it must be," she murmured the thought aloud.

"Forgive me, I didn't mean to go on so."

"Oh, pshaw. Perish the thought, Mr. McCoy. I heartily enjoyed hearing your reminiscences. It would be exciting to witness exactly how a photograph is taken. I can piece together the information in my head through what you've told me, of course, but experience is by far the most worthwhile teacher." Oh, dear. Now it sounded as if she were finagling an invitation to join him. "I mean. . ." What did she mean?

He smiled. "I think that can be arranged."

Thoroughly flustered by her ill-mannered gaffe, she quickly stood and smoothed her blue calico skirts. "No, please. I wouldn't dream of imposing. Forgive my tongue for wagging the wrong direction a second time."

He, too, stood. "It would be no imposition, Miss Sager. I would welcome your company."

Vivian eyed him, uncertain. He sounded as if he truly meant it. Studying his earnest expression in the nearby torch-light, she could almost believe that he did.

"This Wednesday, I plan to journey to a spot near the Red River, one I glimpsed from afar during my travels here. I would appreciate having someone to talk with, as the lengthy process of photographing inanimate objects does tend to get lonesome at times. If the possible lack of chaperones distresses you, I can persuade my uncle to ride along with us and take Mrs. Chamberlain, too." He grinned as if at a private joke, and two crescent dimples appeared in his tanned cheeks.

"Well. . .I. . ."

"Please. Say you'll come." His gaze was almost tender, and she felt drawn in by his expressive brown eyes. "Who can tell? You might enjoy the prospect of photography so well that you'll be inclined to seek a profession as one of the first women photographers in the West."

If she did decide to go, her interest in the art of chronicling wouldn't be the sole reason for changing her mind. Taken aback by that errant thought, she took a slight step sideways—and promptly connected with the edge of the boardwalk. His hand shot out to grab her upper arm, preventing her from a fall and further disgrace.

Warmth radiated through her sleeve where he touched her, but it couldn't rival the heat that sailed even to her ears. "I—" She took a quick step back, loosing herself from his hold. "Perhaps, I might. That is, I will. But for now I—I should go."

With that, she lifted her skirts, managed to turn without breaking a leg, and set off at a fast pace to the familiar shelter of her brother's blessedly empty mercantile a few buildings away.

Travis finished setting up the boxlike camera, the size of a small, potbelly cookstove. It sat on its three-legged stand facing the mighty Red River, the barrier between Texas and Indian Territory. When he'd left Cut Corners, the day was clear, but now only a ray of sun shone through a mass of cottony white clouds that swept by, picking out orange and red streaks in the river and purple in the bluffs surrounding it. It was a shame that cameras weren't able to photograph color.

"This spot is lovely, in its own rugged way," Vivian breathed from nearby. "With all those small sandbanks in the middle of the rushing water. And that stretch of gray grass growing over the one over there—appearing almost as if it were a huge scraggly eyebrow. And those wooded bluffs flush up against the water. I've never been this far out along the river. I find it quite peaceful."

"Don't be fooled, Miss Sager. Looks can be deceptive. Both men and cattle have drowned while crossing this river's depths."

"Yes, I've heard of its dangers." Her voice quieted, as if she were lost on another thought trail. "As brilliant a blue as the sky is today, it's a crying shame that the image you take will only show up in black and white."

Astonished that she'd voiced a thought similar to the one he'd had earlier, Travis lifted his gaze from making sure the camera was secure on its tripod. "One day in the future I'm confident such an achievement will be realized."

"Really?" Reflective, she looked back out over the landscape. "I wonder if it'll happen in our lifetime."

His decision to invite Vivian Sager had given him as much surprise as it appeared to have given her on the night of the dance, but it wasn't often he found someone genuinely interested in his work. After the initial curiosity, most people got a glazed look in their eyes when Travis went into a detailed discourse concerning his profession, but Vivian's face had never lost its expression of eager interest. The thought again crossed his mind that he might very well be inspiring the first woman photographer of the West, and he chuckled. Somehow, as clumsy as she was, he couldn't picture Miss Sager in such a role.

He watched her walk toward the front of the wagon where Lula and Stone still sat—Lula as chattery as a pert mockingbird while his uncle sat off to the side, mute as a cheerless crow. Vivian promptly stumbled over something in the dirt and barely caught herself before falling. Shaking his head, Travis returned to his task.

His uncle hadn't been one bit happy that Travis had volunteered him and Mrs. Chamberlain to be chaperones—not that he was courting Vivian. Far from it. But he did want to protect her reputation. At the dance, Travis had insisted his uncle was being downright rude not to venture even one reel with the

lively widow, and now he seemed further to be proving himself as a miserable companion—not that Lula seemed to take
notice or care. Travis smiled and reckoned she could keep the
conversation going for both of them. He wondered if she and
Peony Wilson were related. That dear lady had nearly talked
his ear off when her sheriff husband, Rafe, had introduced her
to Travis at the dance.

Sensing someone behind him, he looked over his shoulder.
Vivian smiled. "What are you doing now?"

"I've prepared the plate and put it in its holder." Travis again
focused on his work. "Now I'll place it within the camera."

"Is there anything I can do for you?"

"No." He quickly straightened and turned partway, almost
as if he would stop her if she tried to come forward. The image
of her bumping into him and the precious glass he now carried
lying in shards on the rocks entered his mind. "This equipment
is highly delicate."

Her expression clouded. "Oh. I only meant to ask if you'd
like me to bring you the canteen or if you'd like anything to eat.
I wasn't offering to help with your equipment."

He forced himself to relax. Of course she wasn't. Seeing
the eager light had been doused from her features, he felt like
a cad. "You're welcome to watch," he offered, in an effort to be
kind. If she stayed her distance, he could foresee no catastro-
phes arising.

"I'd like that." She advanced.

"Well, I didn't mean—"

But it was too late; she had come to a stop a little behind
him, at his elbow. He tried to focus on his work, withdrawing
the glass slide, inserting the plate holder, raising the slide, and
after a count of six covering the lens—but the lingering scent of

rose water proved to be a constant reminder of her presence.

"Would you mind explaining what you're doing?" she asked.

He welcomed the distraction as he forced the slide down with gentle firmness and withdrew the plate holder. "I've just taken the photograph and am now preparing to enter my dark tent to complete the process." He wasn't expecting her to follow him, but after almost snapping off her head earlier, he didn't have the heart to tell her to wait outside. He did, however, tell her not to come too close since he was working with acid.

In the dusky glow of the dark tent lined with orange calico and reeking of the medicinal smell of ether and other chemicals, Travis quickly set to work before the collodion could dry. He poured a solution of pyrogallic acid over the glass. Within seconds, an image appeared, rapidly increasing in brilliance.

"Oh, my," Vivian gasped in wonder, stepping closer. "It's the river—and there are the sandbanks and bluffs—and in such vivid detail, too!"

Travis smiled, though he spotted a blur in the corner near the bluffs, depicting a failed attempt. Perhaps a prairie animal had raced across the grasses while he'd closed the shutter. Nevertheless, he rinsed the developed plate well with clean water, then poured potassium cyanide over it, afterward again washing it in water. He would keep it for his collection.

"Light that candle over there, would you?" After giving the low command, he wondered at the intelligence of his words. Would she drop the lit match and set the tent on fire?

Vivian managed to strike the match against the large matchbox and light the candle without mishap. Travis thanked her and rapidly moved the plate over the flame, continuing this maneuver until it was dry. While the plate was still warm, he varnished it.

"This is all so amazing," she said. "I don't see how it can be done, to transfer such a detailed image to glass, but there it is." She was quiet a moment. "It is a messy process, though, isn't it?"

"Actually, I'm using the wet-collodion process, which is almost obsolete. In recent years, pretreated, gelatin-coated plates have pioneered a much faster dry process, dispensing with the need of a dark tent like this to develop the photograph immediately. Unfortunately, a crate of treated plates I ordered never arrived at my destination spot last spring, so I must resort to old methods until I can purchase them."

"How awful. We have no such items at the mercantile, but we do have a catalog, and I can see about ordering them if you'd like."

"That won't be necessary." He smiled to show his gratitude. "I'll be leaving for Dallas within several weeks, and I'll procure the plates there."

"Of course." She tipped her head as though pondering a dilemma. "Odd, though."

"What?"

"It seems as painstaking as this process appears—and since you said there are other plates that are so much better—that you would wait until you got those plates and not put yourself through such tasking methods."

Incredulous, he said. "And give up chronicling?"

"Only for several weeks until the new plates arrive."

He busied himself closing bottles. "Not even for that short time will I consider quitting. I strive for excellence, Miss Sager. To have my work recognized. To be the best at any given craft or job, one must work hard at it every day."

"Yoo-hoo," Mrs. Chamberlain called from outside the tent. "What are you two doing in there?"

"It's alright, Mrs. Chamberlain," Vivian hastily called back. "Mr. McCoy is just showing me the process of developing a photograph."

The tent parted, and the plump woman took a step inside, wrinkling her nose. "Oh, it is odorsome, isn't it?"

"One of the drawbacks of the trade," Travis said lightly. "I would like to attempt another photograph, if you have the time. This one is marred and not fit for publication." He showed Vivian the blur.

"We're here by your generous invitation, Mr. McCoy," Vivian said quickly. "I have no need to get back any time soon since Lionel said he would watch the store. Actually, I could stay here all day. Despite my earlier comment, I consider this quite exciting and have enjoyed viewing how it's done."

Mrs. Chamberlain frowned at her exuberance. "Yes, well, Mr. Creedon has expressed his desire for supper."

"Please," Travis said. "Go ahead without me. I'll eat after awhile. I know we spent some time reaching this destination and then hunting and picking out what I felt was the perfect spot, and I imagine you both must be starved."

"If it's alright with you," Vivian said, "I'd prefer to watch the process from the beginning. I'm not all that hungry yet, and I wouldn't feel right eating without you."

"Very well." Mrs. Chamberlain exited the tent.

Again Travis gently warned Vivian to keep her distance as he poured the viscous collodion over a new plate, then immersed it in a bath of silver nitrate. At her request, he described every step along the way and why he was doing it. He'd never had such an interested pupil.

Once he slipped the wet plate, now a creamy yellow, into its holder, he exited the tent to make another attempt at a perfect photograph, something the *Atlantic Monthly* would consider worthy to publish. He so desired to be as accomplished a photographer as the famous Matthew Brady, Alexander Gardner, and T. H. O'Sullivan. But as he'd told Vivian, to be the best at any craft took countless hours of tedious work and a constant striving for perfection. Except for Sundays, he worked every day.

Vivian walked beside him, asking questions and recounting all he'd told her, as if to double-check facts. He was amazed to discover she had such a keen mind, quick as a steel trap, and one that recorded details so well.

As they neared the camera on its tripod, Vivian suddenly stumbled on some loose rocks. "Oh!"

Without thinking, Travis dropped the slide and grabbed her before she could fall headlong down the cliff and into the rushing muddy water. Her arm flew around his waist in an effort to prevent her fall. He stared down into her flushed face, inches from his.

"Oh, Mr. McCoy, I'm ever so sorry! I certainly never intended. . . I never meant. . ." Her face went rosier. "It's these horrid boots. Well, that's not the entire truth—I'm also hopelessly clumsy. Please forgive me."

Travis didn't respond. He'd grown lost in her eyes. . . eyes so big, so blue. Framed with long lashes that curled at the tips. Never had he noticed how lovely they were. At the harvest dance, the lighting had been dim, even with the torchlight all around. And in the store, the area had also been poorly lit, with a counter separating them. But now her eyes stared up at him, only inches away. So big. . .so bright. . .the color of a crystal-clear lake shimmering amid the mountains farther West. . .

"Mr. McCoy?" With her forefinger, she pushed the dislodged spectacles back up the bridge of her nose.

He released her. "Boots?" His voice sounded as if it had a frog in it, and he cleared his throat.

She averted her gaze to her skirts and smoothed them. "Yes, well, never mind. I apologize for ruining your glass plate, especially when you had to go through such painstaking methods to get it ready. Of course, I'll have it replaced."

"No, never mind. It's not necessary." Travis hunkered down to retrieve the cracked glass. He needed the action to try to clear his head, to think, to separate himself from the vision of twin blue lakes. "I'll just go and prepare another. I have hundreds."

This time she didn't follow him to the tent.

The second attempt to take a photograph didn't go much better, though he did produce a presentable piece of work. Throughout the entire process, she didn't speak a word to distract him, but Travis couldn't keep his mind—or gaze—from wandering to the tall, rail-thin woman who stared out over the Red River, her attention rapt.

Chapter 3

Vivian could scarcely believe that Travis had agreed to accompany her to a picnic after the church meeting. As was often the case on warm days, families gathered with neighbors to sit beneath the oaks that stretched along the creek behind the church.

After the mishap, when her tumble caused him to crack his glass plate, Vivian felt sure Travis would want nothing more to do with her, but she later felt the necessity to be polite and return the favor of an outing by inviting him on a picnic. While she tucked a checkered cloth around the fried chicken in her basket, she silently mocked her own thoughts. Be polite? Want to return the favor? If she were honest with herself, she would admit that she was thoroughly smitten with Mr. Travis McCoy. Visions of a fourth Christmas wedding daily filled her thoughts since she'd met the man two weeks ago, visions she repeatedly told herself were far-fetched and ridiculous. Something only she would think up, in all probability spurred by the idealistic dime novels she read.

She stilled her motions with the cloth and lifted her gaze. If only. . .

The noise of her brother's boots thudding across the planks snatched her from impossible daydreams. Embarrassed to be caught woolgathering again, she hastily patted down the cloth, though it was already secure.

Lionel sniffed the air appreciatively. "Something sure smells good in here."

"It's for the picnic with Mr. McCoy," she explained, "and his uncle and Mrs. Chamberlain."

"I figured that. If I weren't accompanying Matilda, I'd join you." He poked at the cloth as if to get a look at what was beneath it. Vivian playfully slapped his hand away. "I'm sure Matilda Phelps's food will be just as delightful."

"Yeah, I reckon. She's just about as good a cook as you are." He swallowed hard, his Adam's apple bobbing up and down. "Fact is, I might be asking her to marry up with me. Today even, if I can work up the nerve."

"Oh?" Vivian studied him in surprise. She'd known all along her brother had been planning to propose to Widow Phelps, of course; she just hadn't realized it would be this soon.

"And unless I'm missing my guess, I won't be the only one marryin' up in the near future. You and Mr. McCoy certainly have been keeping time together."

Heat rushed to Vivian's face. "He merely invited me to view his work and see how it's done since I showed such an interest at the dance. And I repaid the favor by asking him to a picnic. I would hardly call that 'keeping time together.' "

Lionel's bucktoothed smile grew wide.

She hadn't fooled him one bit.

"Oh, just take this, will you?" She thrust the picnic basket at him. "We'll be late for the church meeting if we stand here lollygagging any longer."

"Yes, ma'am." The grin remained on his face.

As Vivian and her brother commenced their short walk to the church on the corner, Lula and Stone left the boarding-house, also wearing their Sunday going-to-meeting clothes. Travis appeared behind them, and Vivian took in a deep breath. His black sack suit fit nicely to his slim form. Above his pin-striped, buttoned vest, he wore a dark tie wrapped around his stiff winged collar, making him appear the embodiment of charm. She'd never seen him look so handsome.

He didn't join her but instead kept company with his uncle. Vivian harbored her disappointment and turned to catch up with her brother, who walked a few feet ahead. Catching sight of her, Travis tipped his tall crowned bowler hat. Giddiness sailed through her, and she offered a shy smile before pulling her wool shawl more securely about her and hastening to Lionel's side. As they approached the church, she noticed Rafe Wilson stood in a huddle with his father, Eb; his cousin, Jeff; and Erik Olson. Both Lionel and Travis moved toward them, and the other men raised their voices in greeting. The younger men's wives had formed their own ring and motioned for Vivian to join them.

"What a lovely dress," Peony said. "Is it new?"

In confusion, Vivian stared down at the button-down, blue frock with its frilled bustle plumped out in the back, the same dress she'd owned for almost two years. "No, it's what I wear every Sunday. The dress Lionel asked you to make me."

"Oh, yes, of course," Peony agreed. "I recognize it now. It's just that you look so different today. Your face is absolutely glowing."

"It certainly is," Anna added with a grin. "And I like what you've done with your hair, too. Having those tendrils hang down near your temples suits you."

Vivian wasn't sure how to reply. She offered an uncertain, embarrassed smile and continued inside, selecting the same pew she and her brother always took. One with a beautiful carving of Jesus raising Jairus's daughter from the dead. Erik Olson, the town's gifted carpenter, had crafted each pew from oak, each with a different biblical carving on the end that faced the center aisle. The gift of engravings he'd given to the church.

To Vivian's shock, Travis and his uncle filed into the pew directly behind hers, even though Stone Creedon always sat on the other side.

She didn't miss her brother's knowing grin as he slid in beside her but refused to acknowledge it. Instead, she tried to cover her clunky boots with her skirt hem as best she could, not wanting Travis to catch a glimpse of the ugly things. To think, the day he'd saved her from her fall into the river, she'd almost made yet another social gaffe and blurted that her feet were so large women's boots didn't fit her. She wore serviceable men's boots instead. But the mercantile didn't have a size that fit well, so she'd chosen them overly large instead of painfully tight. Now she wished she'd given in to vanity and ordered a custom-made pair. Soft kid boots with button tops like Mary Jo wore. With rounded toes and not old-fashioned square ones. . .

My, where was her mind trailing now? Why should she be thinking of boots, of all things, when her focus should be on worship?

"All please stand," Pastor Clune said from the front.

Along with the rest of the congregation, Vivian did so. She

concentrated on singing the worship hymns and listened to the message that followed—a message that gave her pause and caused her to examine her heart.

Travis sat with his long legs sprawled out and his back against an oak's trunk, watching as Vivian spread out food over a blanket. She'd seemed quiet after the service, and he wondered what was bothering her.

All around, townspeople gathered in spots over the grass, some seeking shade under the trees, others taking advantage of the bright spots—that is, when the weak sun peeked from beyond its covering of thick white clouds. Neighbor talked with neighbor as the womenfolk prepared the food for their individual families and the children played tag. Beyond the trees, a creek shimmered, and a few dragonflies darted over the water, late summer guests now that autumn was here. With the thick copse acting as a wind barrier, the day wasn't too cold for a gathering.

"This is a nice place," Travis said. He closed his eyes in contentment.

"Yes, it is. Many of us gather here after services when the days aren't too cold and the weather's nice." Vivian worked to unscrew the band around a glass top from a jar of pickled beets. "Of course, there probably won't be many more days like this. It gets pretty cold in Cut Corners." She pressed her lips together as she twisted and pulled. Suddenly, with a loud *pop* the lid came off—and beet juice spattered onto her skirt.

"Oh, dear." Quickly she set the jar down and worked to mop up the stain with a napkin.

Travis sympathized. "I should have offered to open that."

"It's not your fault. Likely I would've spilled something

else if it hadn't been that." As if it heard her, the jar of beets toppled from its precarious stance on the uneven ground and fell, splashing red juice onto the blanket.

"Mercy!" She set the jar upright. "I hate being so clumsy. It's no wonder people don't want to be around me." Her face went as red as the beets, and she lifted her gaze to his. "Please, forget I said that. I really don't know what I'm saying." She took a deep breath and smiled, though it seemed a tad shaky. "Would you care for some potato salad with your chicken, Mr. McCoy?"

"Please." He grew thoughtful as he watched her scoop large servings of potatoes onto the plate beside three golden brown chicken pieces. Her hands trembled as she offered him his dinner, and he quickly grabbed it before his trouser legs were christened with the yellow lumpy concoction.

Travis looked around the area for his uncle and Mrs. Chamberlain but didn't spot them. He offered to say the blessing, and Vivian agreed. Afterward, he went into a deep study, thinking about how to broach the topic he wanted to discuss.

"Miss Sager, if you'll permit me saying so, I believe you're much too hard on yourself."

Her expression seemed guarded. "Oh?"

"Take, for example, the minister's message earlier on how we're not to give great heed as to what others think about us but instead how we should only strive to please God." He took a bite of chicken. "This is delicious, by the way."

"Thank you." She forked a modest amount of green beans into her mouth. "Please, continue."

Travis thought a moment. "Relating to this morning's message, allow me to demonstrate further. Sometimes, as humans with flaws, we tend to see those flaws as if they were enhanced, like the detailed image that appears once a negative has been immersed in silver nitrate. But that's all we see, and we're certain that's all others see in us."

She furrowed her brows and pushed her spectacles higher on her nose with one finger. "I'm not certain I understand."

"The image of the river you viewed the other day was just that—an image. You concentrated on a small fraction of everything that river and those bluffs actually are. A small frame of a larger picture. Nor could you see what was hidden within the river. Or beyond its bluffs. Those who've never been west and view that photograph will see the image, not the whole panorama. They'll think of that river in no other way—though at least they'll have the ability to view a portion of its magnificence, even if it is in monochromatic grays and ivory."

He smiled sheepishly. "But I digress. Sometimes we as humans tend to do the same regarding our flaws. They're the only image we see—gray and white—and we take no notice of the complete colorful beauty of all that lies beyond. We worry so about what people think of us, we see nothing but those flaws we feel are separating us from a pleasant union with others and concentrate on them alone. As a result, though we often try to hide what we view as our shortcomings, they come to the forefront each time."

She sat back, regarding him with wonder. "I perceive, sir, that you're a professor in disguise."

He laughed. "Hardly that. I've had the hard hand of experience as my teacher."

"Hard?"

Travis thought back to his childhood and was silent.

⸎

Vivian shouldn't have asked the question. His pleasant

expression faded, and a grim one took its place, clouding his eyes. She wondered if she'd offended him. Before she could apologize, he cleared his throat.

"I had a horrible stuttering problem in my youth, something my father could not and would not tolerate."

Vivian was amazed. He spoke so confidently, even eloquently, at times.

Travis settled back against the tree trunk, his forearm propped atop an upraised knee, a chicken leg dangling from his hand. "The one image I saw of myself in those days was of a boy with huge, flapping lips. I had nightmares of that very thing. It wasn't until my grandfather took an interest in me that I thought of myself as anything but a stutterer. When I was around those I wanted to please most—those people I wanted to think well of me—I invariably found my tongue tripping against the roof of my mouth and wound up making a fool of myself."

Thinking of her clumsiness, Vivian could relate to his embarrassment.

"My grandfather was teaching me about cameras one day in his studio—he was a daguerreotypist, which is how I got the interest in photography—and he could tell I was upset. I told him about some boys who'd poked fun at me and how I hated myself because I stuttered. I was only thirteen," he explained with a boyish grin, one that brought out the crescent moons in his cheeks. "Anyway, he said, 'Travis, there's a lot more to you than just your mouth. So stop putting all your efforts into trying to please others, who are just as flawed, and trying to make them like you, when you should be striving to please your Maker instead.' " Travis chuckled. "Grandfather once thought of becoming a preacher."

"So what happened?" Vivian asked.

"I got to thinking about what he had said and did just that. I spent more time listening during church services instead of playing with the things I carried in my pockets, and I began to talk with God while I was fishing at the creek. The next time someone made fun of me, I thought about how everyone was flawed one way or another, and the taunts didn't hurt as much as they used to. I stopped seeing only the image of myself as a boy with big flapping lips and began to see traits I approved of. I'd already shown a propensity toward photography, and my grandfather told me I would make a good photographer someday. I spent countless hours in his studio, assisting him and watching him make miniatures of his customers. One afternoon, I realized I'd spoken for five minutes to a stranger—a situation that normally would have made me nervous—and I hadn't stuttered once. So I suppose you could say that I got over my problem by no longer caring what negative things others thought of me but by instead focusing on the full panorama—the view of how God pictured me."

His words gave her a lot to think about, ideas to ponder later when she was alone in her room. The more she grew to know Travis McCoy, the more impressed she became with the man.

"How is it that you never married?" She hadn't realized she'd murmured the thought aloud until she saw surprise cross his face. "If you don't mind my asking," she quickly uttered. "It's just that you're so much different than your uncle and don't seem the bachelor type at all."

Oh, dear. That sounded worse.

He took a large bite of chicken and washed it down with a swig of ginger ale before answering. "Some see my profession as a flaw. I live the life of a nomad, traveling and living out of my wagon much of the time. I never stay in one place long enough to set down roots. My dream is to become one of the best chroniclers in the business."

"And?" Vivian shrugged, not satisfied with his answer.

"What sane woman would embrace such a life?" His words were incredulous.

"I would." She spoke without thinking. "I mean—" She scrambled for words to save herself. "I'm certain there's a number of women who would consider it a privilege and an adventure, besides. Um, yes, well, I think it's time to go. It looks like rain." Hurriedly she began gathering the items to replace in the basket.

"Miss Sager." Travis's words were solemn. He laid his hand over her wrist as she tucked the cloth around the food. The warmth of his touch made her feel a little light-headed.

After taking a few seconds to compose herself, she looked up into his sober eyes.

"I never intend to marry. For some, it's the natural way of things, I suppose. But I fear I'm more like my Uncle Clive—Stone, as you know him. His true love married another, and he made the decision to remain a bachelor. For me, my love is photography."

"Of course." She smiled, hoping to portray indifference, though inside her heart felt weighted with iron. "You must travel the course planned for your life, Mr. McCoy, as we all must. I was merely curious as to why you came to such a decision. You've satisfied my curiosity quite well." She looked toward the creek, and he dropped his hand from hers as if just realizing he still grasped it. "I wonder where your uncle and Mrs. Chamberlain have gotten to. I thought they'd planned to eat with us."

His attention remained fixed on her. "There's one thing I do miss in all my travels, and that's companionship. Perhaps it's presumptuous of me to ask this, in light of our recent conversation, and I'll understand if you refuse, but I should very much like for us to share a friendship while I'm in Cut Corners. I'm comfortable talking with you, and given the fact that I don't partake of social conversation to a great degree, and when I do, I don't do it well, that's saying a lot."

Vivian was surprised. "Why should you think I'd refuse your friendship? And that you must seek my permission?"

He hesitated, as if he might not speak. "In my few days here, I've learned a lot about the town. I've come to realize that my uncle is one of four men who like to meddle in others' affairs and they've all played the roles of matchmakers, as you doubtless know already. An odd state of affairs, if you ask me, since three of the men are old bachelors. But I think you should also know, they've been playing the same game with us, manipulating us, like they do their checkers and dominoes—and I heartily apologize for my uncle's interference. I hope it didn't cause you undue distress."

She hardly knew how to reply. On the one hand, she was embarrassed that he should correctly surmise her interest in him; on the other, she was grateful for the manner in which he framed his apology so as not to cause her further humiliation. At least he hadn't come right out and said, "I have no interest in courting you, Miss Sager."

But a rejection was still a rejection, and Vivian felt deflated. Her gaze searched the area, anything to keep from looking at him. The wind had picked up, scattering those leaves that had fallen, and gray clouds made a slow sweep over the sky. "There's your uncle now," she said, catching sight of the old man and

Mrs. Chamberlain walking together toward them, both deep in conversation.

Travis turned his head to look, and his mouth dropped open in surprise.

"I do apologize for missing your picnic, Vivian," Lula said as they approached. "But Clive and I had a few things to talk over. Since the weather looks as if it's taking a turn for the worse, I feel we should head on home. I have a mincemeat pie among other foodstuffs, so you have no need to concern yourself about us. We'll get along just fine."

Clive? Since when did Lula address Stone by his given name?

"Time's a wastin', woman," he said, seeming jumpy. " 'Stead of jawin' about the goods, let's put 'em to use afore they spoil."

"Oh, hush up, old man," she said in mock exasperation. "You'll get plenty. The good Lord knows that I baked enough to feed King David's army."

"You think I'm bein' smarmy?" He pouted like a little boy. "Never. I ain't no apple polisher."

Mrs. Chamberlain rolled her eyes to the storm clouds. "Whyever won't he use that ear horn of his?" she asked, addressing the heavens.

Once the two had left, Vivian hurried to pack the basket. "We should be going, as well. Thank you for a lovely afternoon, Mr. McCoy."

"Please tell me I haven't h–hurt you with my slipshod apology," Travis said. "Perhaps I m–m–misconstrued the matter."

Hearing him stutter, Vivian looked at him in surprise. His eyes had closed. After a long moment elapsed, he opened them, shrugged, and his lips tugged into a faint smile. "Sometimes, when I'm upset, the s–stuttering returns. Once I calm, it disappears."

Hearing his boyish-sounding admission, she felt closer to him than ever before. If she couldn't have his love, she would take the next best thing.

"I should dearly prize a friendship with you while you're in town, Mr. McCoy."

"Travis. . .please."

"Alright, then. Travis." Her face warmed as she repeated his name. "And you must call me Vivian." She hoped she wasn't breaking all codes of etiquette by asking such a thing.

"Vivian it is." His smile was wide, bringing the crescent moons out in his cheeks, while his rich brown eyes positively danced.

Vivian held back a sigh. What peculiar twist on life's path had brought her to the point of truth she now faced? She was falling hopelessly in love with a happily unattached chronicler.

Chapter 4

"Mark Olson, you get over here right this minute." The exasperated voice of Anna Olson came to Travis's ears as he set up the camera for the town photograph. Anna shrieked. "Oh, my! Whatever did you get in to this time?"

Travis looked up from pushing the plate holder into the camera. The young boy had mud from the bottom of his trousers to the waist of his untucked shirt. "See what I found!" he exclaimed in delight.

He thrust a dripping frog her way, obviously expecting an enthusiastic response. Anna screeched, as did Mark's sister, Molly, who backed away.

"Now, now," Erik soothed, calming his wife. "Mark, put the frog away. Tuck in your shirt and yust stand behind Molly. That way your trousers will not show. We have already taken too much of Mr. McCoy's time."

"Aw, it's just a frog. It ain't hurtin' nobody." But the boy placed the amphibian within his shirt and obediently took his place in the second row of the group of forty-two townspeople, counting babies, lined into three rows.

Travis kept his focus on the camera until he was sure he could look up without breaking into laughter. Idiosyncrasies aside, he was becoming fond of this small town and toyed with the idea of extending his stay several more weeks, as his uncle had urged him to do, until the New Year. Other than his parents, Uncle Clive was his only living relation, and business in Dallas could surely wait.

"Everyone hold as still as a tree," Travis said. Rapidly he managed the camera, going through the steps necessary to take the photograph. He pulled out the plate holder. "Finished. You have permission to breathe again."

The sound of relieved laughter and jovial voices raised in conversation followed Travis while he rushed into his nearby dark tent. As he poured the pyrogallic acid over the plate and the image grew more vivid, he noticed a blotch and peered more closely. He chuckled.

What appeared to be a frog peered out from the collar of Mark Olson's white shirt.

The tent flap opened, and a stream of unwelcome sunlight illumined him, covering the plate as an intruder entered and walked his way. "No!" Travis commanded, upset, sure the negative was now damaged. "Leave this tent at once!"

He glimpsed Vivian's astonished face as she whirled around to go—and caught her foot on the center stake. The tent gave a protesting *whoof* as it pillowed down atop their heads.

⁂

Vivian stood as still as a stunned squirrel, unable to see anything but orange cloth before her eyes. Humiliation warred with remorse. These past two weeks she'd done well to avoid accidents or stumbles while in Travis's company. Having heeded his words concerning his personal experiences, she'd grown more at ease around him and less inclined to embarrassing acts of clumsiness. But now this—her worst blunder yet!

The canvas shifted as Travis pulled on it, and she heard the crunch of his boots coming closer. She wished she could dig a hole, sink into the ground, and cover herself from what was sure to be his accusing stare—but too soon, the weighty canvas lifted from her head, the tent resumed its upright position, and she looked up into Travis's face.

Her spectacles had been knocked off, but he was close enough that she could make his features out clearly. He didn't appear angry, just bemused.

"I do apologize," she said, her words no more than a breath. How many times had she used that phrase in reference to him?

She felt a tear slide over her bottom lashes and, embarrassed, lifted her hand to whisk it away. Before she could bring her hand all the way up, two of his fingertips slowly brushed the wetness from her cheek. She held an astonished breath.

"I shouldn't have yelled," he said quietly, his words oddly distant. "I startled you."

"No, I. . ." She couldn't think when he was staring at her in such a manner. "I should have been more careful and watched where I was going."

He didn't respond, only continued to study her eyes, her face, her mouth. His hand moved so that his palm lightly cradled her cheek. He stared at her a moment longer before his head lowered a fraction toward hers.

Vivian inhaled a soft breath, certain he would kiss her. Tilting her face upward ever so slightly, she let her eyes flutter closed. But the kiss never came, and the warmth of his hand left her jaw.

Confused, she opened her eyes again. He had straightened and appeared disconcerted, now unable to meet her gaze. He bent down, retrieving her spectacles. "They don't appear broken."

"Thank you." She took them from him and slipped them back over her ears.

He turned away. "If you wouldn't mind informing the others that a second photograph will need to be made, I'd appreciate it." He righted an overturned bottle on his table. She was relieved to note that the lid was still intact and nothing had spilt. "Once I prepare for another shot, the sun will be too low in the sky for a worthy image. Please inform everyone that we'll try again tomorrow."

"Of course." She clasped her hands at her waist. "I just want to say—"

"Please." He awarded her a glance. "No further apology is necessary. I was as much at fault as you." He presented his back to her as he worked at securing the center stake that was once again holding up the tent.

Vivian stared at him a moment longer then moved to go. Suddenly remembering the reason she'd come into his dark tent in the first place, she stopped and pivoted. "Actually, I came to tell you the most amazing news," she said before he could order her to leave again. "News I thought you might like to know. Lula just announced to everyone that your uncle proposed."

"What?" Travis jerked upright, his hand still around the stake.

The tent pillowed down atop their heads once more.

Seconds of silence elapsed—then Vivian giggled. The giggles turned into unstoppable laughter, and as Travis unearthed them a second time, Vivian was grateful to see him smile.

Chapter 5

Feeling melancholy, Travis sucked on what was left of his lemon drop while he stood outside the boardinghouse and stared at the mercantile across the street. The sheriff's wife, Peony Wilson, bustled through the door, holding her little girl's hand. Behind him, another door opened.

"Thought I'd find you out here," his uncle muttered as he came to stand beside him. "You ought to go on over there and talk to that gal, the way you been starin' over there and moonin' all mornin'."

Turning his full attention on his uncle, Travis cocked an eyebrow. "Are you referring to me? I'm not the one getting hitched."

Even Stone's ears turned red. "Yeah, well, maybe you should think on it some."

"And what about you? Are you really going through with it?"

His uncle shrugged. "Don't see why not. Widow Chamberlain's been after me to marry up with her since I moved into the boardinghouse. She's got a right carin' heart beneath

319

all that chitter-chatter, and she kin throw fixin's into a kettle and come out with somethin' to please any man's belly. Like no ther woman I know, exceptin' maybe Lacey Wilson. And Miss Sager."

Travis ignored the not-so-veiled reference to Vivian and waited, sensing there was more.

"Fact is," Stone said, scratching his whiskered jaw, "she ain't so hard on the ears once she stops blabberin' about other folk and their problems. Sometimes it helps bein' partial deaf." He cackled at that.

Travis shook his head at his uncle's remark but couldn't help the smile that spread across his face. One thing he'd learned—the gossip had died down in Cut Corners since Lula joined his uncle Stone as a chaperone. After their first two disastrous meetings, his uncle had actually seemed to enjoy the widow's company. "Well, then, I can honestly say I'm glad you found yourself a good woman, even this late in your years, Uncle. But that kind of life isn't for me."

His uncle snorted. "And just why not?"

"Because I've got other plans, plans that don't include a wife."

"Balderdash. I reckon every young buck thinks like that at some point in his life. I told you about Erik Olson, didn't I? And Rafe Wilson?"

Travis was getting mightily tired of hearing about the town's "mule-headed young men" and how they'd finally "wised up" and proposed to their gals at Christmastime.

He crunched down on his lemon drop and swallowed it. "My mind's made up, Uncle. You're not going to change it."

Before Stone could argue, a shout came from across the street.

"Hey, Stone," Eb called. "We're just shufflin' the dominoes. Get on over here."

Travis motioned with his arm toward the mercantile, where the other three meddlers now sat in chairs on the boardwalk, with a square board on a barrel between them. "Your cronies are waiting for you, Uncle. And for the record, it would be best for everyone concerned, especially Miss Sager, if you four dispense with hatching any further plans of trying to 'pair us up and get us hitched,' as I overheard Swede say last night. My course in life is set, and there's no room for a wife. Good morning, Uncle." Travis settled his hat on his head and headed north down the boardwalk.

"Where you headin'?" his uncle called after him.

"While I'm still here, I plan to visit Lacey's Diner, after having heard so much praise about the food there," Travis answered without turning around. "I'll be leaving Cut Corners earlier than planned—this coming Monday. I've decided I want to reach Dallas soon, after all."

"What?" his uncle called in shock. "What about your plan to stay through Christmas, like you said last week?"

But Travis kept on walking. He'd just made the decision and reckoned it was the wisest course to take. Having seen the determined gleam in his uncle's eyes, he was positive the old-timer wouldn't give up, nor would his friends; and Travis wanted to spare Vivian any further embarrassment. It was best for all concerned that he cut his visit short and leave town before the four old coots could cause more damage.

Vivian looked over her shoulder to make certain no one was in the store before giving in to the desire to turn the cheap wood-pulp pages of the latest novel that had arrived. Another shocking detective yarn with a strong, virile hero named Old Sleuth—whose favorite disguise was that of an agedman—involved a spine-tingling mystery regarding the trail of a missing woman. . . .

"Miss Sager, did you hear what I said?"

Startled, Vivian threw the thin book up in the air. It landed on the floor with a rustle, front side up, showing the black-and-white illustration of a terrified woman in a frozen scream.

Mrs. Chamberlain's brows sailed to her bonnet.

"I—I was just straightening the shelves." Vivian grabbed the duster she'd left near the cash till.

"Ahem. Yes." Lula stooped to retrieve the dime novel and laid it on the counter. "I have no earthly idea why your brother would sell such trash in this store. Pure drivel. I really should have a word with him. . . ."

Vivian hoped her face wasn't as red as it felt, betraying her guilt. Mrs. Chamberlain was one of a few ladies in town who thought such novels unfit for decent Christian folk. Yet to Vivian, they offered a glimpse of excitement in her otherwise dreary existence. She saw nothing really evil about them.

"Well, back to why I came. I'd like for you to come to my wedding." Lula adopted a flustered look, batting her eyelashes as a young girl might. "Since Mr. McCoy is leaving day after tomorrow, Clive decided we might as well not tarry. We're saying our vows tomorrow morning in front of Parson Clune—just a quiet gathering, nothing fancy. I do hope you can be there. As you know, I haven't any family nearby; and since if it wasn't for you and those outings we took, Clive may have never gotten the idea into his head to marry me, I want you there to share in my happiness."

Vivian only stared, while shock wrapped around her

mind like cotton wool, and she grappled with what Mrs. Chamberlain told her. Travis had changed his plans again and was leaving early—two weeks before Christmas. He was leaving Cut Corners in two days.

"Vivian?"

She blinked and swallowed hard. "Yes, of course. I'd consider it an honor to attend your wedding. I look forward to it."

Once Lula left the store, Vivian allowed her shoulders to droop. Why hadn't Travis mentioned he was leaving when she'd spotted him eating a meal in Laccy's Diner yesterday? He hadn't said a word to her about going. Just nodded in acknowledgment and invited her to sit with him. Of course, she'd declined, thinking others might look upon them sharing an unplanned meal together as much too forward on her part. But, oh, how she'd wanted to stay!

Now he would never know how much she loved him. Not that she ever planned on telling him so.

Sighing, she replaced the novel on the shelf. Even Old Sleuth and his daring escapades couldn't rouse a spark of interest right now. Despite what Travis had said about remaining unattached at the picnic weeks ago, Vivian had hoped against hope for a Christmas proposal to top Cut Corners' tally of three.

The day progressed as slow as molasses on a cold morning. When the hour finally came to close up, Vivian did so gladly. After supper, she meandered to her room and turned up the smoky glow of her kerosene lamp, but the stack of dime novels waiting for her beneath her bed didn't appeal. Regardless, she pulled them out, more out of habit than from any desire to read one. For a long moment, she stared at the illustration of a woman posed in a frightened stance with the hero's hand protectively at her back as they both stared in horror at something the reader couldn't see. In a rare fit of frustration, Vivian kicked the stack over, losing her balance. She fell to a sitting position on her patchwork quilt. Tears clouded her vision as she stared at the mess on the bedside rug.

"Oh, Father in heaven. Why? Why can't I find happiness like Lacey and Anna and Peony—and even old Mrs. Chamberlain? Am I doomed to a life of caring for my brother only? But soon I won't have even that." Removing her foggy spectacles, she swiped the tears from her cheeks with her fingertips. She wouldn't cry again.

"Why is it that men run when they see me coming? Not all the women of Cut Corners are ravishing beauties—such as the ones in those novels—yet most all have found husbands. I still have every one of my teeth, and they're straight, too, unlike Mrs. Chamberlain's." Remorse niggled at her conscience for making such an unworthy comparison. "I just don't understand it. Why is it that no man finds me the least bit dear to claim as his wife?"

No—not *no* man. *The* man. The only man she desired for a husband. Travis. Mentally she whispered his name, as if by doing so she might treasure it all the more.

With Travis, she'd found companionship, something she'd never had in great quantity with anyone else in town. They'd shared similar dreams and laughed together. He'd helped her to see herself as God saw her, and as a result she didn't feel the necessity to try to satisfy everyone else—a thankless task since no one was ever wholly pleased with the way she was or the way she did things. He'd taken her on mental journeys with him out farther west—regaling her with scenic wonders of striking red sandstone cliffs in their odd formations, hot desert sands, and magnificent, towering, snowcapped mountains.

And now he was going back to them and other places like them and leaving her behind.

Well, she would no longer make a fool of herself over the man nor cause him further distress. She would allow him to slip out of town as quietly as he'd come in.

Clicking her tongue against her teeth in self-reproval concerning her former fit of weakness, she replaced the novels and scooted them back into position under the brass rail of her bed. The books were pleasurable reading, but lately they failed to quench an ache that had been growing inside her. She readied herself for the night then reached for God's Holy Word and opened it to where she'd left off during her last quiet hour with her Savior. Too long ago.

As she read His words of instruction and promise from the book of Hebrews, they convicted her but also acted like balm to her troubled soul. One verse stood out: "Let your conversation be without covetousness; and be content with such things as ye have: for he hath said, I will never leave thee, nor forsake thee."

Recognizing her earlier murmurings as a thin veil for coveting what her neighbors had, Vivian repented. "Lord," she whispered, head bowed, "help me to be content with what I already have, with who I am, and with what You've blessed me with. We observed Thanksgiving a few weeks ago, but I see now that I've hardly been grateful. I take comfort in Your promise that You'll never leave me and will always be there for me. I love You, my sweet Jesus."

As she hugged her Bible to her chest, tears again pricked her eyes at the gentle words that responded deep within her heart.

"I love you, dear daughter. And I have only your best in mind."

Chapter 6

All through the ceremony at the front of the empty church, Vivian avoided Travis's gaze. He supposed he couldn't really blame her for treating him like an oncoming plague of locusts—he'd never known her to avoid him so—but still it smarted after the easy friendship they'd shared.

Couldn't she understand that his dream of being the best chronicler in the West was the most important thing in his life? It was imperative that he reach Dallas—and soon—to get on with his photography business. He needed those treated glass plates. At least that's what he told himself was what spurred his desire to leave earlier than planned. That and his wish not to see her get hurt more than she already must be.

Despairing of ever catching her eye, Travis returned his attention to the beaming couple and those clustering around them now that the service was over. Lacey's great-aunt Millie, her hair flying in all directions even beneath the beribboned bonnet, took Lula's hands in hers as if they were schoolgirls and kissed her on both cheeks.

The other Meddlin' Men clustered around his uncle, offering their congratulations and best wishes. Swede slapped Stone's back with an open palm. Mayor Chaps Smythe, with lingering British correctness, stood tall and shook Stone's hand. "Bully for you, old boy!" He cited words about a good life and prosperity in his precise English accent, while Eb Wilson, with suspicious moisture in his eye, winked at Travis and loudly joked, saying now that Stone had been firmly lassoed to the matrimony wagon, they had tackled their most stubborn pair yet. Then he wished Stone a marriage as happy as his own had been.

"Don't know about bein' stubborn," Stone said in his quiet gruff way. "But I reckon mulishness runs in the family. 'Cause I know someone even more set in his ways than me."

Travis had no doubt his uncle was talking about him, since he stared straight at him as he spoke. Before he could defend himself, Lula cleared her throat.

"Now, now. Let's not get into a discourse on who's the most stubborn of the bunch. Each of you old goats has your fair share of that trait, if you want the truth." Lula said the words lightly, casting a smiling glance Travis's way, as if she were his ally. "I made three lovely pies yesterday—one of them pecan. For a wedding present, your dear daughter-in-law gave me her recipe, Eb—the same pie she serves at the diner—and you're all welcome to come over to the boardinghouse and sample a slice or two and let me know what you think. Parson Clune, you and your wife and children must come, too."

Everyone agreed. As the hubbub once more increased, Travis watched Vivian slip quietly away from the circle and head down the middle aisle. He waited a moment then hurried to catch up with her. As his boots hit the boardwalk outside, he caught sight of her tall figure stepping off the same boardwalk and onto the muddy strip of land before the other walkway began. The clouds had grayed and looked as if they'd drop more rain sooner than later. Travis hoped the weather would stay clear for his departure.

"Aren't you coming over to the boardinghouse?" he called after her. She halted and hurriedly lifted a hand to her face, then dropped it to her side and turned. He moved to join her. "Mrs. Chamberlain will be mighty disappointed if you don't sample her pecan pie."

Her blue eyes shimmered behind the glasses. "I'd like to." She gave a weak smile. "But I promised Lionel I'd get back as soon as possible after the ceremony to mind the store."

"Oh." Travis was disappointed.

"I'm happy for your uncle and Mrs. Chamberlain. . .er, Mrs. Creedon," she went on to say. "As you likely know, Stone Creedon is the last person anyone ever thought would marry, and I'm truly happy for both of them. Please extend my apologies for missing out on the festivity, and wish them well for me." Her voice caught. "I really must go now. Good-bye, Travis."

He wanted to stop her, to talk to her awhile longer, but what could he say? Truth was, nothing he could say would change things; so instead he helplessly stood in the middle of the road and watched her hurried trek toward the mercantile.

Inside, he felt lower than a worm.

Vivian wiped the counter with a vigor that should have taken away the oak grain. She heard Lionel's boots scuff on the planks behind her.

"Travis McCoy is leaving town this mornin'," he said.

"So I hear." Under the window glass's black-painted

words DRY GOODS, she could clearly see the commotion surrounding Travis's wagon in front of the boarding-house. Despite the light rain that sprinkled the ground, a number of people had ventured out to tell him good-bye. Vivian knew from overhearing talk in the store that many of the townsfolk admired him. Small wonder.

A long pause ensued. "Well, I reckon it's the right neighborly thing to do to wish him well and bid him Godspeed. Don't you?"

"I reckon it is." She scrubbed harder when her cloth encountered a patch of stubborn dirt.

Lionel snorted and headed for the door, mumbling something under his breath. Once he was gone, Vivian lessened her brisk scrubbing, straightened, and massaged her aching shoulder. It wasn't that she intended to scorn Travis or that she didn't want to tell him good-bye; it would just hurt too much. Rend her heart to pieces and bring home to her the realization that her dreams of a Christmas proposal were now firmly buried in the ashes of all her other unfulfilled hopes. Yes, she wanted him to realize his ambitions and nightly prayed that every last one of his dreams would be realized—even if, for that to happen, she must sacrifice her own desires.

But she would not say good-bye.

Trading the cloth for a broom, she began a brisk sweep of the mercantile.

A tinkling above the door announced Lionel's return. "I'm glad you hung those bells over the door last week," she said, her back to him. "It's nice to know when a customer enters the store."

"I'm not a customer, but I like those bells, too."

She froze then whirled to face Travis. His expression was

grave, and she dropped her gaze to the top button of his long frock coat, unable to meet his eyes.

"On second thought, I am a customer." He hesitated. "Give me a penny's worth of lemon drops."

She raised her eyes to look at him. "You want lemon drops," she repeated, doubting it.

"Sure do. And a penny's worth of those, too." He pointed to a jar of horehound drops.

Her actions forced and erratic, Vivian moved behind the counter to gather his purchases. She handed both small paper parcels into his hand and waited, but he didn't offer any change. Finally, she looked up. Raindrops dripped from his hat brim. She lowered her gaze to his face, and the sadness in his brown eyes made her heart catch.

"I couldn't leave without saying good-bye," he admitted.

She nodded once. "Then I'll be wishing you well." Vivian shifted her feet. "That'll be two cents, please."

He dug the coins from his pouch and laid them in her palm. Her nerve endings tingled at his touch, and she pulled her hand quickly from his.

"I'd like to write you, if I may," he said after a moment.

She averted her gaze to the counter. To what purpose would it serve, except only as a continual reminder of all she'd lost? "I'd rather you didn't."

"Why?"

"Now that you're leaving, I just think it'd be best if each of us goes our own way and forgets about one another."

When he didn't move, didn't speak, she again inched her gaze upward. She couldn't place the look in his eyes. But his mouth was drawn tight enough that the crescents in his cheeks appeared.

"Then I guess there's nothing more to say." His words came

clipped. "Except for good-bye, Miss Sager." He nodded once then strode out of the door and out of her life. For good.

Soon she heard his wagon's harness and the creaks of the huge spoked wheels as he drove hurriedly away. Inside, she crumpled and wanted to give in to the moisture that heated her eyes. Instead, she brushed at her lashes and resumed her efforts to give the floorboards a thorough whisking with the broom. Regardless, the tears continued to fall.

The bells tinkled as the door opened. Hurriedly, she wiped her face with the back of one hand before facing her customer. "Oh. Hello, Molly. Mark. What can I do for you today?"

The two children eyed her as if uncertain. "We come to get some stick candy," Mark said. "Uncle Erik said we could."

"Of course." Vivian briskly moved to the counter and laid aside her broom. Knowing their favorites, she pulled the snow-white peppermint sticks from a jar.

"Were you crying?" Molly asked, her pale blue eyes anxious. She let go of her brother's hand to relinquish her two pennies.

The last thing Vivian needed was for those two to tell everyone they'd caught her in tears. She tried to smile. "What makes you think that?" She handed the children their treats.

" 'Cause your cheeks are all wet and your glasses are foggy."

Vivian busied herself with putting their pennies in the till.

Molly looked down at her stick candy a moment then cupped her hand over Mark's ear and whispered something to him. He looked at his sweet and nodded. Both children snapped off the tops of their candies and handed the sticky chunks to Vivian.

"Uncle Lars says sugar candy always make a body feelbetter," Molly explained. Her smile was wide as she grabbedMark's hand, and together they ran, giggling, out the door.

Touched, Vivian looked after them then at the stubs of

candy in her hand. Not for the first time, she wished she could have children as dear as those two. Obviously it was never meant to be. She must accept the plan God had for her, whatever plan that was, and stop hoping for impossibilities.

Chapter 7

Vivian and Lionel shared a light supper late on Christmas Eve, a full two weeks after Travis's departure. Earlier in the day, Lionel had taken part in the elaborate bachelors' pot roast luncheon that Lacey's great-aunt had started as an annual celebration—his last year to partake of it, since he was marrying Widow Phelps in the spring. Later, Lacey opened up the diner to the entire town, her third year to do so, and doled out scrumptious desserts free of charge.

Determined not to let Travis's absence ruin her Christmas, Vivian had walked over to the diner to join in the fun and had even managed to smile and sample some mincemeat pie and delicious fudge. All of the women—especially Anna, Lacey, and Peony—had been so kind, and the memory of their gentle words and sympathetic smiles caused tears to cloud Vivian's eyes even now. From their hesitant way of speaking, Vivian realized they, too, had thought Travis might propose.

She simply must get her mind off that man.

Forking a last bite of potato pudding into her mouth, she

shot up from her seat to set the butter in the sideboard and collect the dishes to wash them.

"I declare, Vivian." Lionel leaned back in his chair, eyeing her. "These past two weeks you've been as fidgety as a jackrabbit with an itch. Sit down a spell and drink your coffee while it's hot."

Keeping her hands in motion helped her to stop thinking on things she had no business thinking about. But there was one matter she needed to discuss with her brother. Might as well be now. Smoothing her hands down her apron, she reclaimed her seat.

"Actually, we do need to talk, Lionel. You'll be marrying up with Matilda come spring." She cleared her throat. "And I noticed an ad for employment in the last mail-order catalog we received. They're looking for a bookkeeper in Kansas City. I've sent a letter applying for the position. I feel it's time I move on."

"What?" Lionel's cup hit the saucer with a bang, startling Vivian into lifting her gaze. His brows were bunched together. "Never. I won't hear of it."

This wasn't the answer she expected. "Why not?"

"Don't you like it here?" His tone became uncertain.

"It's not that, but soon Matilda will be living here, too, and it's time I made other arrangements."

"Vivian." He reached across the table to lay his hand over hers in an uncharacteristic show of affection. "You're always welcome in my home. I talked with Matilda, and she agrees. After all, you're all the family I've got left."

Tears pricked Vivian's eyes at his warm response. All this time she'd thought his was a grudging hospitality and that he wanted her out from underfoot. She shook her head, still unsure. "But didn't you help Stone Creedon and the others in trying to pair me off with Travis McCoy? I saw you talking to the old men the day he arrived."

Lionel's face reddened, and he cleared his throat, pulling his hand back. "Well, yes, I did. But only with your benefit in mind. Before Ma died, she made me promise to look after you, and as your big brother, that's what I thought I was doing. Looking after you by helping to find you a husband. I'm sorry it turned out so badly. I never would've figured. . ."

"Yes, well, never mind that." Vivian shifted in her seat, her attention going to her coffee. She took a sip. "Thank you for talking to me about all this, Lionel. I've always thought of myself as an imposition."

"Never." The word came out fast and sure.

She smiled. "Then I can leave Cut Corners all the more content, knowing I'll have a home to return to if things don't work out."

He seemed troubled. "You're still planning on going?"

She nodded. "I'm tired of reading about other people's adventures. I want some of my own."

"Those stories all tend to lean on the melodramatic side, Vivian. Nothing like real life—or real people."

Shocked, she set her cup down fast, spilling her coffee. "You know?"

"About your liking for dime novels? Sure. I never had a mind to read, not like you. Seems you've had your nose stuck in a book since you were in pigtails. Course then it was the classics you were drawn to."

Vivian cleared her throat. "How'd you find out?"

"I do inventory each week, remember, and it seemed too much a coincidence that whenever a new crate arrived, one of them novels would always disappear off the shelf that day, regardless if we had one of the few customers with a liking for them visit the store or not."

So her secret was out. A wave of shame lapped through her, though of course she'd put coins in the till for them and hadn't taken them outright. "How long have you known?"

"Since Old Sleuth made his debut, I reckon. Aw, don't look so humbled, Vivian. There's a lot worse things in life, and I'm not sure I cotton to what some of them persnickety old women say about them books being evil. Far-fetched definitely. But evil?" He shook his head. "Their gossiping tongues always a-yappin' and spreading poison about others is more evil, to my way of thinking. As long as you don't get fooled into believing them stories are what life's truly about, I don't see how they can do any harm."

"I know they're not real. I'm not that naive. But I always wanted a smidgen of adventure, Lionel. Ever since Pa used to tell of his skirmishes with the Apaches when he first traveled west, and his encounter with those wolves that time, and meeting up with those crooked fur traders, and—"

Her brother laughed and stretched out his long legs, his back pressing flush against the chair. The wood creaked, protesting the added weight. "No quiet hearth at home for you, huh? Yep, I remember them bedtime stories of Pa's. Liked to have scared me witless, but, oh, how we clamored for more, didn't we?"

They continued to reminisce a while longer in harmonious union before Lionel rose from his chair and stretched.

"I'm going to call it a night. I suggest you do the same. The church bell will be ringing before we know it, gathering everyone for Christmas services."

"I just want to do some straightening first."

"Don't stay up too long." He stooped to hug her, and surprised, she hugged him back, then watched as he headed to his sleeping quarters.

An hour passed. Then two. Vivian couldn't have slept had she tried.

Once the dishes were washed and put away and the kitchen was fully straightened, she headed downstairs and transferred her whirlwind cleaning to the store. She was glad for the soft kid boots with the fashionable heels that she'd finally broken down and ordered from the most recent mail catalog. All she'd needed to do was send in her measurement by drawing an outline of her foot on parcel paper, and weeks later she'd become the proud owner of a pair of *ladies'* boots that actually fit. What a difference it made in the way she walked and even carried herself! Oh, she was still clumsy at times, but her stumbles had greatly decreased with the advent of her new boots.

With the shelves straightened, dusted, and put in order, she grabbed the broom. Minutes later, she looked up from her whirlwind whisking to see a sight that made her mouth drop open. Broom in hand, she hurried to the door and swung it open, certain her eyes must be playing tricks on her.

A fine dusting of snow fell from a soft, powder gray sky. She stood, amazed, and lifted her face to let the cold flakes kiss her cheeks. Snow—in Cut Corners, of all places.

Only once before could she remember them receiving snow at Christmastime—the year Lacey Wilson got married—and some winters they didn't get snow at all. Surely, this was a night for miracles. Even the sky seemed hushed, stilled, as if to remind her of the awe-inspiring miracle that had taken place almost two thousand years ago on a night much like this one.

"Oh, Lord, You are wondrous, and Your ways are wondrous to behold."

The whisper had barely left her lips when she heard the

vague sound of a creaking harness and the rapid clopping of horses' hooves coming from a distance. She turned her gaze toward the railroad tracks to look. Possibly Doc was out to deliver a baby. Anna's was due any day.

A wagon came rumbling and clattering around the bend of Ranger Road. And for the second time that night, Vivian stood speechless.

"Whoa!" Travis pulled on the reins as he drove up in front of the mercantile, and his focus went to the woman silhouetted against the light coming from the store. Vivian stared at him as if he were an angel come to announce the birth of the Savior. Nothing so dramatic, but he did have an important announcement, and he was bound and determined to get his words out before his lips froze to his teeth. He prayed he wouldn't stutter. He was more nervous than a plump goose on Christmas Day.

"Vivian," he called out, low enough so as not to wake the entire town. "I've been a fool. It took me a whole week in Dallas to recognize the truth—that what I really want in life I left behind in Cut Corners. I came as soon as I could get away."

Still clutching a broom, she took a step forward until she stood at the edge of the boardwalk. The light from the overhead clouds illumined her face. "Travis?"

"Yeah, it's me." He pulled up the brake lever and wrapped the reins around it. Swallowing hard, he stepped down from the wagon. After the curt way he'd behaved when he last told her good-bye in the store, he wouldn't blame her if she turned her broom on him and shooed him out of town. But he must answer to the strong desire that was even now playing a song within his heart at the very reality of seeing her again. He'd driven all day and night; he wouldn't play the coward now that the moment had finally arrived.

He pulled off his hat, bringing it to his chest, and dropped to one knee on the ground just beginning to collect patches of snow. Icy water soaked his trouser leg, and he shivered at the contact.

"Vivian Sager, I've been a downright fool, and I wouldn't blame you if you never wanted to see me again. But I'm going to say my piece, come what may. I love you." With those words out in the open, the rest came easy. "There's no way I could ever live my life and forget you like you said I should. I've come back because my life has been empty and dull without you by my side. So I'm asking—begging—would you do me the honor of marrying a dim-witted nomad like me and share in my life of chronicling the West?"

Her broom dropped to the planks with a clatter. "You want to marry me?"

"Yes. With all my heart." His knee in danger of turning to a hunk of ice, he stood unsteadily. "Will you be my wife?"

"Will I!"

"Yes?" He took an uncertain step forward.

"Yes!"

She ran off the boardwalk toward him. Throwing his hat to the wind, he planted his hands at her waist and hoisted her high in the air. She clutched the tops of his shoulders as he swung her around, and both of them laughed. All at once, his shoe slipped on an icy patch, and he lost all balance. Before he knew what hit them, they tumbled into an undignified heap on the frozen ground.

"Are you alright?" he was quick to ask.

She rubbed her hip, but she was smiling. "How can I be anything but glad when you've just fulfilled my every dream?"

Her eyes sparkled, and she removed her dislodged spectacles, now speckled with snow.

Suddenly she laughed aloud. His heart full of joy, Travis joined her.

"Vivian, you're beautiful."

"Beautiful?" This time her laugh sounded choked. "Me?"

"Yes, you. You have the loveliest blue eyes, the sweetest smile, the most tender heart."

Drawing close to her, he cradled her satin jaw in his palms and saw the response of love in her eyes before they fluttered shut. The touch of her warm lips against his cold ones was all he thought it would be—and more.

"You two ever gonna get up off that ground and stop your carryin' on so we decent folk can get some shut-eye around here?" Stone yelled from a top window of the boardinghouse. The point of his striped nightcap lay slung over one eye.

"Uncle," Travis called, unable to wipe the smile from his face. "Wish me well—I'm getting married!"

"Buried, you say? You look healthy enough."

"He said 'married,' " Lula loudly proclaimed from behind him.

"Well, glad to hear you finally wised up," Stone said. "But unless you're plannin' on marryin' her tonight, could we get some sleep now?"

Lula stuck her head with its frilled nightcap out the window. "Oh, don't mind him. Come on up, Travis, and I'll ready a room for you quick as a wink. First I received that letter from my brother today, saying as how he and his dear Indian wife and family will be visiting in the spring, and now this. It's all so exciting." Her bubbly voice trailed away.

"A night for miracles," Vivian added, her voice soft.

"Amen to that." Travis stood to his feet and, taking hold of her hands, helped Vivian up from the ground. They stared at one another a moment longer, until he slowly drew her close for a parting kiss. Travis could hardly wait for morning to roll around when he'd see her again. He wondered if dawn was too early to come courting.

Epilogue

I now pronounce you husband and wife." Pastor Clune's voice boomed throughout the church decked in all manner of greenery. He grinned. "You may kiss your bride."

Vivian felt lighter than air as Travis gave her a tender kiss that curled her toes. Her heart leaped an excited little beat at the loving look of promise in his eyes before they both turned their attention to family and friends, who stood nearby with wide smiles, and accepted their well wishes. The Meddlin' Men clapped one another on the back and shook hands as if congratulating each other. Vivian knew it was the Lord who'd brought Travis back into her life, but she wouldn't begrudge the four old men their fun.

"I'll surely miss you, little sister," Lionel said as he hugged Vivian.

She embraced him just as hard, realizing that in a few short hours she would be leaving him, their first time ever to be separated. "I'd stay longer, but Travis has to return to Dallas—he has clients waiting there. Then, as soon as the weather clears, we're traveling farther west, on to New Mexico and Arizona and even up through Colorado. But when the time comes to settle, years on down the road, we plan to return to Cut Corners and make our home here."

"I know. He told me. I guess you're getting that adventure you always dreamed of."

"Yes." She drew back, taking hold of his hands. "Oh, Lionel. Please be happy for me. I do love him so."

"That's the one thing that makes it bearable losing you. That, and knowing he'll take good care of you. And God'll take care of you both." He squeezed her hands before letting her go.

The next few hours passed in a blur of activity that left Vivian breathless. First came a party at the boardinghouse, with a huge dinner followed by dessert—and both Lula and Lacey plying everyone with their scrumptious cakes, pies, and cookies. A host of well-wishers flocked around the bridal couple. All too soon, it was time to pack up and say good-bye.

Dressed in her new smart traveling clothes of deepest blue, Vivian hugged each of those members of Cut Corners who'd become so dear to her. In past weeks, she'd gained the courage to open up to the three women she so admired and form friendships with them. Now she felt as if they were the sisters she'd never had. First came Anna, who'd delivered a healthy son named Michael four minutes before midnight on Christmas Day. Vivian kissed the top of Michael's downy head poking through the swaddling blanket then bussed Anna's cheek.

"I'll never forget you, Vivian. You must write to us and let us know how you're doing."

"I will."

"Do you hafta go?" Mark asked from beside Anna.

Vivian smiled. "Yes, but it's a good thing. It's not a bad one."

"Will you hafta ride on the train like we did?" Molly chirped up.

"No. We'll be traveling in Travis's wagon."

Mark's pale blue eyes grew wide. "The What-izzit Wagon? With the cam-ruhs?"

"Yes."

Molly and Mark looked at one another then back at Vivian. "But if you go," Mark said, "who'll give us candy?"

Vivian laughed. "I guess my brother'll have to take over that job."

"That's enough, children," Anna chided softly. "Miss Vivian and Mr. Travis have to leave now, before it gets too dark and there's not enough daylight to see."

Molly suddenly moved forward, her small arms going around Vivian's blue skirts. "Good-bye, Miss Vivian. I wish you didn't hafta go."

"Me, neither," Mark added.

Emotion clogging her throat at the unexpected sweet gesture and words, Vivian stooped down to hug both Mark and Molly close. "I'll miss you children. Be good. Stay out of trouble."

Next came Lacey, who, with tears in her eyes, offered Vivian a basket piled high with delicious-smelling food from her diner. "I tucked a dozen of my best ginger cookies in there, too," she whispered before pulling away.

And finally, Peony, large with child, waddled up to embrace Vivian. "You're a special woman, Vivian. Don't let anyone ever tell you otherwise. I'm sure you'll make your husband proud as you chronicle the West together."

They kissed cheeks, and Vivian laid a gentle hand atop little Lynn's curly head. Unable to speak for the tears, she pivoted sharply and offered a hasty good-bye hug to each of the sometimes irascible but always loveable old-timers she would fondly remember as the Meddlin' Men—Stone, Chaps, Eb, and Swede. Lula and Lionel she hugged last, before she moved away.

Travis helped her step up into the wagon. Once seated, she looked out over the cherished people she'd known a good part of her life. Their sometimes-quirky, sometimes-crazy mannerisms and character traits, she would never forget.

Travis clicked his tongue as an order for the horses to proceed.

"Good-bye!" The townspeople called and waved.

Holding her hat, she turned in her seat and waved back, watching as they continued to walk forward and wave. She watched until they were little more than the size of grasshoppers on the prairie.

"Regrets?" Travis asked suddenly, voice somber.

Vivian turned her attention to her new husband. "None. I'll miss them, yes, but I wouldn't choose being with them one more day if it meant I'd have to be without you."

He smiled and reached across the space between them to grab hold of her hand. Bringing her glove to his mouth, he kissed her fingers. "Look in the sack by your feet."

Puzzled, Vivian reached for the burlap bag and pulled the string. Withdrawing a framed object, she gasped. Fresh tears clouded her eyes. In her hands, she held a photograph of all the townspeople of Cut Corners. She smiled at their sober faces, though she noticed a few cheery ones, too. And she laughed aloud when she saw what appeared to be the frog that caused such a ruckus peeking out of Mark Olson's shirt.

Was any woman ever so blessed to have such a thoughtful husband as her Travis?

"I made that picture from the negative I assumed was ruined when the dark tent fell on our heads," he explained when she didn't speak. "I was able to save it, and I thought you'd like to have it. We can make that photograph the start of a family memory book. An album. And we'll add photographs of our children once they start coming, should God bless us so."

At his mention of the little ones they might one day have, her heart soared even as she felt a blush rise to her face. As cold as the day was, the sudden surge of warmth inside felt good. Sliding closer to him, she wrapped her gloved hand through the crook of his arm. "Have I told you yet today how much I love you, Mr. McCoy?" she said, feeling like a young schoolgirl out riding with her beau.

Grinning, he turned his head to plant a swift kiss on her cheek. "A man never gets tired of hearing it, Mrs. McCoy."

She giggled. "Well, I do love you. And I'm sure that today—the start of 1882—is destined to be the best year yet, due to the wonderful way in which it began—with me becoming your wife, and you my husband. I doubt any woman in the whole wide wonderful West could be happier than I am right at this moment."

Travis stopped the wagon. Mystified, Vivian turned to look at him, but before she could ask what was wrong, he drew her into his arms and gave her a lingering, heart-escalating kiss.

"I love you, Vivian," he whispered, pressing his cold cheek to hers. "I was a fool not to realize it sooner."

She held him close, certain no dime novel could ever compare to the wonderful adventure she was about to share with this dear man.

GRANDMA VERA'S CREAMY PECAN PIE
(Guaranteed to be as good as Lula's and Lacey's)

1 cup light corn syrup
1 cup sugar
3 lightly beaten eggs
2 tablespoons melted margarine or butter
1 teaspoon vanilla
1½ cups pecans
9" frozen deep-dish pie crust

Preheat oven to 350°. Stir corn syrup, sugar, eggs, margarine (or butter), and vanilla in large bowl until blended well. Stir in pecans. Pour into frozen crust. Bake 50-55 minutes—pecans should be light to medium golden brown and have "cracked" look to them. Cool and cut. Top with dollop of whipped cream, if desired. Enjoy!

PAMELA GRIFFIN

Award-winning author Pamela Griffin makes her home in Texas, where snow makes a rare visit at Christmastime, but she doesn't let that fact dampen her holiday cheer. Christmas is her favorite holiday, and she enjoys viewing the lights with her kids, making homemade candy and other goodies, watching old Christmas movies, and all the rest of the gala that this festive time of year brings—especially friendly get-togethers and family reunions. She loves to write and has written several stories set during the Christmas season.

Multi-published, with close to thirty novels and novellas, she gives God the glory for every amazing thing He's done in her writing career. She invites you to drop by and visit her website at: http://users.waymark.net/words_of_honey.

A Letter to Our Readers

Dear Readers:

In order that we might better contribute to your reading enjoyment, we would appreciate your taking a few minutes to respond to the following questions. When completed, please return to the following: Fiction Editor, Barbour Publishing, Inc., P.O. Box 719, Uhrichsville, OH 44683.

1. Did you enjoy reading *Lone Star Christmas*?
   ❑ Very much—I would like to see more books like this.
   ❑ Moderately—I would have enjoyed it more if ＿＿＿＿＿＿＿＿
   ＿＿＿＿＿＿＿＿＿＿＿＿＿＿＿＿＿＿＿＿＿＿＿＿＿＿＿＿＿＿
   ＿＿＿＿＿＿＿＿＿＿＿＿＿＿＿＿＿＿＿＿＿＿＿＿＿＿＿＿＿＿

2. What influenced your decision to purchase this book?
   (Check those that apply.)
   ❑ Cover   ❑ Back cover copy   ❑ Title   ❑ Price
   ❑ Friends   ❑ Publicity   ❑ Other

3. Which story was your favorite?
   ❑ *The Marrying Kind*   ❑ *Here Cooks the Bride*
   ❑ *Unexpected Blessings*   ❑ *A Christmas Chronicle*

4. Please check your age range:
   ❑ Under 18   ❑ 18–24   ❑ 25–34
   ❑ 35–45   ❑ 46–55   ❑ Over 55

5. How many hours per week do you read? ＿＿＿＿＿＿＿＿＿＿＿

Name ＿＿＿＿＿＿＿＿＿＿＿＿＿＿＿＿＿＿＿＿＿＿＿＿＿＿＿＿＿

Occupation ＿＿＿＿＿＿＿＿＿＿＿＿＿＿＿＿＿＿＿＿＿＿＿＿＿＿

Address ＿＿＿＿＿＿＿＿＿＿＿＿＿＿＿＿＿＿＿＿＿＿＿＿＿＿＿＿

City＿＿＿＿＿＿＿＿＿＿ State＿＿＿＿＿＿ Zip＿＿＿＿＿＿

E-mail＿＿＿＿＿＿＿＿＿＿＿＿＿＿＿＿＿＿＿＿＿＿＿＿＿＿＿＿

If you enjoyed
LONE STAR CHRISTMAS
then read:
angels
for christmas

*Crafty Little Angels Put Their Charm
Into Four Holiday Romances*

Strawberry Angel by Pamela Griffin
Angel Charm by Tamela Hancock Murray
Angel on the Doorstep by Sandra Petit
An Angel for Everyone by Gail Sattler